MURDER TO MUSIC

The Libby Sarjeant Series
by Lesley Cookman

9781905170159

9781905170845

9781906125028

9781906373306

9781906373771

9781907016080

9781907016462

MURDER TO MUSIC

LESLEY COOKMAN

Published by Accent Press Ltd – 2011

ISBN 9781907726545

Printed and bound in the UK

Cover Design by Zipline Creative

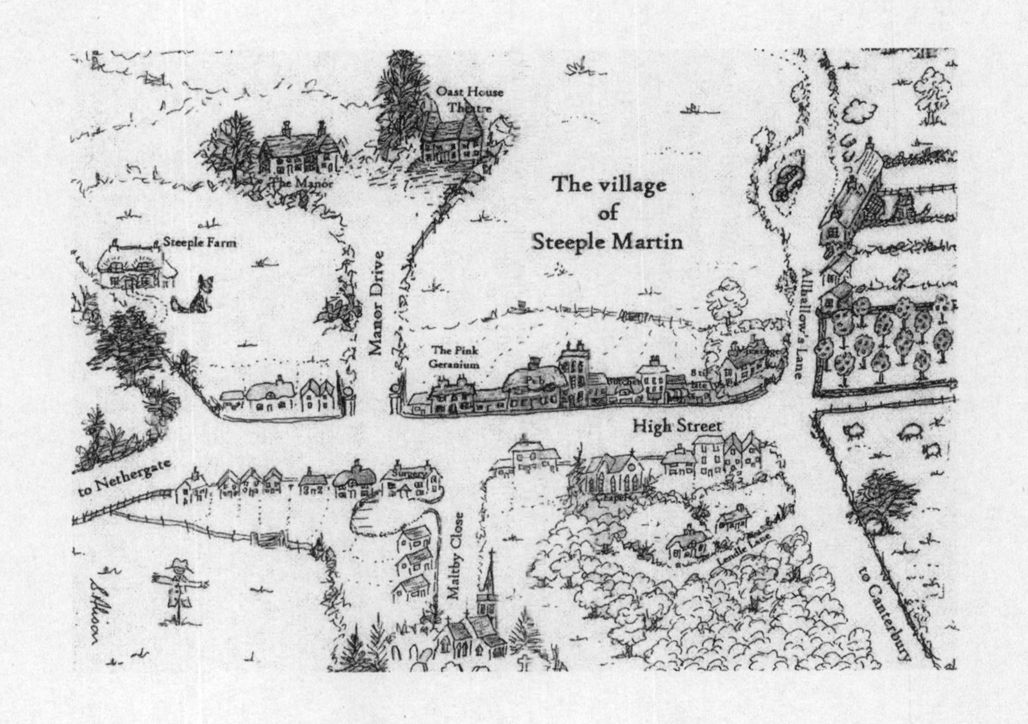
The village
of
Steeple Martin
Oast House
Theatre
The Manor
Steeple Farm
Manor Drive
The Pink
Geranium
Pub
Allhallow's Lane
High Street
Surgery
Maltby Close
to Nethergate
to Canterbury
Lendle Lane
S.Alison

Chapter One

THE WIND BLEW GREY clouds rimmed with silver across a darkening sky and the house was revealed in a flash of lightning. A light shone briefly from a window on the left, turned into a flickering strobe by a whippy birch. The music came to a sudden stop and the light went out.

Fran parked her car as close to the hawthorn hedge as she could.

'I can't get out now,' said Libby.

'You'll have to slide across, then,' said Fran, climbing out herself. 'The lane's too narrow to park anywhere else.'

Libby levered herself across the gear stick and caught her jacket on the handbrake.

'Blimey,' she said, blowing out her cheeks. 'This woman makes things difficult, doesn't she?'

'Difficult? Why?'

'No buses, nowhere to park. Doesn't she want visitors?'

Fran laughed. 'Not everyone lives in the centre of a village, Lib. Just because it's a little off the beaten track doesn't mean she's unsociable.'

Libby looked round. The lane ran between fields that stretched to further hedges, small hills and a few clumps of trees. High summer: there was a smell of meadow with an undertone of cowpat.

'Come on then,' she sighed. 'Let's get it over.'

'Don't give me that,' said Fran, leading the way

to a small slatted gate set in the hedge. 'You were just as keen to meet her as she was to meet you.'

'She's a celebrity seeker,' sniffed Libby.

Fran laughed even louder. 'She's a famous novelist, Lib! I hardly think she thinks of you as a celebrity.'

The cottage stood, like a Victorian painting, at the end of a short path bordered by hollyhocks, roses, lupins and a few early dahlias. All that was needed was a child in a bonnet and a kitten in a basket.

The door opened and a woman beckoned them in.

'Come in, come in,' she said. 'Hello, Fran. And you must be Libby.'

She held out a hand and Libby shook it. The woman was only a little taller than she was herself, and not as tall as Fran. Her hair was fashionably streaked in shades of blonde, but was obviously white underneath – and distinctly untidy. She favoured, Libby was pleased to see, the same long and floaty clothes she did herself, although baseball boots peeped out from beneath the wide harlequin trousers. She looked at the woman's round face and found herself being equally minutely studied.

'I'm Amanda George,' she said, 'but only on the covers of the books. Mostly people call me Rosie.'

'Hello,' said Libby, suddenly feeling a little shy. The woman was at least ten years older than she was, successful and confident.

'Well, come on in, then,' said Rosie, standing aside for them to pass her. 'Go through to the garden. I thought we'd have tea out there.'

The back garden was as traditional as the front. A vegetable patch appeared to be tucked away behind a ceonothus hedge and yes – here was the cat. A black and white monster who rolled on his back as soon as they appeared.

'Oh, ignore Talbot,' said Rosie. 'He's shameless.'

'My Sidney's just grumpy,' said Libby, squatting to rub Talbot's stomach. He stretched his back legs to their full extent and purred a little.

'Can I do anything to help, Rosie?' asked Fran.

'No, nothing. I'm going to boil the kettle. Do you prefer tea or coffee?'

'Tea, please,' they said together.

'Nice,' said Libby, as they sat down on the cushioned chairs. 'Lovely garden.'

'A lot of work,' said Fran.

'Too much for me,' said Libby. 'I expect she's got a gardener. All right for some.'

'You're letting your prejudice show again,' said Fran. 'I don't know what you've got against her.'

'I haven't got anything against her,' said Libby uncomfortably. 'She actually seems quite nice.'

Fran snorted, and Rosie came out carrying a tray with teapot, milk jug and mugs.

'I've got sugar if you want it, and I've put my sweeteners on there,' she said. 'We'll just wait for it to draw.'

'I do like tea from a teapot,' said Libby. 'I'm fighting a rearguard action against teabags in mugs.'

'I so agree,' said Rosie, and Libby suddenly knew what people meant when they said somebody "twinkled". 'Mind you, it's handy on occasions, when you haven't got much time.'

'So, what's the mystery?' asked Fran, leaning forward with her arms on the table.

'Straight to the point, eh, Fran?' Rosie laughed. 'Reminds me of my writing advice "get straight into the story". Don't fanny around with the back story.'

'But that's what we want to know, isn't it?' said Libby. 'The back story?'

Rosie leant forward and picked up the teapot. 'Of course it is. I'll just pour this out and then we can get on with it.'

When they all had their cups, Rosie leant back in her chair and looked at Libby.

'Not that I didn't want to meet you anyway,' she said, 'having read about you in the newspaper and knowing you were a friend of Fran's.' She took a sip of tea. 'But it did seem to be a heaven sent opportunity.'

Libby looked across at Fran and raised her eyebrows. Fran shook her head.

'An opportunity for what?' she prompted.

'Well.' Rosie sighed. 'There's this house, you see. I know where it is, and I know it's been boarded up. But I need to find out more about it.'

'For a book?' asked Libby.

'No, although I suppose I might turn it into a book one day. No. You see, I dream about it, and it feels as though I lived there.' Rosie looked from Libby to Fran and made a face. 'Sounds mad, doesn't it?'

Fran shook her head. 'Not to me, it doesn't,' she said. 'You know about my experiences.' Fran was writing her account of how she came to be living in

Coastguard Cottage.

'That's what made me think of asking you.' Rosie turned to Libby and smiled. 'You know Fran's writing about Coastguard Cottage?'

Libby nodded, although she knew little about the creative writing classes Rosie taught and Fran attended.

'When we talked about it, she told me how you had stayed there as a child, too, and about the picture. She said you painted similar pictures.'

'Yes. She could have shown you a postcard. Her husband makes postcards of some of the paintings.' Libby glanced at Fran, who was looking at the cat.

'Oh, she has. I've now got several.' Rosie was twinkling again, and Libby warmed to her. 'Anyway,' she went on, 'it gave me the idea of trying to find out about the house and why I dream about it. I'm sure I've never been inside it.'

Libby frowned. 'But surely you must do research for the books you write? Couldn't you find out about it?'

'I could, but I think I might get sidetracked and start researching that instead of writing the next book. I don't suppose you've got any more free time than I have, but you might be less likely to let it take over your life.'

'I doubt that,' said Fran. 'You don't know Libby when she's got her teeth into something. Nothing else matters.'

'Oh, dear.' Rosie looked back at Libby. 'Perhaps I shouldn't be asking.'

Libby laughed. 'Fran's exaggerating,' she said. 'And she's as bad anyway.'

Fran smiled ruefully. ‘She’s right.’

‘So what do you think, then?’ said Rosie. ‘Would you like to look into it?’

Fran and Libby looked at each other and nodded.

‘Oh, I think so,’ said Libby. ‘After all, it’s not a murder or anything like that. It would be good to look into something just for interest’s sake.’

Rosie sighed. ‘Thank you.’ She looked down at the table and straightened a spoon. ‘It’s been bothering me slightly. There’s such a strange atmosphere about the dreams.’

‘Where is the house?’ asked Fran after a pause. ‘Is it local?’

Rosie looked up. ‘Oh, yes. Just on the outskirts of Cherry Ashton.’

Fran raised her eyebrows at Libby.

‘Towards the coast the other way from Nethergate,’ said Libby.

‘Near Creekmarsh?’

‘Further over than that. Quite lonely.’

Rosie nodded. ‘The house is on one of the lanes in from the main road. On its own.’

‘Has it got a name?’

‘White Lodge,’ said Rosie. ‘And I think it may once have been the lodge for a bigger house.’

‘Who lives there, now? Do you know?’ said Fran.

‘No one,’ said Rosie. ‘It’s boarded up.’

‘Oh.’ Libby looked at Fran. ‘It’ll be difficult to find anything out about it then, won’t it?’

‘We’ll find a way,’ said Fran. ‘You know we will.’

‘And you will let me know if you start incurring

any expenses, won't you?' said Rosie.

'I don't suppose we'll have any of those,' said Libby with a grin. 'But if we suddenly get a fine for trespassing, you can pay it.'

'Trespassing?' said Fran. 'Are we going to?'

'Well, we'll have to go and look at it, won't we? And up close. So I expect we'll trespass. Not inside, though. It'll be all locked up, and I've never been good at breaking and entering.'

Fran sighed and shook her head. 'See what I'm up against, Rosie?'

Rosie laughed. 'And why she's the perfect person to investigate. More tea?'

'Not for me, thanks,' said Libby. 'Could you just tell us about the dreams?'

'Yes.' Rosie leant back in her chair. 'I thought you'd want to know about those.'

'Well, that's why you want us to look into it,' said Fran. 'Where are you in the dream? Inside or out?'

'Both. Sometimes I'm in a garden – coming through a gate in a wall. It has a sort of old wooden lintel,' she frowned, 'which seems odd in an outdoor wall. And it's a bit overgrown. There are stones, there, a bit like grave stones.'

Fran looked at Libby. 'And where else?'

'Inside. There's one particular place which has very long windows but no furniture. Although I can hear a piano. And you know how it is in dreams, sometimes I just look round and the whole scene has changed to something else. There's a kitchen, but it seems to be upstairs and rather shabby. Sometimes it has a bath in the same room.' She shivered. 'And this atmosphere. Yet I feel almost certain it's – or it was – a happy place.'

'And you have some kind of connection to it?' said Fran.

Rosie nodded. 'It won't let me alone, you see. I seem to dream about it almost every night, and I can't shake it off during the day. That's why I need to find out, to lay it to rest.' She turned to Libby. 'And why I can't do it myself, or it would completely take me over. Do you see?'

'Yes.' Libby smiled. 'Don't worry. We'll find out. Won't we Fran?'

Chapter Two

'WHAT DID YOU THINK?'

'About Rosie or the quest?' Libby squeezed back into the passenger seat of Fran's tiny car.

'Both.' Fran started the car. 'You liked Rosie, didn't you?'

'Yes, OK, I liked Rosie. Have you read any of her books?'

'Of course I have. She's my writing tutor.'

'But you might not read her books. They might not be the sort you like.'

Fran shot a quick glance sideways at Libby. 'What's the problem, Lib? What are you getting at?'

'Nothing.' Libby fumbled for the seat belt catch. 'I just wondered. Would I like them?'

'As I've never seen you read a book, I have no idea what you like.'

'I read.' Libby was indignant.

'What, though? Magazines? Scripts?'

'Sometimes. I like home magazines. And scripts if I have to.'

'Books?'

'Some. You know I do. I like crime and romance –'

'Oh, not chick-lit?' Fran snorted.

'Don't be judgemental,' said Libby. 'Not all women's fiction is chick-lit, and not all chick-lit is badly written.'

'Oh.' Fran shot her friend another quick look in surprise. 'So you do read.'

'I lent Cy books last winter when he was holed up at Peter and Harry's. I have an eclectic range. And I love the mobile library.'

'I miss that,' said Fran. 'I have to go to the main library in Nethergate now.'

'Well, surely they've got a better selection than the mobile one,' said Libby.

'But the mobile one stops right outside Harry's caff,' said Fran.

Fran had lived briefly in Libby's home village of Steeple Martin, staying in the flat over The Pink Geranium, the vegetarian restaurant owned by their friends Harry and Peter. Harry was the chef, Peter a sleeping partner who occasionally helped out in extremis.

'Actually,' said Libby, 'the library comes tomorrow. I shall see if they have any of Rosie's books. Do you call her Rosie in class?'

'No,' said Fran. 'She's a tutor because she's Amanda George, so that's what she's called in class.'

'And is she good? As a tutor?'

'Oh, yes.' Fran smiled. 'Well, I think so, in that she's inspiring, but I've never been to a writing class before, so I don't know.'

'And is she weird?'

'What?'

'Well, dreams and asking us to find out about a house …'

'So I'm weird, now, am I?'

'Eh?' Libby turned to look at her friend. 'What do you mean?'

'That's exactly what I did,' said Fran. 'And you

helped me.'

'Oh. Yes.' Libby thought for a moment. 'And that's what you're writing about, isn't it?'

'Exactly. And at least we know where this house is, so we've got a starting place,' said Fran.

'Although why Rosie hasn't started research herself I can't understand,' said Libby. 'It's almost as if she's scared of it.'

'Oh, she is.'

'Definitely?' Libby turned to look at her friend again.

'Oh, yes. And that wasn't even one of my moments. It was coming off her in waves. Couldn't you feel it?'

'Not a thing,' said Libby. 'And even if it wasn't a moment, you pick up those sort of things when normal people don't.'

'So I'm back to being weird again,' said Fran.

Libby sighed.

Fran parked opposite Libby's cottage in Allhallow's Lane, just behind the increasingly decrepit Romeo the Renault in which Libby frightened the roads of Kent.

'More tea?' asked Libby.

'Why not?' Fran got out of the car and locked it.

Sidney the silver tabby sat in the window to the left of the front door and watched their approach before disappearing as Libby put the key in the lock, and shot between their feet as she opened it.

'That cat'll be the death of me,' said Libby, leading the way through to the kitchen, where she filled the electric kettle.

'Does he trip you up on the stairs?' Fran leant

against the table.

'Of course. You know how he waits on the third step up.' She set two mugs beside the kettle. 'Go and get my laptop and we'll see if we can look up White Lodge, shall we?'

Fran obediently fetched the laptop, sat down at the table and opened it.

'Shall I just put White Lodge, Cherry Ashton into the search engine?' she asked.

'See if anything comes up.' Libby poured water into the mugs.

Fran pressed some keys and sat back with a laugh. 'Well!' she said. 'You'll never guess what.'

'What?' Libby put a mug down beside her, and leant over her shoulder.

'It's for sale. Look.' She clicked through links and came up with an estate agent's website. 'Oh, no, it's not. It must have been removed.'

'Go back to the original link,' said Libby. 'See what the date is.'

The original link turned out to be the estate agent's description of the property when it was registered a year previously.

'Seven bedrooms,' read Libby, 'fab. No pictures.'

'Cellars, walled garden – and look – there's a barn.'

'Rosie said it was boarded up. She must have been to see it,' said Libby. 'Do you think she saw it and then it triggered off the dreams? Or she dreamed it and went to find it?'

'If she dreamed it first she wouldn't know where it was.'

'No, but perhaps she just stumbled across it?'

Fran looked up. 'Why didn't we ask any of these questions when we were with her? They seem so obvious now.'

Libby shrugged. 'Surprised, I suppose, and keen to get on with another mystery. Didn't she give you any indication of what she wanted to ask us?'

'No.' Fran shook her head. 'I though it must be to ask us about one of our cases –'

'Cases!'

'Investigations, adventures, what you like. I thought it would be that, to use in a book.'

'I wonder who bought it?' Libby turned the laptop to face her. 'And how long ago Rosie saw it? It sounds as though it was recently.'

'Perhaps it wouldn't sell, so they took it off the market.'

'Complicated isn't it?' Libby clicked back to the search engine. 'Let's see if there's anything else about it.'

There were, in fact, several references to White Lodge, but only in passing, and many of them turned out to be nothing to do with the house at all, until Fran clicked on a reference to Cherry Ashton workhouse.

'Look!' she pushed the laptop back towards Libby. 'It was part of a workhouse!'

'Blimey.' Libby peered at the page. 'Demolished in – what? 1909? Why is the house still there?'

'I should think it was the – oh, I don't know – warden's house? Too good to demolish?'

'Let's look up the workhouse,' said Libby.

It wasn't until Ben appeared in the kitchen over

an hour later that Fran realised what the time was.

'Guy will think I've left home,' she said standing up and giving her friend's partner a quick kiss. Libby went to see her off.

'So what have you been doing?' Ben was looking at the computer screen.

'Fascinating, actually,' said Libby, 'and I haven't even thought about dinner.'

Ben leant back against the sink and folded his arms. 'I sense a mystery.'

'Well,' said Libby, looking guilty, 'it is sort of.'

'It must be at least six months since you've been involved in something, so I suppose I shouldn't be surprised. Tell all.'

Libby smiled in relief. 'OK. How long is it since we ate in the caff?'

'About a week.' Ben grinned. 'And now we might as well take out a season ticket. We end up eating there every other night when you're sleuthing.'

'It's not normal sleuthing,' said Libby. 'Come on, let's have a drink and I'll tell you all about it. But first give Harry a ring.'

Over glasses of red wine, Libby filled Ben in on the afternoon's activities. 'And then,' she finished up, 'we started looking into the Cherry Ashton Workhouse.'

'And what did you find?'

'Nothing really. It was there, set up by the Poor Board or something, and there were elected Guardians. So we had a look at workhouses in general. There were some horrible stories, Huddersfield, Andover and Fareham, but no mention of Cherry Ashton. We did wonder, though, because it said in one of the general descriptions that the Master and Matron had apartments in the building. White Lodge is a separate building and it states that the workhouse was demolished 1909.'

'Perhaps the workhouse was built round it. On land that belonged to it?'

'Oh, I suppose that could be it. But from what Rosie said and the estate agent's description it sounded a bit grand for a Master's lodging.'

'Well, tomorrow you could call the agents and ask if it's likely to come on the market again, or if they know anything about who bought it.'

'Oh, so we could.' Libby brightened. 'And we could drive over and see if we can find it. I said we'd look round.'

'Be careful,' warned Ben. 'Don't go getting yourself into trouble.'

'As if I would,' said Libby. Ben sighed.

Later in The Pink Geranium, Donna the waitress brought over the menu.

'No Adam tonight?' asked Libby.

'No, we're not busy,' said Donna, 'and he's been working hard over at Creekmarsh. Shall I see if he's in?'

Libby's son Adam lived in the flat over the restaurant, where once Fran had stayed, and occasionally helped out if Harry was very busy. His proper job was as an assistant to a landscape designer who was currently working on restoring the grounds of a local mansion owned by television personality Lewis Osbourne-Walker.

'No, don't worry, Donna.' Libby suddenly put

out her hand to Donna. 'Is that a ring?'

Donna, unflappable, organised and efficient, blushed. 'Yes.'

'Your doctor?' asked Libby. 'Oh, congratulations!' She stood up to hug Donna to the imminent danger of the table.

'What's all this?' said a voice, and Harry appeared, grinning, over Donna's shoulder. 'Destroying my restaurant?'

Ben stood to kiss Donna, too. 'You know what our Libby's like,' he said, sitting down again. 'Hello, Hal. Is Donna allowed champagne on duty?'

'Oh, no,' said Donna, flustered. 'Thank you, but I've got to drive to Canterbury when I've finished.' She coloured faintly again. 'But thank you, all the same.'

'Her chap's a doctor at the hospital, isn't he?' said Libby, after Donna had gone to fetch a bottle of red wine.

'Yes. Nice bloke, but very unsociable hours,' said Harry, sitting down astride a chair. 'Just hope she's not going to start breeding and leave me.'

'Harry!' Libby slapped his arm. He grinned.

'So, to what do I owe the pleasure?'

'Libby forgot to do dinner,' said Ben.

'You could have done it,' said Harry, with a lifted eyebrow.

'I know, I know, but she suggested we came here.' Ben made a face at his beloved.

'Oh, no, you aren't?' Harry peered at Libby's face. 'Not another investigation?'

'I don't know why you should think that,' said Libby huffily. 'We eat here all the time.'

'There's something about the way Ben said you forgot to do dinner,' said Harry. 'Come on. What's it all about?'

Libby relented and explained.

'So you see, it isn't a proper investigation. It's just to find out something about the house.'

'Well, it'll keep you out of mischief,' said Harry, standing up. 'I shall now go back to my arduous duties in the kitchen.'

Adam appeared just as they were finishing their meal.

'Hi, Ma,' he said, kissing her cheek. 'Hi, Ben.'

'Hello, darling.' Libby peered round his shoulder. 'Hello Sophie.'

Fran's step-daughter Sophie squeezed past Adam to kiss Libby.

'Hi, Lib. Sorry I've been keeping him out till all hours again!'

'Shocking. Why it's almost ten o'clock,' grinned Libby. 'Will you have a drink with us?'

'Yes, please,' said Adam. 'I'll go. Red wine? Sophie?'

When they were all settled with fresh drinks, Adam tackled his mother.

'What's all this Harry's telling me about a new investigation?'

'Oh, for f – goodness' sake,' said Libby. 'Hasn't anybody got anything better to do than poke their noses into my business?'

Adam and Ben roared with laughter.

'That's rich, coming from you,' said Ben, wiping his eyes.

'Look, once and for all, it's simply to find out

about a house for Fran's writing tutor. She hasn't got time herself and knowing Fran's – um – intuition – thought she'd be the ideal person to look into it.'

'With you,' said Adam.

'Of course with me. She couldn't do it without me.' Libby slid a quick glance at Sophie and saw her grinning.

'So there we are. That's it and all about it. So now shut up and, Ad, tell me about Creekmarsh.'

Chapter Three

THE FOLLOWING DAY, LIBBY called the agent on whose books White Lodge had been.

'That monstrosity,' he said. 'Sorry, I hope it's nothing to do with you, but I've never handled a property that was so difficult.'

'Oh.' Libby sat back in her chair, surprised. 'Really? It looked rather a grand place.'

'Have you seen it?'

'Well – no, not actually seen,' said Libby.

'You're welcome to go and look at it if you like,' said the agent, surprisingly. 'We've still got the keys, but I'll have to trust you to go on your own. I can't spare anyone to go with you, and frankly, even if I could, no one would.'

'Really?' Libby's metaphorical ears pricked up. This seemed to confirm Rosie's dream impressions. 'Why? Is it haunted?'

There was a short silence. 'I daresay it's nothing,' the agent said eventually, sounding uncomfortable, 'but do you know exactly where it is?'

'Ah!' said Libby. 'Do you mean the Cherry Ashton workhouse?'

'Yes.' The agent sounded relieved. 'It was the atmosphere, you see. We took a few prospective purchasers to see it, but no one would go in to the attic rooms. Most didn't even get as far as the kitchen.'

'I see.' Libby thought for a moment. 'I would

like to see it, if possible, and if it's all right with you. What about the vendor? Somebody still owns it, don't they?'

'It's a probate sale,' said the agent, 'and very complicated.'

'Who was the owner?' asked Libby.

The agent became wary. 'I'm not sure I can tell you anything else,' he said.

'No, no, of course not,' said Libby hastily.

'And could I ask you what your interest is in the property?'

'A friend remembered it and asked if it was still on the market,' lied Libby. 'She seemed to think it was boarded up.'

'It is, I'm afraid,' said the agent. 'Will she be coming to see it herself?'

'Oh, yes,' Libby lied again.

'Well, you can pick up the keys any time from the office. You'll have to sign a receipt and probably leave a deposit – because of squatters, you know.'

'Oh, yes, of course,' said Libby, wondering how usual it was for estate agents to let viewers go unaccompanied to empty houses.

'So,' she said later to Fran on the phone, 'we can go any time. Today?'

'You were going to go to the library, and I was going to pop in and see Jane this afternoon,' said Fran. 'She's finished work now.'

'Oh, yes, I'd forgotten,' said Libby. 'She's almost due, isn't she?'

'A week or so, I think. Look why don't you come, too? She's as bored as hell and very uncomfortable.'

'OK, and perhaps we can go and see White Lodge tomorrow.'

'Tomorrow's Saturday,' said Fran, 'and I shall be helping in the shop. Guy's busiest time, a summer Saturday. I might even sell one of your pretty peeps.'

'Oh, right. Monday, then, I suppose. Shall I ring the agent and make an appointment?'

There was a short silence. Then, 'No,' said Fran slowly. 'Don't do that.'

'Why? What's the matter?'

'I don't know,' said Fran. 'But he did say any time?'

'Yes.'

'Can you go and pick them up on your way to Nethergate this afternoon?'

'The agent's *in* Nethergate,' said Libby.

'Riley's?' asked Fran.

'Yes.'

'Then I'll pick them up on the way to Jane's.'

Libby explained about the receipt and the deposit, 'So I'd better go,' she finished.

'Park here,' said Fran, 'and we'll go together. I can be the friend who wants to view.'

'Brilliant.' Libby beamed. 'What time shall I be there?'

'Why did you not want me to make an appointment?' Libby asked, as Fran pulled her front door closed behind her.

Fran shook her head. 'Something –'

'Something what? Did you have a "moment"?

'I don't know. I just felt that if you made an appointment something would happen to prevent you keeping it.'

'Prevent me?'

'Well, prevent it from happening.'

'But why?'

'I've told you,' said Fran, irritated. 'I don't know. Did you go to the library?'

'Yes. They had two of Rosie's books.'

They walked along Harbour Street next to the low sea wall, the other side of which families played with buckets and spades, balls and frisbees as though the words "computer games" had never been invented. They waved at Lizzie in her tiny ice-cream shop and at Sophie rearranging items in her father's shop window.

'She was with Adam last night,' said Libby.

'Yes, I know,' said Fran. 'I didn't think it would last with her being away at uni.'

'It's survived over a year despite that,' said Libby. 'Are we founding a dynasty?'

'They're much too young,' said Fran firmly. 'Come on, Riley's is up the high street.'

The high street climbed sharply away from the square where the venerable Swan Inn stood. A little way up on the right-hand side, Riley's presented a bland front to the tourists and shoppers. A young man in his shirtsleeves looked up from a desk when they came in.

'Hello, my name's Sarjeant,' said Libby. 'I rang earlier.'

'Oh, right.' The young man opened a drawer and took out a set of keys attached to a large brown luggage label. 'If I could just ask you to sign here.' He pushed an open ledger towards her and indicated a space next to the printed name "Mrs Sergeant". Libby altered it and signed.

'And here,' he said proffering a piece of paper, 'and I'm awfully sorry, but I'll have to ask for a £50 deposit on the key.'

Libby produced her credit card. The piece of paper was offered as her receipt for the deposit and he handed over the keys.

'Do you know where it is?' he asked. 'Oh, you said your friend had seen it, didn't you?' He nodded towards Fran, and they both smiled.

'He didn't even ask if you were the friend,' said Libby, as they made their escape down the hill and turned right up towards Cliff Terrace and Peel House.

'It was a reasonable assumption for him to make,' said Fran.

'So when are we going to see it?'

'We could go after we've been to Jane's, unless you've got to get back early,' said Fran.

Libby's eyebrows rose. 'You're keen all of a sudden.'

'I just feel we should go as quickly as possible.'

'Before something stops us?'

'I think so,' said Fran awkwardly. 'I know it's silly.'

'What would stop us? Not the ghosts!'

'No – I don't know.' Fran looked up at the front of Jane's attractive terraced house. 'Come on. I hope they've moved down on to a lower level now. She won't want to be hauling a pram up to the top of the house.'

'She won't want to be hauling herself up to the top of the house,' said Libby, climbing the steps to the front door, 'let alone a baby and a pram.'

Jane Baker answered the door quickly and beamed. 'I'm so pleased to see you both,' she said, stepping aside for them to squeeze past her large bump.

'Oh, you've moved back down here,' said Fran, as they went into the large room on the left of the hall. For some time the sitting room had been on the top floor of the house.

'Well, the kitchen's here, and the bedroom's only one floor up,' said Jane, 'and I couldn't face the climb to the top!'

'We were saying that just now,' said Libby, going to the window, 'and you've still got a lovely view.'

Libby and Fran had met Jane Maurice, as she was then, two years previously. She had subsequently married her tenant, Terry, and credited Libby with getting them together. Libby didn't mind. It meant Jane, in her position as chief reporter and deputy editor of the *Nethergate Mercury*, could occasionally be useful if Libby wanted information about practically anything. Also, Terry, her husband, was large, silent and mechanically gifted, not to mention having a sister who was an accomplished singer, songwriter and pianist and useful person to know.

'So how are you?' asked Fran, following Jane into the kitchen. 'Apart from bored?'

'Oh, you know. Tired, uncomfortable and my

feet swell.' Jane indicated the mugs set out on the table. 'Tea or coffee? Instant coffee, I'm afraid.'

'Tea for me,' said Fran.

'And me,' said Libby. 'No, don't bother with biscuits.'

They carried their mugs into the sitting room and Jane lowered herself thankfully into a corner of a sofa and swung her feet up. 'You don't mind, do you?' she said waving a hand at the feet.

'Why should we mind? I remember what it was like trying to get comfortable at this stage of pregnancy. Night times were the worst,' said Libby.

'Dreadful,' agreed Jane. 'I get hardly any sleep.'

'I think it's nature's way of preparing for the sleepless nights to come,' said Libby.

'Is nature that cruel?' asked Fran.

'Of course. Red in tooth and claw,' said Libby. 'It's also why old people get grumpy and grouchy and unpleasant, so their children won't miss them as much when they die.'

Jane let out a peal of laughter. 'They'll be glad to get rid of them instead?'

Libby, pleased with this evidence of understanding, nodded happily.

'I don't know, Libby,' sighed Fran. 'You have the strangest outlook on life sometimes.'

'Anyway, speaking of children and parents,' Libby went on, ignoring the interruption, 'how's yours?'

'My mother?' Jane wrinkled her nose. 'Well, she's here. You knew that.'

'She took some persuading, didn't she?' said Fran.

'A lot. Partly because she was unhappy about Aunt Jessica leaving me Peel House and she didn't want to live in it.'

'She overcame her scruples, though, didn't she?' said Libby. 'Once she realised she wouldn't have to pay any rent, rates or services for the flat.' Libby, having met Mrs Maurice more than once, was disinclined to attribute any of the nicer qualities to her.

Jane looked uncomfortable. 'Well, yes. And she did say she'd be able to help with the baby.'

'Really? Will she look after it if you go back to work?' asked Fran.

'No, I wouldn't expect her to,' said Jane, 'and anyway, I'm going to work from home. I'll only need to actually go out now and then. And while the baby's young I can take him or her with me.'

'Don't know what it is, then?' said Libby.

'No, neither of us wanted to,' said Jane. 'So tell me what you've both been up to.'

Fran reported on her recent trip to France with Guy, Sophie and Adam.

'And what about your Chrissie?' asked Jane. 'She's pregnant, too, isn't she?'

'She's being an absolute monster,' said Fran. 'I almost feel sorry for Brucie-baby. She just lays about on the sofa and doesn't do anything, as far as I can make out.'

'Well, she hasn't gone out to work for years, has she?' said Libby.

'No, but at least she did the washing and cooking and kept the house clean,' said Fran. 'Now she won't even do that. And she's only four months.'

'What about Cassandra?'

'Oh, the cat's the only one who understands her, apparently.' Fran snorted. 'It spreads itself across her on the sofa and refuses to move.'

'It's going to be severely upset when the baby arrives,' said Libby.

'I told her that when she said she wanted a baby,' said Fran, 'but there, she's never taken any notice of me.'

'What does Lucy say about her?' asked Libby, referring to Fran's other daughter, already mother to Rachel and Tom.

'Scathing, as you can imagine. Actually, *she's* stopped being such a pain towards me now. So much so that I'm letting her come down for a week with the children.'

'Where's Guy going?'

Fran looked surprised. 'He's staying here, of course. He doesn't mind them half as much as I do, and, I must admit, it's much easier with a grandma *and* a grandpa. They don't wear me out so much.'

'That's another reason I don't want Mum to have to look after my baby too much,' said Jane. 'She's on her own.'

'But at least she's on the premises,' said Libby, 'and she doesn't work.'

'But she's got her own life,' said Jane. 'She's actually made some friends down here. She joined some club at the library and now she seems to be out all the time.'

'Perhaps she's found a new man?' said Libby with glee.

'Mum? Don't be daft!' Jane laughed. 'Anyway,

what about you? What have you been doing?'

Without hesitation Libby launched into a description of the past two days' activities.

'Amanda George? She's your writing tutor?' Jane turned to Fran. 'Do you think she'd agree to do an interview with me for the paper? Or for our colour mag?'

'I didn't know you had a colour mag,' said Libby. 'How posh.'

'It's only monthly and goes across the whole group.'

'I'm sure she would. All authors love a bit of free publicity,' said Fran. 'Shall I ask her?'

'Yes, please,' said Jane. 'Give her my email address, would you? And do you suppose she'd let me use your investigation in the piece, too? It would be terrific local interest.'

'I don't think so,' said Fran. 'In fact, if you do speak to her, don't mention that we've told you anything about it. We don't know what's behind it, yet.'

'No, I suppose so,' said Jane, 'but Cherry Ashton is a very emotive subject locally.'

'Because of the workhouse?' said Libby.

'Well, yes.' Jane nodded and turned to look out of the window. 'And the children.'

Chapter Four

LIBBY AND FRAN LOOKED at each other.

'The children?' echoed Libby.

Jane turned back. 'Didn't you know about the children?' she said. They both shook their heads. 'It's not very nice. Didn't you look it up on the internet?'

'Of course,' said Libby. 'That's how we knew White Lodge was – or had been – part of the workhouse.'

Jane shook her head. 'I can't believe it didn't come up anywhere. Even I knew about it, and I didn't come here to live until three years ago.'

'But you work in the meeja. You get to hear things.'

'You used to stay with your aunt, didn't you?' asked Fran. 'Did you hear about it then?'

'No. I can't actually remember when I first heard about it, but it comes up periodically in the office.'

'So what is it, then?' said Libby.

'You don't have to tell us,' said Fran quickly, noticing the look on Jane's face. 'I'm sure we can find out some other way.'

Libby looked puzzled and Fran made a face at her. 'We can ask Campbell, can't we?'

Jane's expression relaxed. 'That's a good idea. He'll know.'

An hour later, after much conversation about the coming baby and viewing of the cot, Terry came home and Libby and Fran left.

‘So tell me what that was all about?’ Libby stomped off down Cliff Terrace.

‘Oh, Lib.’ Fran sighed. ‘You saw her face. Whatever it is, it’s about children – buried there, I would guess. And Jane’s hormones are all over the place. She was getting really distressed.’

‘Oh.’ Libby scowled at her feet. ‘Sorry. Yes.’

‘I don’t think you’re really insensitive,’ said Fran, laying a hand on her arm, ‘just a bit thoughtless sometimes.’

‘I know.’ Libby glared at the beach. ‘Bull –’

‘In a china shop,’ Fran finished for her. ‘Not quite. Just a mind above other things.’

‘That’s a laugh. My mind is very firmly rooted in the everyday mire.’ Libby turned to her friend. ‘But nice of you to try and make me feel better. Now, are we going to call Campbell McLean?’

The local television news reporter had helped Fran and Libby in the past and never seemed to mind their occasional pleas for help.

‘I’ll ring the office,’ said Fran, fishing out her mobile. ‘We don’t want to disturb him in the middle of a broadcast.’

Kent and Coast Television promised to get a message to Campbell as soon as they could, but warned that as he was out recording a piece about bulls for the evening bulletin it might be some time.

‘Do you think he’s having to get up close and personal with some hulking great beast?’ asked Libby, as they arrived at Coastguard Cottage.

‘Remember him at that farm we went to looking for illegal immigrants?’

Libby laughed. ‘He hated that, didn’t he?’

'He got a good item out of it, though,' said Fran. 'Come on, if we're going now. You can drop me back here, can't you? It's on your way?'

'Oh, are we still going? I thought you might want to wait to talk to Campbell.' Libby fished in her basket for Romeo's keys.

'Not chickening out, are you?' Fran waited for Libby to unlock the passenger door, and climbed in.

'Course not.' Libby started the engine. 'Now, as far as I remember, we drive right past Creekmarsh towards the saltings.'

'But we don't know if it's on the main road, do we?' said Fran.

'There aren't many roads in Cherry Ashton. We'll find it.'

The road followed the river past Lewis Osbourne-Walker's house Creekmarsh, then turned inland on to the windswept saltings.

'There,' said Libby, pointing at a spire above a slight rise. 'That must be Cherry Ashton.'

'Is this the only road in?'

'Don't know. Look, that's it, I bet you.'

Ahead of them, against a sky darkening with rain clouds, stood a house. A solitary tree stood opposite on the other side of the road, but that was all. Libby stopped the car.

There was complete silence. The house, part half-timbered and part tile-hung, felt dead, its windows, as Rosie had said, boarded up. A tall wall ran along the front.

'Come on then,' said Libby, after a moment. 'This is what we've come to see.'

Fran followed her across the road, and through

the archway in the wall.

'It doesn't feel right,' she said.

'As though we're trespassing, you mean?' said Libby. 'Yes, I feel a bit like that, too. But we're not. Look.' She waggled the keys before going up to the front door and peering at the locks.

'No, I didn't mean that,' said Fran. 'There's something not right about this place.'

Libby swung the door wide. 'Fine time to have one of your moments,' she said, and stepped inside.

'Exactly the right time, I'd have thought,' said Fran. 'I'm not sure I can go inside.'

Libby turned round. 'You don't have to. I'll look round on my own, if you like.'

Fran took a deep breath. 'No, I'll come.' She stepped gingerly forward and shivered.

The hall was long, wide and very dark. Past the sweeping curve of the staircase could be seen a little light, which Libby soon discovered to be a door into the back garden.

'Well, they didn't board this up,' she said, rattling the door handle. 'I wonder if one of my keys opens it?'

'Shouldn't we finish looking round inside first?' said Fran. 'If I go outside I won't want to come in again.'

'That bad, huh?' Libby cocked her head on one side. 'What's the feeling exactly?'

'I'm just spooked.' Fran looked round. 'It feels as though something's here.'

Libby frowned. 'Don't say that.'

'Sorry.' Fran moved back down the hall and made for a pair of double doors. 'This is the room with the long windows and a piano.'

Libby raised her eyebrows but said nothing as Fran opened the doors.

The boards over the windows had not been fixed particularly well, and there was enough light to see that the room indeed matched Rosie's description, including, in the corner, a baby grand piano.

'Nothing else,' said Fran. 'Let's find the kitchen with a bath in it.'

'That would have just been Rosie's dream making things up,' said Libby.

'Well, it didn't make this up, did it?' said Fran, and led the way up the stairs. The higher they got, the colder Libby felt.

Some of the windows at the back of the house hadn't been boarded up. The very modern tiled bathroom and a large room next to it were as bright as the general oppressiveness would allow, but Libby's legs still felt as though she was teetering on the edge of a very high cliff.

'You're right, you know,' she said, as Fran opened another door into a pitch dark room, 'it is very nasty here. Shall we go?'

Fran stopped so suddenly Libby bumped into her. 'What?'

'Look.' Fran stepped aside and Libby peered round her.

Inside the room, which was long and narrow, she could just make out a large roll topped bath with claw feet, and on the other side of the room a deep porcelain kitchen sink. Fran pulled the door shut with a bang.

'That's it,' she said. 'Come on. This is weird.'

As fast as they could in the semi-darkness, they went down the staircase and out of the front door. Libby let out a breath she didn't know she'd been holding.

'Now we'll go round to the back,' said Fran. 'Find the door we were going to go out of.'

Libby led the way round the right side of the house through an unkempt garden, in which brambles snaked across a path with a vicious tendency to nip at uncovered legs. Libby's jeans did better than Fran's skirt.

'Oh, my God.' Fran stopped dead as they rounded the corner to the back of the house. In front of them a rotting wooden door, with a wooden lintel above it, was set into a tall wall of what looked like very old stone.

'You know,' said Libby, 'Rosie must have been here. This is exactly what she described. The room with the piano, the bath in the upstairs kitchen and now this. There's no other way she would have known. She isn't psychic. That's why she wanted you.'

Fran turned slowly. 'You're right. Even I can't conjure up this amount of detail without some prior knowledge.'

'So why was she here, and why doesn't she remember? And come to think of it, it must have been since the house was empty, because that's how she described it. And that can't have been long ago.'

'No. A year, the agent said, didn't he? And it's a probate sale. So it could actually have been empty for a lot longer if the owner was in a home, or something.'

'And supposing it had been left to someone before then, maybe years before, and they never lived in it. He did say a *complicated* probate sale.'

Fran looked up at the wooden lintel above the door. 'This looks even older than the house.' She gave the door a tentative push. It moved a little way and stuck. 'Come on, there's enough room for us to squeeze through.'

The garden they squeezed into was as overgrown as the one at the side. To their left, in the middle of the back wall of the house, they saw the door into the passage and, further along, the long windows of the room with the piano. To their immediate left, two more boarded-up windows.

'Stones, look.' Libby pointed.

Half-hidden by undergrowth and brambles, stones leant at awkward angles, mostly against the further wall of the garden, but a few lying in the middle.

'Gravestones.' Fran closed her eyes. 'The children.'

'Workhouse children?'

Fran shook her head. 'I don't think so.' She opened her eyes and looked at Libby. 'Jane didn't seem to be referring to children in relation to the workhouse, did she? No, it's something else.'

'More recent?'

'Not by the look of the gravestones.' Fran moved forward and tried to clear the nearest. 'Look, there's nothing on it. Not even a faint mark.'

'How do we know they're gravestones, then?'

'The shape, for a start, although some of them just look like boulders, don't they? I just know they are.'

Libby looked round the garden. 'I wonder how long it took for it to get this overgrown?'

'Not long,' said Fran, moving to another of the stones. 'But the stones have been here for a long time.'

'Not that long.' Libby's voice was muffled. 'Look over here.'

Fran joined her standing over a cleared patch of stubbly grass.

'This has been cleared quite recently.' Libby bent and dug a finger at the ground. 'Although not *that* recently. It almost looks as though it's been dug over.'

Fran looked up suddenly. 'Listen.'

'What?' Libby glanced warily over her shoulder.

'That music.' Fran looked back at Libby. 'Piano music.'

'I can't hear anything.' Libby frowned. 'It's just you.'

'No, no, listen. Clear as anything.' Fran moved back towards the house.

'Oh, God.' Libby backed away towards the gate. 'I *can* hear it. There's someone in there playing the piano.'

Fran walked cautiously towards the long window and peered round the edge. Then she looked back at Libby.

'No,' she said. 'There isn't.'

Chapter Five

THEY STARED AT EACH other.

'That's it,' said Libby. 'We're getting out.' She turned, squeezed through the gate and almost ran down the side of the house. Fran followed more slowly, thoughtfully rubbing at the scratches on her bare legs.

'That was no ghost,' she said, as she caught Libby up at the car. 'That was real music. Someone knew we were there.'

'All the more reason to get out quick,' said Libby, turning the key in the ignition.

'It was to scare us off,' said Fran, peering over her shoulder at White Lodge as Libby turned the car round. 'I wonder if that's what scared off prospective purchasers? Not to mention the estate agents.'

'Surely he'd have mentioned it?'

'Not necessarily. Remember he was almost eager for us to see it. He wants to get rid of it, and if he really thought we were *bona fide* viewers he wouldn't tell us anything to put us off.'

'But he did. He told me on the phone it was a monstrosity and about people being spooked. Why not tell us about the piano as well?'

'Perhaps he thought it would be over-egging the pudding?'

'Maybe. But it's odd. In fact, it's more than bloody odd,' said Libby, 'it's terrifying. If that disturbed part of the garden is a recent grave it isn't a legal one.'

'Murder.' Fran stared at her friend.

'Oh, bloody hell, not again,' said Libby.

They took the keys back to Riley's, which was just about to close. A young woman took Libby's credit card and refunded the deposit.

'Have a nice day,' she said, as she locked the door behind them.

Fran and Libby looked at each other in surprise.

'She didn't ask us anything about it,' said Libby. 'Why not?'

'They're obviously used to people not wanting the place after they've seen it. It must be a regular thing for them to let viewers go on their own.'

'But not recently. It doesn't come up on their website, remember. They're hardly advertising it.' Libby looked thoughtful as they turned back down the high street. 'And you'd have thought they would be pushing it to get rid of it. I wonder if they've told the police?'

'If they've heard the piano music, they should have done.'

'No, I meant about the grave.'

'If no one's been to view they wouldn't know. It hasn't been there long.'

'Well, do we tell the police, then?'

'Would they listen?' Fran looked dubious.

'Ian might.'

'Oh, poor Ian.' Fran laughed. 'We can't do it to him again.'

'He's our pet policeman,' said Libby. 'We can just ask him a question.'

'He isn't our pet policeman. He's a friend.'

'Poor bugger. But he was – and still is – a policeman first. He only became a friend because he fancied you.'

'Well, yes, I suppose so. But he wouldn't be able to do anything. I would imagine White Lodge is out of his jurisdiction. He's still working out of Nethergate.'

'We could just ask him a question, as I said. Hypothetically.'

'And he would immediately ask why we wanted to know.'

'I don't care. I'll ask him if you won't.' They stopped outside Coastguard Cottage. 'I'll ring him tonight. Better if I do it, anyway. Then Guy won't be jealous.'

'Don't be daft,' said Fran. 'Guy never gets jealous.'

'Hmm.' Libby unlocked the car. 'Well, anyway. I'll ring you later and tell you what he says.'

It occurred to Libby that she ought to ring Ben, having been far longer than she had expected that afternoon.

'It's all right,' he sighed. 'I guessed you were out on the trail with Fran. Find anything?'

'Well, sort of,' said Libby. 'I'll tell you when I get back. And,' she added as an afterthought, 'get your advice.'

She arrived back at Allhallow's Lane to find Ben preparing his signature stir fry, a glass of red wine already poured for her.

'Rice is on,' he said, 'so come and sit down and tell me all about it.'

So Libby told him. 'And what I want to know,' she finished, 'is should I phone Ian to tell him?'

Ben frowned. 'If you heard that music then it isn't, as Fran said, anything paranormal. So someone's there. And if that is a grave, then you must tell the police.'

'Fran thought they wouldn't listen to us.'

'That's why you wanted to tell Ian.' Ben nodded. 'I think you should.'

Libby sighed and drained her glass. 'I'll do it after dinner, then.'

An hour later, she rang Detective Inspector Connell's mobile number.

'Libby? Is this a nice surprise or a nasty one?'

'I'm sorry, Ian. Am I disturbing you in the middle of something important?' asked Libby as sweetly as she could.

'Only the first night off I've had to myself.'

'Oh.' Libby was genuinely regretful. 'In that case, I really am sorry.'

'That means you weren't before. Come on, what is it? You only call me when you want something.'

Guiltily, Libby acknowledged this. 'But honestly, Ian, I really think I ought to tell you, and so does Ben.'

Ian's voice sharpened. 'Ben does? All right, what is it?'

Libby outlined the facts as succinctly as she was able. 'And we don't *know* that it was a grave, just that it had been cleared comparatively recently.'

'And that was the only patch like that?'

'I'm afraid we didn't look any further. We were spooked by the piano music.'

Ian was silent for a moment. 'And you're sure it was real? And no one was playing the piano?'

'Yes.'

'Then it was probably one of the only sensible things you've done. Someone was trying to scare you off the place.'

'So will you look into it?'

Ian sighed. 'I suppose I'll have to, although strictly speaking we haven't much to go on. If I take it to the Chief he might not want to waste any time on it.'

'Really? When it might be a murder?'

'I might have to do a bit of snooping around on my own.'

'Snooping? Oh, we're good at that!' said Libby.

'I know you are, but you stay out of it until I say so. Why were you there in the first place, anyway?'

Libby told him about Rosie and the dreams.

'Then she needs to be questioned. You said even Fran thought she must have been there in the fairly recent past.'

'But why would she want Fran to investigate? Or me, for that matter?'

'I don't know. Perhaps you should go back and ask her. Meanwhile, I'll bring it up with the Chief and see what he says. I'll get back to you.'

'Well, that's that,' said Libby, switching off the phone. 'I suppose Fran and I should go back to Rosie.'

'Perhaps not until Monday?' suggested Ben. 'Then we could have a nice relaxing weekend.'

'We always have nice relaxing weekends,' said Libby. 'Except that, if you remember, we invited your mum and dad to Sunday lunch here for a change.'

Libby and Ben usually went up to the Manor for one of Ben's mother Hetty's legendary Sunday lunches, sometimes with Peter, who was Ben's cousin and Hetty's and Greg's nephew, Harry, of course, sometimes Peter's younger brother James and very occasionally Adam. However, on summer Sundays Harry kept The Pink Geranium open, so neither he, Adam nor Peter would be there and James was somewhere in Europe with his latest girlfriend.

'Why won't that be relaxing?' asked Ben.

'Because I'll have to cook and I shall be nervous in front of Hetty. She's the gold medal winner of Sunday roasts and I'm certain I won't do it properly.'

'Then cook something else. It doesn't have to be a roast.'

'They'll think it's sacrilege,' said Libby.

'No, they won't. Tell you what – compromise and do that lamb shanks thing you did for Fran and Guy. That's a roast in a way.'

Libby brightened. 'Oh, good idea. And I can do dauphinoise spuds and – what veg have you got in the Manor garden?'

'I'll have a look tomorrow,' said Ben. 'And now, phone Fran and tell her what Ian's said and then come and watch television.'

Fran agreed they should go back and talk to Rosie and volunteered to ring her the following morning.

'We'll have to leave it to her to suggest the time.

She's very busy.'

'I thought your creative writing classes had finished for the summer?'

'She does write books, Lib, she doesn't just teach.'

'Oh, yes. OK, I'll leave you to make the arrangements.'

'Oh, and let me know if you hear from Ian.'

'I have a feeling I will,' said Libby. 'I think he took it seriously, even if his Chief might not.'

Sure enough, while Libby was doing her Saturday morning blink-and-you'll-miss-it dust and vacuum ritual, the phone rang.

'I was right,' said Ian. 'I had to phone the Chief at home and he didn't think we'd got enough to make an official enquiry. He did say, though, that if I can come up with anything more he'll review it. Which means – do it on your own time, Inspector Connell.'

'Well, that's good, isn't it?' said Libby.

'I'm glad you think so. I do have a private life, you know.'

Suppressing a desire to ask exactly what private life, Libby apologised. 'But you know what I mean. Fran and I are going to see Rosie again, and we could always ask for a return viewing of White Lodge.'

'That would be just plain daft. If someone was trying to scare you off yesterday they might get even heavier a second time.'

'You know,' said Libby thoughtfully, 'that's a puzzle. Because how did they know someone would be viewing the house?'

'Two reasons come to mind,' said Ian. 'One, they've fitted up some kind of trip switch to start up a mechanism when it's triggered, or two, and more worrying, is that someone in the estate agent's office is passing information.'

'Oh, I don't think so. After all, they seem to be keen to allow people to view the property unaccompanied. To then scare them off is a bit of a contradiction in terms.'

'Possibly.' Ian didn't sound convinced. 'Anyway, no going back there unless I'm with you.'

Libby sighed. 'You know best,' she said, privately thinking that he didn't. 'But I've had an idea. I told you about Jane mentioning children, and Fran being sure they were buried in the garden? And that she didn't think they were workhouse children?'

'Yes?' Now Ian sounded wary.

'Well, I thought, how about County Records? See if there's a historian or something in the archives? Or an archaeological survey or something?'

'You're not getting *Time Team* in, Libby.'

'No, I know,' said Libby, wishing she *could* ask television's favourite archaeology programme to come and do one of their three-day investigations, 'but don't you think it would be a good idea?'

'You can go and root about in County Records all you like,' said Ian. 'Just stay away from White Lodge until I say so.'

Chapter Six

FRAN CALLED TO SAY Rosie had agreed to see them on Monday afternoon and the lamb shanks in red wine went down very well with Hetty and Greg on Sunday. On Monday morning, Libby went online to see what she could find out about County records. Unfortunately, searching the archives meant physically going to Maidstone and the County Library. She looked up “Archivists”, but no names were given. Stumped, she went back to looking up Cherry Ashton and White Lodge, hoping that something would leap out at her.

Eventually, she had the brainwave of putting “Cherry Ashton child deaths” into the search engine. However, all this produced was a proliferation of genealogy sites. “Infant mortality” simply produced unconnected articles containing mainly statistics. “Workhouse deaths” came up with a mixture of the two and several of the pieces she’d found before.

‘I know,’ she said out loud. ‘Archaeology societies.’

This produced enough results to keep her busy for an hour, jotting down names and numbers. Before going any further she decided she ought to confer with Fran, but, wary of pushing too hard, felt it would be better to leave it until the afternoon.

‘Well,’ said Fran that afternoon, while driving toward Rosie’s cottage, ‘it’s an idea. What we really want is a local amateur historian. They always find one on *Time Team.*’

'That's the second time *Time Team's* come up.'

'Oh?'

'Ian mentioned it. But I had thought how great it would be if they could come in. I mean, they're always finding remnants of things they didn't know were there, and bodies that don't match the evidence.'

'That's what you're thinking, is it? About the bodies – the children?'

'Yes. And I don't understand what's so mysterious about them. If Jane knows about it, and Campbell McLean knows too, even though he didn't come back to us, he must, it must be general knowledge, so why isn't it coming up in searches?'

'Someone will tell us. Perhaps Rosie knows.'

'In that case why didn't she tell us in the first place?'

'Why,' said Libby darkly, 'didn't she tell us a lot of things?'

Rosie received them a little less enthusiastically than the first time, but took them through to the garden again, where once more tea things were set out.

'Have you made any progress?' she asked, after pouring tea.

'In a way,' said Fran, 'but we've got several questions.'

'Questions?' Rosie looked wary.

'First,' said Libby, 'when did you first see the house?'

Rosie seemed taken aback. 'Oh, years ago. Then I was driving that way to see a friend and I saw it again. And it was after that I started dreaming about it.'

'See, the thing is,' said Libby, 'in your dreams you saw the place empty, and described it to us exactly as it looks now. And we don't think it's been empty more than a couple of years. So how would you know?'

'You've been there?' Rosie avoided the question.

'Yes, we've been there.' Fran kept her eyes on Rosie's face. 'And, as Libby says, it's exactly as you described it. And if you're a psychic, why did you ask me to investigate?'

'I'm not a psychic.' Rosie avoided their eyes and took a sip of tea.

When no more seemed forthcoming, Libby said, 'In that case you have to tell us what's behind all this. And why you don't know the history of the house. It was easy enough to find out, even for us.'

'At least, part of it was,' said Fran.

'What do you mean, part of it?' asked Rosie, looking up. *Ahh*! thought Libby.

'That White Lodge was part of the Cherry Ashton workhouse.'

Rosie looked embarrassed. 'Yes, I knew that.'

'Right,' said Fran, 'so now tell us the rest of it.'

'The rest of it?' echoed Rosie.

'Yes,' said Libby firmly. 'How you know exactly what the house looks like, inside and out, and why you bothered to get us involved. Are we some kind of research for one of your novels? How to hoodwink two gullible middle-aged ladies?'

'Libby!' said Fran, shocked.

But Rosie was looking even more embarrassed. In fact, a slow blush was creeping up her neck.

'All right, I'll confess.' She leant back in her chair and cradled her cup in her lap. Her long hair had escaped from its clip and drifted over her shoulders. She looked, thought Libby, like the good witch from a fairy tale.

'First, what I told you was quite true. I'm positive I have a connection to White Lodge, although I have no idea what it is. As soon as I saw it – oh, must be a year ago now – I remembered seeing it before, years before, as I said. But then I started dreaming about it. Not empty, as I told you, but mainly the outside and that garden, although it wasn't overgrown. So I looked it up, as you must have done, on the internet, and found it was for sale.'

She paused for another sip of tea. 'So I made an appointment to view. The agent who took me seemed strangely ambivalent about the viewing, as though she didn't want to go, but on the other hand was keen for someone to buy it.' She looked at Fran and Libby. 'Is that how it seemed to you?'

They nodded.

'So we went to see it. I knew the minute I went inside I'd been there before. And all the time we were going round the house I was aware that the agent was very uncomfortable. I was fine. Whatever she felt, I knew the house had been happy at one time.

'She didn't want to take me upstairs, so I went on my own, and saw that room with the bath and the kitchen sink. And then –' she paused 'then I thought I could hear piano music.'

Libby and Fran both drew a deep breath and

Rosie nodded. 'So I went downstairs to ask the agent if she could hear it, but she was already outside the front door. I insisted we go round the back and, very reluctantly, she let me lead the way. Then we saw the garden.' Rosie stopped and looked away towards the trees, although Libby felt she wasn't actually seeing them. 'And I heard the music again – very faintly. So I turned to ask the agent if she could hear it, and there she was, the other side of that rotting gate, looking terrified. Of course she could hear it.

'Anyway, she said she knew nothing about it, knew nothing about the house except that it was a probate sale, and hightailed it back to her car. I stayed and prowled round the garden for a bit, but the music had stopped and I couldn't find anything else except those stones.'

'So why didn't you tell us all this to start with?' asked Libby.

'I didn't want to prejudice you. I thought if I told you about the music you would be expecting to hear it, or you'd think I was a mad old fool.'

Libby's expression could have told anybody that was exactly what she did think.

'And about the workhouse?' asked Fran, after giving Libby a warning glare.

'Yes, of course I knew about that. But it was closed at the beginning of the last century.'

'Demolished, actually,' put in Libby. 'In 1909.'

'Right.' Rosie looked at her with respect. 'So what did you mean about half the history?'

'The children,' said Fran. 'Everyone else seems to know about the children, except us. And they're nothing to do with the workhouse.'

'How do you know?' Rosie was wide-eyed.

'I don't know, but everybody else does. So what about them? Who are they?'

'Actually,' said Rosie, after a minute of staring at her feet, 'nobody *does* know. It all stems from one body being unearthed years ago and unsubstantiated rumours about a child's ghost in the garden.'

Libby looked dubious. 'Is that all? When was this body unearthed, and how?'

'By accident, as far as I can tell, when something was being done to the garden. Must have been sometime in the fifties, or perhaps earlier.'

'And why did they think there were more?'

'It was the other gravestones. I think it was assumed that they were the bodies of workhouse children, but you don't think so?' Rosie turned to Fran.

'What age was the body?' asked Libby. 'I mean, when did it date from?'

'I don't think they could date it very accurately in those days,' said Rosie, 'but they thought it dated from the workhouse period.'

'And where is it now?' asked Fran.

Rosie looked surprised. 'I don't know. Re-buried, I suppose.'

'Who would know?' Libby leant forward. 'And if you know all this, why on earth did you want us to find out about it? This is all very suspicious, Rosie, you must see that.'

Rosie sighed. 'I know. I did a certain amount of research after I'd been to see the house, and that is all I came up with. But I couldn't come up with any more, and the estate agents wouldn't talk to me about the music. And then I started dreaming again.'

'The same dreams?' said Fran.

'The ones I told you about. But there was always music – piano music. And it began to frighten me. And I couldn't go back to the estate agents, I'd already pestered them enough. I couldn't seem to get any further with my research, and the only documents at the county archives seemed to be about the workhouse. Although it did appear to have been a merchant's house before it became part of the workhouse.'

'So then you called us in,' said Libby. 'Tell me, would it have hurt to have told us all this in the first place?'

'I didn't want to prejudice you, I've told you,' said Rosie, although the blush was staining her neck again. 'I'm sorry if I misled you.'

'Well, it was rather a childish thing to do,' Libby sniffed.

'I thought it would interest Fran,' said Rosie.

'So you invested it with a whiff of the supernatural just to season the dish.' Libby frowned.

'It's all right, Lib,' said Fran. 'Now, Rosie, why didn't you go on with the research yourself?'

'Because of your reputation,' said Rosie, sitting up straighter. 'You see, I know all about your career as investigators.'

'I'd hardly call us that,' said Fran.

'Bunglers, more like,' said Libby.

'Anyway, when Fran enrolled for my classes, I was delighted, especially when she told me she wanted to write about her Coastguard Cottage experiences.'

'Ah!' said Libby. 'So you made your experience as much like hers as possible to get her interest.'

'Oh, God.' Rosie leant forward and put her head in her hands. 'It really does sound awful when you put it like that.'

'Yes,' said Fran. 'And now tell us about the music.'

'Piano music,' said Rosie, sitting upright once more. 'When I heard it while I was upstairs in the house I thought it was coming from that piano downstairs, and how funny it was the same music as in my dreams –'

'In your dream?' said Libby sharply. 'In the first dreams?'

'Yes. Didn't I say?'

Libby shook her head.

'Oh, yes, there was always music. Debussy, mainly. The music that day was *L'après-midi d'un faun* – do you know it?'

'On the day we visited it was *The Girl with the Golden Hair*,' said Fran. 'Still Debussy.'

'Now, how would they have known that?' asked Libby, of no one in particular.

'They?' asked Rosie.

'Didn't it occur to you that someone was playing that music?'

'Well, of course.'

'And you never questioned it?'

'No.' Rosie looked bewildered.

'Yet you asked us in to find out about it?' Libby went on mercilessly. 'Not even when you realised that, by doing so, you'd be putting us in danger?'

Chapter Seven

'DANGER?' ROSIE REPEATED. 'HOW?'

Libby made a sound suspiciously like a snort. 'For a writer you're being remarkably dense. Or are you? Perhaps you know all about it already?'

'I really don't know what you mean,' said Rosie, looking bewildered.

'We've reported it to the police,' said Libby, ignoring Rosie's gasp, 'because if the piano was playing each time someone visited it means that someone was behind it. Some kind of recording equipment which is turned on whenever someone comes to look at the house, to scare them off. That genuinely hadn't occurred to you?'

Rosie was now looking aghast.

'There's something else, too,' said Fran in a gentler voice than Libby's accusatory tone. 'You said you'd been in the back garden and seen the gravestones.'

Rosie nodded.

'And did you see that the ground had been cleared?'

'No. It was completely overgrown.'

Libby and Fran looked at each other.

'That means it was within the last year,' said Libby.

'What was?' asked Rosie.

'We think – a new grave.'

Rosie turned white. Fran reached forward to steady her, but she stayed upright. Libby took her cup.

'Here,' she said. 'More tea.'

Rosie took it obediently and sipped, her colour returning.

'I'm so sorry,' she said.

For a moment they sat in silence, then Rosie put down her cup.

'I seem to have made a complete mess of things,' she said. 'First of all I should have told you everything I'd found out. And now I've unwittingly put you in danger.'

'Only while we were at the house,' said Fran. 'But you understand why we had to inform the police. If what we found is a new grave, then the music is being played, presumably, by someone keen to keep people away, and therefore someone involved with the death.'

'But I didn't see the grave,' said Rosie. 'You said it had only been there since I saw the house. Why keep me away?'

'Perhaps there are others,' said Libby. 'There has to be a reason, and it isn't ghost music. I do wonder why on earth the estate agents didn't report it, though.'

'Others? You mean other graves?' said Rosie.

'Apart from the old ones, I mean,' said Libby. 'Anyway, we need to talk to the agents and see what they have to say. And find out about those children's graves, too.'

'We were thinking we should try and find a local amateur historian,' said Fran. 'I don't suppose you know anyone, do you?'

Rosie thought for a moment. 'Actually,' she said

slowly, 'I think I do. There's a chap who runs adult ed classes in local history. I don't know him personally, but he's there on the same day I am. I'll go and get the brochure.'

She stood up and went into the cottage. Libby looked at Fran.

'Now what?' she said.

'I suppose we tell Ian what Rosie's told us, but it won't do him any good. And I want to find out about this Debussy connection.'

Rosie returned with the thick Adult Education brochure, flicking through and finding a page.

'There,' she said. 'That's him.'

The page had brief biographies of the tutors. Professor Andrew Wylie was listed as a retired Professor of History at one of the northern universities who now ran local history sessions and occasional walks.

'How would we get hold of him?' asked Libby. 'Look in the phone book?'

'Yes,' said Fran, 'but I think Rosie should make the approach as a fellow tutor.'

Rosie nodded. 'And what do I tell him?'

'The truth,' said Fran, 'but perhaps keep the modern part of the mystery to yourself. Just say you want to find out about the history of the building in the early part of the twentieth century, particularly after the workhouse was closed down. Don't tell him about the dreams or the music, though.'

'If he wants to go and see it he'll find out for himself,' said Libby.

'Shall I tell him about asking you two to help?'

'Oh, I think so,' said Fran. 'He can liaise with us.

Unless you want to become more involved yourself?'

'I don't know,' said Rosie. 'I think I'm a bit too old for that.'

'Oh, don't be daft,' said Libby. 'Go on, why don't you ring him now?'

Rosie stared at her for a moment, then smiled. 'All right. I'll go and find the phone book.'

She returned a few minutes later with the telephone directory and a phone.

'Right,' she said, her briskness seeming to have returned. 'Here we are – Prof. A Wylie. Oh, he lives in Nethergate. Canongate Drive. Do you know it?'

Fran and Libby looked at each other and smiled. 'Yes,' said Libby, 'we know it.'

'Oh?' Rosie's raised eyebrows asked the question.

'Funnily enough,' said Fran, 'someone who lives there helped me when I was trying to find out about my cottage.'

'Not to mention knowing someone who lived in the flats at the other end,' said Libby.

Fran frowned at her. 'Lives,' she corrected. 'Edna's brother.'

'Oh, yes, who travels in stationery.' Libby giggled. 'Do you suppose he still does? Seems like an obsolete profession to me.'

'Go on then, Rosie, try the number,' said Fran.

Rosie punched in the numbers and waited. Eventually, she adopted the expression of someone listening to a recorded announcement.

'This is Amanda George, Professor Wylie,' she said. 'I teach adult education classes on the same days as you do. I wonder if I could ask your advice?' She left her number and switched off the phone. 'There. That's all we can do for the moment.'

Fran sat back in her chair. 'I'm sorry if we've given you a shock,' she said, 'but we were a little suspicious –'

'And so were the police,' put in Libby.

'Goodness! Were they?' Rosie looked worried.

'Because it seemed that you'd been to White Lodge comparatively recently and denied it.'

'Omitted to tell us,' corrected Fran.

'Oh, yes. I suppose they would be.' Rosie looked uncomfortable. 'Will they want to talk to me?'

'Maybe. They've got to find out a lot more to make an investigation viable,' said Fran, 'but we'll keep you informed.'

Rosie looked at her curiously. 'And they keep you informed?'

'We have a contact in the police,' said Libby, a touch proudly.

'Oh, I remember reading about that,' said Rosie. 'He calls you in, Fran, doesn't he?'

'In a way,' said Fran, 'but he doesn't like admitting it. He's always furious if it gets into the paper.'

'Anyway,' said Libby, 'he's going to do a bit of preliminary digging. Mainly into the new grave, if it is one.'

'Not physically, I hope,' said Rosie, now appearing quite recovered. 'Well, if you've quite forgiven me, how about some more tea? Or a glass of wine?'

Libby looked hopeful, but Fran shook her head. 'I'm driving,' she said, 'and I really ought to get back.'

'Right.' Rosie stood up. 'Will you ring me as soon as you hear any more?'

'Of course,' said Libby. 'And you'll let us know when you hear from the prof?'

'I will,' promised Rosie, 'but it just occurred to me – he may be on holiday.'

'Oh, bother,' said Libby. 'Of course. High summer. I bet he goes away on obscure archaeological digs in the Greek islands.'

Fran shook her head. 'With your imagination it's you should be the writer, Lib.'

'I am,' said Libby. 'I write pantomimes.'

'Do you?' said Rosie.

'I used to,' aid Libby. 'There's only so many variations on "It's Behind You" a girl can take.'

'Well, that's made things a bit clearer,' said Fran, as they drove back to Steeple Martin.

'As long as she's told us the truth, now,' said Libby.

'I think she has,' said Fran. 'And she was very shocked about the new grave.'

'I want to go back to the agents,' said Libby. 'And the house.'

'We can't until Ian says we can,' said Fran. 'Wait until you hear from him.'

However, the first thing Libby heard was a phone call the following morning from Fran, to say that Professor Wylie had called Rosie back. He was, apparently, intrigued by the opportunity to research a historic building, and, as a member of the Kent Archaeological Society, had access to their library at Maidstone.

'Rosie said he sounded quite enthusiastic and wondered if he was bored.'

'Should have gone on that archaeological dig to Greece,' said Libby. 'Did he say when he would get back to her?'

'As soon as he could,' said Fran, 'but it means an actual visit to the library, so we can't expect it to be that soon. He also suggested a geophysical survey in the garden.'

'That's all well and good, but we know – or at least, we think we know – that there are children's bodies there. Anyway, we couldn't afford it, and Ian wouldn't let us.'

Ian called later in the day.

'I went and had a look,' he said, 'and sure enough that music was playing. I've been trying to get the agents to let me see all their correspondence on the house, but they're being remarkably reticent. Without a warrant I can't see it, although I've told the boss about the music and that I'm sure someone's scaring people off, but he's still being uncooperative. But there is another piece of news.'

'Go on then, what?'

'The cleared patch of ground you saw does look like a grave, and there was a bunch of flowers when I went.'

'No!'

'Yes. I'm going back tomorrow, and if you're very, very good, I'll let you and Fran come with me. I don't think there's anyone actually in the house, the music is obviously some kind of mechanism with a trip switch, as I said, but I want to find that. If the agents refuse to give me the keys again, I'll threaten them with the full weight of the law.'

'Would they refuse? They seemed keen enough for me to view it.'

'But they know I'm investigating, not a prospective purchaser.'

'Oh, right. Well, I've got some news for you.'

'Oh, no. What have you done now?'

'Nothing, except what you asked us to do,' said Libby indignantly, and told him about their visit to Rosie.

'And finally, she's got in touch with a historical professor who's going to research the house for us.'

'How?' Ian sounded suspicious.

Libby told him. 'And he suggested a geophysical survey in the garden.'

'Which would no doubt show all sorts of anomalies, and as we know, or rumour suggests, there are bodies there, it wouldn't do us any good.'

'Yes, that's what we thought,' said Libby, a trifle gloomily. 'I just wish we knew what those bodies were. Fran's still sure they aren't anything to do with the workhouse.'

'Which does seem the likeliest explanation,' said Ian. 'Do we know what the house was before the workhouse?'

'A local merchant's house was the best we could come up with. And I also want to know why Rosie remembers it. Now she's told us the truth, her memories – the early ones – seem to have been from when she was very young. Otherwise, she'd remember it far more clearly.'

'I'd rather like to know why she was so careful with the truth,' said Ian. 'I think I shall have to see her for myself.'

'We did say you might want to,' said Libby, 'but I think I believe her now. What about this professor? Will you want to see him?'

'Let's see what he comes up with first,' said Ian.

'OK,' said Libby, 'and see if he comes up with an explanation of the Debussy, as well.'

'That's fairly simple,' said Ian. 'They only had a Debussy CD when they set up the speakers.'

'Oh, how disappointing. You're far too prosaic. Will you let us know when and if you manage to go tomorrow?'

'Of course. Regards to Ben, by the way. How is he?'

'Oh, fine. Same as always. You know Ben.'

'Not annoyed with you for getting involved again?'

'Not so far,' said Libby, 'but that's because it started out as a research project and he thought it would keep me out of mischief.'

Ian sighed. 'Even I know you better than that,' he said.

Chapter Eight

WHEN LIBBY CALLED FRAN the next day to tell her they were to meet Ian at White Lodge at mid-day, Fran also had news.

'Prof Wylie called Rosie. I think she was right, he is bored, because he went straight to the library yesterday and did some research. He's come up with some interesting information, he said.'

'What?'

'He said he'd rather tell her in person. So she said we were handling it, would he tell us.'

'And did he say yes?'

'She said he sounded rather surprised, so she said we would explain. He's asked us to go to his flat.'

'When?'

'He said this morning, if we liked.'

Libby looked at her watch. 'That'd be cutting it a bit fine. It's ten now, and we're meeting Ian at twelve.'

'But think how good it would be if we could have this information when we went to the house. Shall I call Ian and ask if we could make it later?'

'All right,' said Libby reluctantly. 'I expect he'd do it for you rather than me. I think he regards me a bit like a mosquito.'

'But mosquitoes aren't lovable with it,' laughed Fran. 'Don't be daft. Did he ring you from his mobile?'

'Yes. Get back to me as soon as possible, eh?'

In fact it was less than five minutes later when

Fran called back.

'He said get there when we can, and you'll never guess what!'

'What? Of course I can't guess.'

'He says if he'd like to come, the professor can come with us.'

'Blimey! Is he getting soft in his old age?

'Well, he did say if the information was interesting and useful. So we'd better go and find out. I'll ring him now.'

'The prof? Say as soon as possible and I'll meet you there.'

The professor would be delighted to see them whenever they cared to come, Fran reported. 'Rosie's right. He's been bored.'

'I bet we've given him a new lease of life,' said Libby. 'Does he sound as dry as dust?'

'No, quite normal. Bit of an accent of some kind. Anyway, if you leave in the next ten minutes you'll be there by eleven, won't you?'

'Quarter to, I'd say. See you there. What number is it?'

The professor's flat was in a block next to the one Fran and Libby had visited a few years ago in the course of another investigation. Canongate Drive was a newish development, built above Nethergate by Jim Butler, a friend of Ben's. At the other end he'd built himself a large bungalow in which he lived with his ancient dog, Lady. Although neither Fran nor Libby were fond of new houses, they could both see the advantages of the site. Jim's bungalow and several of the houses at his end of the drive had spectacular sea views over Nethergate

Bay, as did the upper flats in the three blocks this end.

Libby parked Romeo behind Fran's Smart car and joined her at the end of the drive, where she was looking at the view.

'I just hope,' said Fran, 'that they don't start building any more below here. It would ruin the view.'

'I don't suppose people who need houses are worried about the view,' said Libby. 'Anyway, I think Jim Butler gifted the bottom field to the town in perpetuity as long as it wasn't built on.'

'What happens if it is built on?'

'Whoever builds on it, they and the council have to pay the legatees the current value of the land plus hefty compensation. A neat trick.'

'If it works,' said Fran. 'I bet the lawyers would find a way round it.'

'Come on, let's not worry about it now,' said Libby. 'Let's go and beard the professor in his eyrie.'

'Shouldn't that be "den"?' asked Fran, as she followed Libby across the road.

'I don't go in for clichés,' said Libby loftily and mendaciously.

The professor's flat was on the top floor of his block, with a view of the bay from all windows.

'Come in,' he said, standing aside and waving them through. Shortish, dapper in pale trousers and a collarless shirt, he was nothing like Libby's expectations. His grey hair was cut very close to his head, and his goatee, reminiscent of Guy's, a darker grey. And far from being desiccated and ancient, he appeared to be much the same age as Rosie. No wonder he was bored, Libby thought.

'It's very good of you to do this for Rosie, Professor,' said Fran, as soon as they were seated on the brown leather sofas in front of the picture windows.

'Please, call me Andrew,' he said, and Libby placed the accent. Very faintly Scottish. 'And why am I talking to you instead of Rosie?'

'It's rather hard to explain,' said Libby, who still wasn't entirely sure herself, 'but she asked Fran and me to look into the history of the house because she thinks she might have links with it herself.'

'Then why didn't she look into it herself?' asked Andrew.

Fran and Libby looked at each other.

'We're not absolutely sure,' said Fran, 'but we think she's frightened.'

'Frightened?' Andrew frowned. 'Well, I don't pretend to understand, but I suppose we'd better get on with the business in hand. Oh – I should have offered you coffee.'

Fran and Libby hastily declined, aware of their promise to meet Ian at White Lodge, and Andrew got up to fetch a blue folder full of notes and photocopies.

'To cut a long story short,' he said, laying the folder on a coffee table, 'the house was built on the site of a former building, a fourteenth-century mansion. Or an important house, anyway. That appears to have been partly destroyed by fire, and one can only assume the person who bought the remains and the land had it knocked down in order to build this rather grand Tudor house.'

'Who was that?' asked Libby.

'A wealthy farmer who owned land all over the marshes. He obviously fancied himself as gentry, although I doubt his grand house gave him entry to the social circles he aspired to.'

'No, it wouldn't,' said Libby, remembering her Austen.

'The family had died out by the mid-nineteenth century, which was when the Poor Board was set up and the house purchased, with the land, in order to set up the workhouse.'

'Yes, we found that much out,' said Fran, 'and that the workhouse was demolished in 1909, although the house remained. But we don't know anything after that.'

The professor's face was alight with glee. 'Ah!' he said. 'And I can tell you why!'

'Yes?' prompted Libby.

'The main house of the workhouse, which, of course, wasn't called White Lodge then, contained apartments for the master and the matron, who were usually a married couple, and were in this case, and the rest was used as an infirmary.'

'Oh,' said Libby. 'I didn't realise they would have had an infirmary. I got the impression that if they got sick they were just left where they were.'

The professor shook his head. 'No. If the sickness spread they would have had all the inmates unable to work, and if they ignored the problem, the Guardians, as they were called, would have investigated. I'm sure in some cases things were swept under the carpet –'

'Yes, I found some appalling cases,' Libby interrupted.

Andrew nodded. 'But in most cases patients were isolated from the rest of the inmates and, if not cured, at least treated slightly better than the rest. I doubt anybody was cured, in fact.'

'So the bodies in the garden could be from the workhouse after all?' said Fran.

'Some of them, possibly.'

'But not all?' Libby leant forward.

Andrew's expression registered triumph. 'Definitely not all.' He turned over a piece of paper in the folder.

'There. See what it says?''

Libby and Fran peered at the document. The heading was all they needed to see.

'The Princess Beatrice Sanatorium,' Libby read out. 'A sanatorium? Wasn't that for infectious diseases?'

'It certainly was,' said Andrew. 'What seems to have happened is that the Guardians decided to close the workhouse – and knock it down – and turn necessity to their advantage.'

'How?' said Fran and Libby together.

'The reason the workhouse was closed down and the buildings demolished was because of infection. They didn't know much about the workings of infectious diseases in those days, but there was an outbreak, and they decided the best thing to do was eradicate the source of infection, as they saw it. So, because the infirmary had already been used to attempt to cure the inmates, they turned it into a sanatorium.'

'For what, though?' asked Libby.

'Haven't you guessed yet?' The professor grinned at both of them.

'No,' they said.

'TB, of course! Tuberculosis. It was rife at that time, and the open-air treatment was being pioneered in Germany. A few enlightened doctors in England wanted to try it, and as TB had been killing the poor inhabitants of Cherry Ashton Workhouse, they decided to make a virtue of necessity.'

'Why Princess Beatrice?' asked Fran.

Andrew shrugged. 'I don't know. I expect they wanted to be taken seriously and remove all memories of the workhouse. Stupid really, as it had been there for over sixty years by then. I doubt if they asked the Princess.'

'So what happened next?' asked Libby.

'The records aren't all that clear, which is hardly surprising, and I've still got more research to do, but it would appear that the treatments weren't terribly successful.'

'The children,' murmured Fran.

Andrew glanced at her with raised brows. 'Children?'

'Not workhouse children, victims of TB,' said Fran.

'In the graves,' Libby explained.

'Do you know they're children?' asked Andrew, looking surprised.

'I think so,' said Fran, blushing faintly. Andrew turned a questioning look on Libby.

'It's a long story, Professor,' she said. 'Let's get on with the story.'

'Please call me Andrew. Professor makes me feel a) old, and b) as if I'm still lecturing.'

'Sorry, Andrew.' Libby beamed at him. 'This is really interesting, and I think you might be pleased to know we have an invitation for you.'

'Really?'

'Our friend Detective Inspector Ian Connell has invited us all, you, me and Fran, to visit White Lodge with him this morning.'

'Really?' Andrew's bushy eyebrows shot up. 'Well, of course, I'd be delighted. I haven't anything else on, and it would be fascinating, but a Police Inspector? Why?'

Fran and Libby looked at each other again.

'Perhaps,' said Fran, 'we'd better let him tell you that. If you don't mind.'

'Certainly, if you think that's best,' said Andrew. 'When do we go?'

'Now?' said Libby. 'If it's convenient and you haven't anything else to do?'

'Delighted,' said Andrew, almost jumping to his feet. 'Shall I take my own car?'

'No, Fran'll take you. Her car's slightly more respectable than mine.' Libby stood up. 'If that's all right, Fran?'

Ten minutes later Andrew was seated in the passenger seat of Fran's roller skate, as Harry and Adam called it, his blue folder on his lap and an excited expression on his face. He looked, Libby thought, like a schoolboy off on an adventure.

White Lodge looked even more tired this morning, bathed in mid-day sunshine. Ian's anonymous saloon was parked on the verge opposite, and Fran and Libby pulled up behind it.

'It's smaller than I imagined,' said Andrew, as they stood looking up at the boarded up frontage. 'How do we get in?'

'I think we'd better go round the back to the garden first,' said Libby. 'See if Ian's there.'

She led the way along the side and through the old gate, which Ian – or someone else – had managed to push right open. Sure enough, Ian was there, talking into a mobile phone. He saw them and switched it off.

'This is Professor Andrew Wylie,' said Libby. 'Andrew, this is Detective Inspector Connell. Andrew's found out quite a bit about the house, Ian.'

Ian shook Andrew's outstretched hand. 'I'm very pleased to meet you, Professor,' he said. 'But somehow, I doubt what you've found out will help with our particular problem.'

Andrew's obvious confusion was reflected in the faces of Libby and Fran.

'What do you mean?' Libby frowned at him.

'I mean, Libby, that what you suspected is probably true. That grave is less than a year old.'

Chapter Nine

'REALLY?' ANDREW LOOKED FROM Libby to Fran. 'You didn't say anything about that.'

'No,' said Libby, and explained how they'd found the grave and informed Ian. 'And it's the music that makes us think someone has something to hide.' She turned to Ian. 'So what are you doing? What's going to happen?'

'I've asked for authorisation to exhume the body –'

There was a collective gasp from the others.

'And a search team for the house.'

'So can't we let the Professor in to have a look first?' asked Fran.

'Actually, that's what I was hoping,' said Ian, with one of his most charming smiles for Andrew. 'Probably strictly against the rules, but I've finally got the Superintendent to sanction the investigation, and I think I'm safe in calling in an expert witness.'

Andrew looked doubtful. 'I wouldn't say I'm that.'

'He calls me an expert witness,' said Fran, 'and I'm even less of one.'

'You?' Andrew frowned and Fran sighed.

'She hates it, but Fran is a bit of a psychic,' explained Libby, 'and before you put on a sceptical face, she used to be employed by Goodall and Smythe to scope out properties in case something nasty had happened there.'

'The estate agents?'

‘That’s them. Their clients are all rich and don’t want nasties in the woodshed. Or anywhere else, for that matter.’

‘Oh.’ Andrew turned and looked at Fran.

‘She’s helped us in a few investigations before now,’ said Ian gently. ‘That’s why I’m always prepared to listen to any suspicions she might have.’

Libby sent him an equivocal look.

Fran was looking distinctly uncomfortable. ‘I don’t like it, you know,’ she said to the professor, ‘and I’ve no idea how it happens, but sometimes things just appear in my head as though they’re facts.’

Andrew nodded, still looking bemused.

‘So, professor, would you care to come inside? One of the things I’m anxious to find out is if anything appears to have been altered recently, and you’d be able to tell us that better than most.’

‘I’m not sure about that,’ said Andrew, ‘I’m not that much of an expert in buildings. I do know a buildings archaeologist.’

‘You’re a member of the Kent Archaeological Trust, though, aren’t you?’ said Libby.

‘Yes, but my particular area is records research. I can do a reasonable visual analysis, but, as I said, I’m not an expert.’

‘That’s probably enough for us,’ said Ian. ‘Is this place listed, do you know?’

‘Oh, yes,’ said Andrew. ‘Only Grade Two, but that’s probably why it’s still standing.’

‘Then we’ll be very careful,’ said Ian, ‘and all the more reason for you to be here.’

Ian led the way to the back door of the house,

with Andrew explaining on the way about the TB sanatorium.

'Those are the children, then, Fran?' Ian turned to her.

'I think so. But I'm still not sure.'

'Do you think you could be tuning in somehow to the modern grave?'

Fran frowned. 'Honestly, Ian, I don't know. I'm not even sure I felt anything any more.'

'How do you know about the grave being new?' asked Libby, as Andrew led the way along the hall, staring around him as he went.

'You thought it was, didn't you? It was fairly obvious. The area would have returned to the overgrown state it had been before if it had been any more than a year old, and, according to one of our forensic experts, it's probably within six months.'

'But the music's been playing for longer than that,' said Fran. 'If the grave's only, say, six months old, why did they need the distraction before then?'

Ian looked serious. 'That's that we need to find out.'

They took Andrew all over the house. The music had started as they went up the stairs, which puzzled Libby.

'*Clair de Lune*,' said Andrew. 'Where's it coming from?'

'That's what we want to know,' said Ian. 'And how it's triggered.'

'Why didn't it start in the garden?' said Libby.

They all stopped on the third floor landing and looked at her.

'Why didn't it?' said Fran. 'What's different

about today?'

'We can't hear it very well up here,' said Libby. 'It's clearest in the garden.'

'So it's the garden that's the key,' said Ian.

'Of course – that's where the grave is.' Libby turned to go back down the stairs. 'That's where we should be looking.'

'But we need to know where the equipment is, and that's definitely in the house.' Ian followed her. 'Professor, have you noticed any, shall we say, anomalies so far?'

'Nothing that would be out of keeping, but it's only a cursory inspection and we haven't much light. If you're right about recorded music, there should be hidden speakers somewhere.' Andrew peered at the panelling on the staircase. 'But not here.'

'But what triggered it?' persisted Libby. 'It didn't start in the garden.'

'What was different about the garden today?' asked Fran, bringing up the rear. 'Had anything been disturbed since we last came, Libby?'

'Only the gate, and I expect you pushed that right open, didn't you, Ian?'

He stopped at the bottom of the staircase. 'No, I didn't. That was how I found it.'

'Do you remember,' said Libby to Fran, 'that when Rosie came to view the house she first heard the music from upstairs?'

'Then there are two triggers,' said Ian. 'One on the stairs and one in the garden.'

'The gate,' said Libby and Fran together.

'We had to squeeze through,' Libby explained,

'which meant we set something off. Ian didn't. The gate was already open. When you came before, Ian, did you have to squeeze through? You said you heard the music.'

'No, it was wide open both times. I heard it going up the stairs, just as we did now.' He frowned. 'There's no point in us investigating before my team get here, we'd ruin any evidence there is, but it certainly means someone's been here.'

'After we'd been,' said Fran, 'and before you came.'

'Which means someone knew.' Libby looked at Ian. 'This is a bit scary.'

'Professor, can you see any evidence of speakers on this staircase?' Ian ignored Libby and turned to Andrew.

'I haven't, but I wasn't looking closely.' Andrew frowned at the dark panelling. 'I think you'd need floodlights to see.'

Ian nodded. 'We'll go outside again then, and wait for the team to turn up.' He started across the landing to the other staircase.

'I don't know why he wanted us to come,' grumbled Libby, following slowly in his wake.

'He said we could come if we liked,' said Fran. 'I don't suppose he actually wanted us.'

'All he wanted was Andrew, really.'

'He didn't know about Andrew until this morning. Neither did we.'

Libby shrugged. 'He wants him now,' she said.

Ian lead them out of the front door. 'Better this way,' he said. 'Less disturbance.' He went back to the side of the house leaving them to contemplate the gloomy frontage.

'He seems very efficient,' said Andrew.

'Oh, he is,' said Fran.

'Just slightly unorthodox,' added Libby.

'I can see that. Will he want me again?'

'Oh, yes.' Libby smiled grimly. 'I think you've just become his favourite expert.'

Andrew looked worried. 'I did say I wasn't an expert,' he began.

'But you know a lot more about old buildings than anyone on Ian's team will,' said Fran.

'Look,' said Libby. 'Here come the troops.'

A minibus, a white van and an unmarked car drew up alongside the house and Ian appeared from the side. Libby, Fran and Andrew watched, fascinated, as the team of men and women assembled equipment and donned blue scene-of-crime suits and disappeared in Ian's wake back round the side of the house.

'Now what do we do?' said Libby after a minute. 'Do you think he's forgotten us?'

'No, I haven't.' Ian poked his head round the corner. 'Come and show us what you did on Friday. Andrew? Will you stay and give us a hand inside?'

Libby and Fran repeated their movements, including their discovery of the "grave".

The men and women watched and listened in silence, then put up the hoods on their suits and the masks on their faces and turned to the undergrowth. Libby saw that a dead bouquet was lying on one of the stones in a plastic evidence bag.

'Is that what you found on the grave?' she asked

Ian.

'It is. I doubt if we'll get anything from it, but we can try.'

'Do you want us any more?' asked Fran.

'No,' said Ian. 'You'd probably be better out of the way, but I may want to talk to you later.'

'Andrew came in my car, will you give him a lift home?'

'Of course.' Ian patted them both on the shoulder. 'Off you go. Don't touch anything on the way back to the cars.'

'They're not going to exhume that body now, are they?' said Libby as they picked their way through the undergrowth. 'In broad daylight?'

'It didn't look like it,' said Fran. 'Perhaps the authority hasn't yet come through. I thought they always did it at night?'

'I suppose that's probably only on the telly,' said Libby. 'I must say, I thought he'd have been a bit more grateful to us.'

'Grateful?' Fran looked at her, amused.

'Well, we put him on to the case, *and* we introduced him to Andrew. He ought to be grovelling.'

'Ian? Grovel?' Fran laughed.

'Didn't he ever grovel to you?' Libby stopped and looked at her friend, interested.

Fran turned a gentle pink. 'No.'

'Not even when he was – um – courting?'

Fran went a deeper pink. 'No.'

'And that's all you're saying?'

'Yes.'

Libby shrugged. 'Oh, well. I'm not saying you

didn't make the right choice, but he is very attractive. And sort of – I dunno – dominant.'

'Domineering,' said Fran, opening her car door. 'And don't you start fantasising about him.'

Libby was indignant. 'I wouldn't.'

'No.' Fran didn't sound convinced. 'You've been a bit ambivalent about him ever since he told you off about the Morris Dancers last year.'

'That is a very confusing statement,' said Libby, going to her own car. 'He assumed I was grubbing around in his murder investigation and told me to stay out of it, as usual. That's all.'

'He does it every time,' sighed Fran. 'And then asks us back in.'

'Predictable, isn't he?' Libby got into her car. 'Let me know if you hear from him before I do.'

Chapter Ten

IT WASN'T UNTIL THE next day that Fran rang Libby.

'Ian just called. He's going to see Rosie.'

'Is that all he had to say?' Libby was frustrated. She'd called Fran at least three times the previous day, finally earning herself an embarrassing telling off. 'Nothing about Andrew? The body? The music?'

'No. I don't think he wanted to talk about any of it, but called me out of courtesy.'

'For her address?'

'No. He already had that. He's a policeman.'

'Well, I do call that ungrateful,' said Libby, sitting down on the staircase.

'You said that yesterday. I'm sure he doesn't mean it.'

'I bet he called you because he knew I'd ask questions.'

'I expect so,' said Fran. 'You'll just have to contain your soul in patience.'

Libby switched off the phone and, resting her chin on her hand, thought. She had nothing to do, unless she did some more to the painting sitting on the easel in the conservatory. The house had been cleaned and tidied for Hetty and Greg's visit on Sunday, and there was a stew in the slow cooker, in case something White Lodge-related had come up and she'd forgotten about dinner again.

But now there was nothing. She stood up and

went through to the kitchen. Never before had she and Fran started an investigation and been shut out so quickly, although there had been occasions where she herself had tried not to continue. But, somehow, that never happened.

She reviewed her options. She could go and visit Adam at Creekmarsh, as she knew Lewis Osbourne-Walker was there. And his mother, Edie, would enjoy a chat. Or she could go and see Flo Carpenter and Lenny, Ben's uncle, in their bungalow in Maltby Close. It was getting on for lunch time, so Harry would be busy in the restaurant, but she could drive down to Nethergate and bully Fran. She made a face. No, that wouldn't do. Fran had already got cross with her yesterday.

Rosie. She stopped dead in the middle of filling the kettle. She could go and see Rosie. No need to say she knew Ian was going too. But, on the other hand, Rosie was Fran's friend and it might seem a little insensitive to go without telling her first. Or even phoning Rosie first, come to that. Libby's friends were used to her dropping in unannounced, and for the most part put up with it, but you couldn't really do it to someone you'd only just met. She sighed heavily and put the kettle on the Rayburn.

There was always the internet. She went into the sitting room and woke up the laptop. "TB" she typed into the search engine. Predictably, it returned over a hundred million references. It was, however, more interesting than she'd thought, especially when she found out that the disease was far more widespread today than she'd imagined. She became engrossed in reading a piece about the incidence in

Africa until the phone rang and alerted her to the fact that the kettle was steaming furiously on the Rayburn.

'Hello?' She moved the kettle off the hotplate.

'The body wasn't new,' said Fran.

'What?'

'Ian just called. Apparently, the grave had just been cleared. Someone had been doing a bit of gardening.'

'Oh.' Libby sat on the kitchen table. 'What a bummer.'

'That's not the attitude, Lib. It's good that there isn't a murder victim in there.'

Libby sighed. 'I suppose so. Did Ian say how old the body was, or what it died of?'

'No, I gather they haven't got all the forensics yet, but it was very obvious that it was old.'

'Well, we've had old before, haven't we? The bones at Creekmarsh. There was a lot of doubt about them. Oh – and I've just thought. How did whoever cleared the grave know it was there?'

'I've no idea. Maybe Ian will tell us, but I think he was a bit cross at having ordered the exhumation and it turning out not to be necessary.'

Libby sighed again. 'Don't tell me. He's blaming us. Or, specifically, me.'

'He just sounded irritated. He was off to see Rosie.'

'We could gatecrash,' said Libby hopefully.

'No, we couldn't. Just wait and see. If we haven't heard by tomorrow we'll give him a ring.'

'Tomorrow?' Libby squeaked. 'I can't wait until tomorrow.'

‘Oh, Libby, for goodness’ sake. It’s nothing to do with us, now. Leave it alone.’

Libby moved the kettle back on to the Rayburn and warmed the brown teapot. Now she really was at a loss.

Who could she talk to about this? Fran was obviously not in the mood. All the objections she had thought of earlier were still in place, although, she thought, brightening, the option of Adam and Creekmarsh was still open. She poured a cup of tea and rang Adam.

‘I’m not there, Mum,’ he said. ‘Neither’s Lewis. They’ve gone back to London and Mog’s decided we have to go and do some plant sourcing today. We’re in Surrey.’

‘Oh.’ Libby felt ridiculously cheated. ‘All right. I’ll see you during the week at the caff.’

Next she rang Flo Carpenter. Flo had been useful several times in Libby’s and Fran’s investigations, having lived in Steeple Martin almost since she came there as a young hop picker during the war. She had ended up marrying farmer Frank Carpenter at the same time that Ben’s mother Hetty had married Greg, the son of the squire. It always made Libby smile to think of East Ender Hetty as Lady of the Manor. It must have been difficult for both Hetty and Greg facing the prejudices of both their social classes, but Hetty had done it. Flo hadn’t faced quite the same problems as there was less of a class distinction between her and Frank, and, luckily, she’d been there to support Hetty. Both women were strong examples of the redoubtable Londoner who had survived poverty, deprivation and the war, but Libby preferred to talk to Flo about the past as Hetty and Greg had been at the centre of a family scandal and murder, and Libby was wary of triggering the memories.

'Yeah, you pop round, gal. Len's just popped down the pub so I'm on me own. Want a bit of dinner?'

'No, thanks, Flo, I've just had a sandwich.' Libby knew that "dinner" to Flo was what you had at lunchtime and was likely to be substantial.

'You driving anywhere?'

'No.' Libby wasn't surprised at this question and knew why it had been asked.

'Good. I'll open a bottle of the Merlot. You liked that, didn't you?'

Frank Carpenter had "kept a good cellar", and Flo had learnt from him. Long before wine was an everyday tipple in practically every household in Britain, Flo was developing her palate.

'Lovely. Thanks, Flo. I'll see you in about ten minutes.'

Maltby Close was the little lane leading to the church. An existing barn had been converted into a comfortable communal sitting/dining room and the remainder into a one-storey cottage, where Flo and Lenny lived. Several more new cottages had been built, all for local residents over sixty. They were owned, not rented, and each paid a maintenance charge for the upkeep and the services of a non-resident warden. Libby arrived to find the door standing open and Flo, cigarette hanging from her mouth and her eyes squinting through the smoke, picking weeds from a window box.

'Go on in, gal.' Flo gestured with a hand full of weeds. 'Bottle's open.'

Flo's sitting room, cluttered and old-fashioned and permanently imbued with the ghosts of long-dead cigarettes, was at least not as stuffy as it would be from October 1st until April 1st, when the heating and the electric fire would be going full blast. An open bottle of Merlot and two glasses stood on a side table.

'So, what's it all about, then?' Flo shuffled into the room and dropped her cigarette into a large ashtray.

'What's what all about?' asked Libby, sitting in her usual armchair by the fireplace.

'You only come and talk to me when you're pokin' yer nose into something.' Flo handed her a glass of wine.

'I don't!' Libby felt her cheeks burning.

'Mostly.' Flo sat down. 'I don't mind. Nice to have a chat. So, what is it?'

'Actually, I'm not sure I do want to know anything,' said Libby, feeling the red tide recede. 'I think I just wanted a chat.'

Flo lit another cigarette. 'Go on. Bet you're doin' something with that Fran. Aintcher?'

'Yes – well, I was. It's just been taken over by the police.'

'Doesn't usually stop yer.'

'No, but this time there's nothing we can do about it.'

'Don't believe it.' Flo sipped her wine. 'Go on, then, what is it?'

Libby reflected that Flo probably enjoyed talking

about her local knowledge as much as she enjoyed listening.

'Well,' she began, 'Fran is taking a creative writing course with a writer called Amanda George.'

'What's that, then? She learning how to write that curly writing?'

'Calligraphy?' Libby giggled. 'No, Flo. It means learning how to write stories and novels.'

'Don't know how you can learn that.' Flo sniffed and drank more wine.

'Well, you can. Anyway, this Rosie –'

'Who?'

'Rosie. Sorry. Amanda George is Rosie's pen name. Or Rosie is Amanda's real name. Whichever way you like.'

Flo looked confused. Libby hurried on. 'Well, she found out that Fran was psychic and asked us to look into this house she dreamt about.'

'More old houses. Is it a real one?'

'Oh, yes. White Lodge at Cherry Ashton.'

'Oh, that place.' Flo's eyes narrowed.

'Do you know it?' Libby was surprised.

'Everyone knows it. Them children.'

'Yes, people kept telling us about the children. It turns out they were TB victims buried in the garden.'

'Haunted, that place.'

'You don't believe in ghosts, Flo.'

'That's as may be. There's no arguing with some things, though.'

'Like what?'

'They used to see a girl. And music playing.'

‘Really? When was this? And how do you know?’

‘They dug a body up there. Years ago.’

‘Yes, Rosie said that. Do you know any more about it? When it was? How it happened?’

Flo lit another cigarette and squinted thoughtfully through the smoke.

‘This bloke that owned it wanted to build a bit more on the back. But someone – government probably – said he’d have to dig something up first.’

‘What bloke? We don’t know about a bloke?’

Flo was disconcerted. ‘I don’t know. It was in the papers. They dug up this kid’s body. Then someone in the house saw this ghost. So he stopped the building.’

‘And sold it?’ Libby leant forward. ‘Who was he, Flo? We haven’t found any references to that, and we’ve all been looking into it. Us, the police, everyone. Even a history professor.’

‘I’m sorry, gal. I just remember about the kids and the ghosts.’

‘You said kids plural. And ghosts plural.’

Flo shook her head. ‘Oh, I don’t remember much about it. But everyone knew.’

‘Yes, so people keep saying, yet no one will actually tell us anything,’ said Libby, and took out her own cigarettes.

‘You looked on the internet?’

‘Course I did. So did Inspector Connell. And the history professor. And he went to his archaeological society’s library.’

Flo frowned. ‘Don’t understand it. Course I wasn’t here when it was a hospital or the workhouse, but we all knew about it.'

'And you say a private individual owned it?'

'Some bloke, I said.' Flo sounded irritated. 'P'raps Het'll know.'

'Or Dolly or Una?' said Libby, referring to two of Flo's contemporaries in the village.

'They might.' Flo shrugged. 'I'll ask 'em at bingo if you like.'

'Would you, Flo? Thank you.' Libby leant back and lifted her wine glass. 'Cheers.'

Later, Libby reported her conversation with Flo to Fran. 'There's a bit of a mystery there, isn't there? Why can't we find anything about it anywhere? Even Andrew only found out about it being a TB hospital.'

'And we never asked when it closed, did we?' said Fran.

'He said he'd got more research to do, remember? I wonder if he's found out anything else? And if he found anything with Ian?'

'All I know is what Ian told me. It wasn't a modern body.'

'Could I ring Andrew, do you think?'

'You could, if you think it's worth it. I'll give you his number. But I don't suppose he'll tell you anything about Wednesday morning.'

But she was wrong.

Chapter Eleven

'IT WAS FASCINATING,' ANDREW told Libby later. She'd had the bright idea of inviting him to Steeple Martin, and followed it up with another bright idea, suggesting that they go to The Pink Geranium for dinner to thank him for his help.

'It's Ian who should be buying him dinner,' grumbled Ben, 'or at least this Rosie.'

'Oh, don't be a grump. He's a nice guy. In fact,' Libby was struck with a third bright idea, 'why don't we ask Rosie too?'

So Andrew picked Rosie up on the way and they all met in The Pink Geranium at eight o'clock. Donna brought them menus and Harry brought a bottle of red wine.

'I see they know you here,' said Andrew, amused.

'This old trout is one of my best friends,' said Harry, throwing an arm round Libby's shoulders. 'But be wary. She gets into things she shouldn't.'

'Harry,' warned Libby.

'Oh, dear,' said Harry. 'This is one of the things, isn't it?'

Rosie laughed. 'I am,' she said. 'I'm one of the things.'

'Oh, you're the author?' said Harry. 'Oh, bugger. I've got to go and cook your dinners, so I can't ask all about it. I shall be back later.'

After they'd all ordered, Libby asked Andrew about his Wednesday morning experiences and he said it was fascinating.

'I've never seen one of those fingertip searches before. And they were so thorough.'

'And did they find anything?'

'No. We didn't even find any speakers, but I gather Inspector Connell is going to look more thoroughly. He has to get permission from the owners and English Heritage because of the listing.'

'So who are the owners?'

'It's rather complicated, apparently.' Andrew picked up his glass of tonic water and frowned at it.

'It's a probate sale, isn't it?' asked Libby. 'The estate agents told us that.'

'I believe so. Anyway, up until Wednesday he had no idea who it was. He was also going to the Land Registry.'

'What I don't understand,' said Rosie, 'is why there seems to be no record of what happened to the building after it ceased to be a TB sanatorium.'

'My friend Flo says some "bloke" owned it, and from what she says, wanted to extend it, probably in the fifties. That was when the body was found.'

Rosie frowned. 'Then why is there no record of it?'

'There must be,' said Libby. 'We just haven't found it yet. Although how it could have escaped Ian I don't know. And what about this folk tale about all "the children"? Where did that come from?'

Ben looked up from his red wine. 'Someone put it about deliberately.'

'Really?' They all looked at him.

'Someone who didn't want anyone looking into

the graves too closely,' said Ben.

'What, back then? They were *murdered* children?' Rosie gasped.

'It makes sense,' said Andrew, turning to her, 'but in that case, why is the music being played now? And why was that grave cleared and the flowers laid on it?'

They all looked at each other.

'A relative who's still living?' hazarded Rosie.

'Could be.' Libby peered into her wine glass. 'But who? If it was a child in the fifties –'

'No – it was dug up in the fifties,' said Andrew.

'Oh, yes. So it would be someone pretty old if it was a relative, and if it was a child who was dug up it's hardly likely to be a descendant,' said Libby. She turned to Andrew. 'Did you manage to do any more research on the building?'

'I haven't been back to the library,' he said, 'and I need to if I'm to go any further.' He turned to Rosie and said diffidently, 'I don't suppose you'd like to come with me? It might be helpful for your research.'

To Libby's interest, Rosie blushed. 'I'd love to,' she said. 'Do I need a pass or anything?'

'No, I sign you in as my guest. Ten o'clock all right? We can have a spot of lunch afterwards.'

'Lovely,' said Rosie and they smiled at one another. Ben nudged Libby.

'Don't stare,' he muttered.

Donna brought a large plate of nachos to share and topped up their wine glasses. Andrew changed the subject and asked about Libby and Fran's previous adventures. Libby, with frequent interpolations from Ben, gave highly coloured accounts, pointing up the mistakes they made and praising the police.

'Especially Ian,' said Libby. 'He's always willing to listen to us – well, to Fran, really. She helped him a lot over the murders connected to Anderson Place.'

'Don't you find it hard, though?' asked Rosie. 'After all, some of the people you suspect could be close friends.'

'Not often,' said Libby. 'Sometimes we know them, which is why we get involved in the first place, but it's rarely people we're fond of.'

'Sometimes it is,' murmured Ben. Libby gave him a quick look.

'Yes, sometimes.' She patted his hand and ignored Andrew's and Rosie's raised eyebrows.

'I mean,' she went on quickly, 'there was that case last summer about the Morris Dancers. I knew several of them, but I wasn't all that fond of them.'

'Morris?' Andrew laughed. 'I can't imagine you involved with Morris.'

'No, I'm not, but it's a fascinating subject. All sorts of weird and wonderful things go on.'

'I've used it as a background,' said Rosie thoughtfully. 'I found there were people who took it so seriously they could almost kill people who mocked it, or joined in as a joke.'

Libby nodded. 'And some people who use it as a cover for some rather nasty goings-on – all covered by the folk tradition.'

'Like The Wicker Man?' said Andrew.

'Very like.' Libby sighed. 'All those pretty

pictures on calendars of Morris sides outside pubs on the village green are very misleading.'

'There couldn't be anything like that involved in the White Lodge, I suppose?' Andrew looked at Rosie. 'You don't remember anything like that?'

'I've already said, I don't *actually* remember anything,' said Rosie. 'But I doubt it.'

'So do I,' said Libby. 'What we really need to do is find out about the grave and the flowers. And the music.'

'I've always loved Debussy,' said Rosie wistfully. 'It seems so sad he should be connected to all this.'

'Do you think Debussy is connected to you?' Libby asked.

Rosie looked startled. 'I don't think so! He died in 1918, didn't he?'

'Did he? That's very precise of you.'

'It's just something I know,' said Rosie frowning. 'Like the dates of the wars, and 1066.'

'That sounds like Fran. Facts in her head that she has no reason to know.'

'But anyone could know Debussy's dates,' said Andrew, his hand moving a little nearer to Rosie's. 'Especially if he's a particular interest.'

'I don't know about that,' said Rosie doubtfully. 'I'm not that musical. I was just introduced to Debussy very young.'

'Oh? Who by?' Libby leant across the table.

'Libby!' said Ben. 'Stop it.'

Rosie shook her head. 'Oh, I don't mind. After all, I started it. But I'm afraid I don't know who introduced me. I assume it was my mother.'

Libby sighed. 'Oh, well. We're not going to get much further with that, are we?'

'Do we need to?' Andrew frowned.

'Ian says it's just that whoever set up the music only had a Debussy CD to hand.'

'It wouldn't have been a CD when Rosie first heard it,' said Ben. 'In her first dream, I mean.'

'No.' Rosie looked at him with an eager expression. 'Of course not. No CDs then. Cassette player, perhaps?'

'When did you have the dream?'

'A year or so back. But the dream wasn't about then, as Libby says. The house has been empty for years, so when I dreamt about it, it was a long time ago.'

'Yes, but the Debussy could just be a sort of overlay in your brain,' said Libby.

'It could, couldn't it?' Rosie was looking more interested than disturbed now. 'I see why you get fascinated with all these investigations, Libby.'

'Oh, don't encourage her,' said Ben.

Andrew gave him a commiserating glance.

'If the Debussy is an overlay, it meant you were listening to it when you were young, but you've already said you were. So does it mean you listened to it in that house?' Libby helped herself to more wine.

'I don't know.' Rosie frowned. 'It's a lot more complicated than I thought.'

'Especially with the addition of bodies being dug up,' said Libby.

'And the flowers on the grave,' added Andrew. He grinned round the table. 'I must say, I'm finding this all quite exciting.'

Ben groaned.

The following day Libby decided it should be a beach day. She was too involved with Rosie and the White Lodge and she needed to do something to take her mind off it. The sun was out, the sky was blue, all she needed was a book and a companion.

Ben was out doing something to Steeple Farm, the house owned by his aunt which he had renovated with a view to living there, but Libby, after havering for some time, had reluctantly decided she didn't want to leave her beloved, although decidedly cramped, cottage. Ben was making sure the house and garden were in a fit state to receive their first tenants in a few days' time.

So Libby packed some essentials into Romeo the Renault and set off for Nethergate. She could always call and see if either Fran or Jane wanted to join her.

However, neither Fran nor Jane were in. On calling in at Guy's shop, Sophie informed her that they had gone to see Chrissie, who, apparently, had a scan picture to show them.

'Couldn't she have scanned and emailed it?' asked Libby. 'Or even come over here?'

'She's too worn out, it seems,' said Sophie, pulling a face. There was no love lost between her and her step-sister.

'And there's poor old Jane heaving herself about in that house and looking after her mother.'

'I thought her mother was supposed to be helping *her*?' said Sophie.

'Jane doesn't want to rely on her.' Libby

shrugged. 'Horses for courses.'

So she ended up sitting on her cushion on the beach by herself. The sun wasn't hot enough to cause discomfort, although she still wore an ancient sunhat, and she'd found a relatively comfortable part of the sea wall as a back rest. After a while the book palled and she found herself watching the few young – obviously middle-class – families on the beach. Suddenly a shadow loomed over her.

'I was told I might find you here,' said Campbell McLean.

Libby struggled to sit upright and clutched her hat. 'Hello. What are you doing here?'

'I was working. The crew have gone now, so I popped in to see Fran, only she's not home. And young what's'ername said you were here.'

'Sophie. Guy's daughter.' Libby patted the cushion beside her. 'Sit down. I can't peer up at you like that. What were you filming?'

'A piece about clean beaches. Some environmental group has complained about sewage in the sea during heavy rainfall.'

'Here?' Libby shuddered and looked round at the peaceful beach.

'Oh, it happens everywhere. It's only supposed to happen a few times in the season, but it's happening almost every day. Not so bad here, as we're dryer than most places in the UK.' Campbell sat down heavily on the beach and took off his jacket. Libby still thought he looked like central casting's idea of a geography teacher. Quite attractive in his way. She wondered why he wasn't married.

'I don't pretend to understand what the significance of the south-east being dryer is, and I don't think I want to know,' she said. 'Have you got a girlfriend, Campbell?'

'Wha–?' His mouth stayed open.

'Oh, sorry. That was a bit of a non-sequitur, wasn't it?'

'Just a bit.' He looked amused. 'What prompted it? And as it happens, no I haven't.'

'I was just thinking how attractive you are.' Libby laughed at him as a blush crept up his neck. 'It's all right, I'm not after you myself. I was just thinking it was a waste. Unless –' She stopped.

'No, Libby, I'm not gay.' He patted her hand. 'I just don't take to commitment.'

'Yet you look just the sort of guy who would.' Libby leant back against the wall. 'Anyway, what did you want to see Fran about?'

'It was just an idea,' said Campbell. 'I hear they're digging up the children's graves at the White Lodge.'

Chapter Twelve

LIBBY STARED. 'HOW DO you know?' she said finally.

'Why? Is it a secret?'

'Well, no, but it's a police operation. I didn't think they'd broadcast it.'

'Things get around. People always want to tell a TV reporter things.'

'I suppose they do.'

'Or ask them things.' Cameron cocked his head interrogatively.

'Oh. You got the message, then.'

'Of course. I didn't get back to you, I'm sorry. But I've been a bit busy this last week. I've been sitting in as anchor.'

'You've what?'

'Anchor. The person in the studio for the news report.'

'Oh. Is that promotion?'

'No, not really. And I'd hate to do it all the time. I prefer to be out and about. But John's been on holiday. So, tell me, what did you want to ask me? Was it about the children?'

'Yes,' said Libby, exasperated. 'Why does everyone else know about them and we don't?'

'There's nothing to know, really. There was a ghost story going round in the fifties when they dug up a body by accident.'

'Yes, that's what Rosie said.'

'Who's Rosie?'

Libby was wary. 'A friend of Fran's.'

'Has she asked you to look into these children?'

'Not really. We just sort of – came across them.'

'And no one knew about them? I find that surprising. It's a well known folk tale around here. What about your friend Jane?'

'She knew but got upset. You know she's pregnant?'

'No, I don't really know her. Very pregnant?'

'Almost due, I think. In fact, she's not home today, so she could even be in hospital as we speak.'

'Well, I'll tell you what I know, but I don't suppose it's any more than you've learnt already. And I assume your interest has led to the police investigation.'

'Er.' Libby cleared her throat. 'In a way.'

'Right. I shall want an exclusive as soon as you know anything.' Campbell leant back on his elbows. 'Go on, ask away.'

'Well, so far, a friend who's a historian has turned up the fact that the workhouse was turned into a TB hospital.'

'The Princess Beatrice, yes.'

'There, see?' Libby was even more irritated. 'It took us an expert to find that out.'

'Why? It's online, surely?'

'I was looking for the White Lodge and the Cherry Ashton Workhouse. It didn't come up at all until our Professor Wylie found the records.'

'Professor Wylie? I know him. We use him as a talking head sometimes,' said Campbell, making himself more comfortable against the wall. 'And the answer to that is simple. It wasn't called White

Lodge until after it was the Princess Beatrice.'

'But it came up on a search as the workhouse,' said Libby.

'Yes, that's a bit odd. Why didn't it say "formerly the Princess Beatrice and the Cherry Ashton Workhouse"?'

'I don't know, although I expect between them Ian and Andrew will get to the bottom of it.'

'Ian and Andrew?' Campbell frowned.

'DI Connell – and Andrew is Professor Wylie.'

'Oh, he's co-opted him, too?'

'Only because we had. So what was the story about the dug-up child?'

'It was when the former owner wanted to clear the ground at the back. That was when they discovered the graveyard.'

'Oh, for f – goodness' sake,' said an exasperated Libby. 'How come none of this is on record anywhere? What former owner?'

'The bloke who bought the hospital after it fell into disrepair. The back garden was so overgrown it needed to be completely cleared. When the child's body was discovered they realised there were several more gravestones and decided they must be from the hospital, so they wouldn't disturb them. Then some idiot who worked there said she'd seen a ghost and the stories grew.'

'Well, that makes sense, but not why the grave was cleared recently,' muttered Libby.

'What?' Campbell sat up and Libby cursed herself.

'Look, that's not common knowledge. Don't you dare use it. It's actually,' Libby said, improvising wildly, 'why Ian's looking into it. Because the grave was cleared.' Well, that was true, wasn't it?

'Why was it cleared?' asked Campbell.

'Weren't you listening? That's what Ian's trying to find out. It can't be someone left who remembers a TB victim, can it? That would be nearly a hundred years ago.'

'When it did it stop being a TB hospital? People were still being put in sanatoria in the 50s, you know.'

'Really?' Libby was startled. 'I thought it had died out by then.'

'No, and it still hasn't,' said Campbell. 'But everyone has the BCG vaccination now. And the old idea of sleeping out in the fresh air whatever the weather came to an end, too.'

'Did they?'

'Oh, yes. And they were in hospital for months and months. Years sometimes. I heard of a small child, two years old, I think, who went in and didn't come out until she was five. Her mother was only allowed to visit every six weeks.'

'That's horrific!'

'But true.' Campbell shrugged. 'Anyway, they don't do it now.'

'So that child could have been quite recent when they dug it up in the fifties?'

'I suppose so. Anyway, it isn't the same grave this time, is it? Can't be.'

'I don't know,' said Libby. 'Perhaps it is. I asked what had happened to the original body, but Rosie didn't know. Perhaps they reburied it.'

'Is that all you know?' Campbell leant his

forearms on his bent knees. 'How did you come to be interested?'

'Oh, this and that.'

'That means you won't tell me. Was it this Rosie?'

'Could have been.'

'But a secret?'

'Well – yes.'

Campbell laughed. 'Honestly, you two. You expect everyone to give you information, yet you won't give any yourselves.'

Libby felt herself going red. 'It isn't that. It just isn't my secret, and anyway, now the police are involved, I couldn't tell you anything anyway.'

Campbell sighed. 'If there is anything, will you tell me?'

'Of course.' Libby patted his arm. 'I really am sorry. When we asked you they hadn't found a body. We didn't know anything.'

'OK. I absolve you from any blame. After all, I did try to get Fran to talk to me about being a psychic detective once, didn't I?'

'And she hated you for it.' Libby grinned. 'So we're quits. But seriously, Campbell, you're sure to get to hear of it. And you can always ring up Professor Wylie and ask him. If he knows anything, of course.'

'Do you think he does?'

'Well, he has been called in as a consultant, mainly because they wanted to investigate the historical records. And look at the building.'

'What did they want to do that for?'

Bugger, thought Libby. 'Oh, to get an idea of its

date, I suppose,' she said vaguely. 'He said he couldn't do a proper visual analysis.'

'But the date of the building is quite well documented. It's early sixteenth century or thereabouts. Of course, there was an older building on the site.'

'Perhaps they want to find traces of that,' suggested Libby.

'I don't know why they would,' said Campbell. 'That was destroyed by fire.'

'Oh, I don't know then,' said Libby. 'Anyway, it's nothing to do with me any longer.'

'Thrown off the case, eh?' Campbell grinned and stood up, brushing himself down. 'Let me know if anything breaks.'

'May I tell Fran what you've told me? About the hospital?' Libby looked up at him, shading her eyes.

'Of course. It's public knowledge.'

Not that public, thought Libby, as she packed her book and thermos into her basket. We didn't find out about it that easily. She stood up, thinking about the poor little two-year-old who'd been sent into a sanatorium. If Jane knew about that sort of thing, no wonder she didn't want to talk about it.

'Sophie said you were here.' Fran was leaning on the railings on top of the sea wall. Libby climbed the three steps to join her.

'I felt like a day on the beach. Only I've had enough. Campbell was just here.'

'Sophie told me. What did he want?'

'He didn't come to Nethergate just to see us. He was here doing some report on sewage outfall.' Libby pulled a face.

Fran nodded. 'Just round into the other bay. It's not that bad here, actually.'

'Sounds awful,' said Libby. 'Would you like some of my thermos tea? I haven't drunk it.'

'Come on. I'll make you a proper cup. I could do with one.'

'That sounds ominous. How was Chrissie?' Libby followed Fran across the road to her front door.

'Dire.' Fran opened the door. 'How I ever spawned that child I shall never know. Thank goodness she doesn't live any nearer.'

'You haven't heard anything from Jane I suppose?' Libby put down her basket and followed Fran into the kitchen.

'No, but I doubt we'd be the first people she'd tell when something happens.' Fran switched on the kettle and opened the back door for Balzac, who strolled in, dark furry tail waving like a plume of feathers behind him.

'I suppose not,' said Libby, 'and we don't want to become those infuriating people who keep ringing up and asking if they're still there.'

'No, we don't,' said Fran. 'In fact I want to become one of those people with as low a profile as possible.'

'Oh, dear. Was Chrissie worse than usual?'

'Do you know what she had the cheek to say?' Fran turned to Libby, brimming with indignation.

'No, what?'

'She thought I ought to move in with her and Bruce a month before the baby's due and stay for a couple of months afterwards.'

'No!' Libby couldn't help giggling. 'And what did Guy have to say to that?'

'I just asked her quite calmly if she and Bruce were going to move out of the master bedroom for us.'

'I bet she loved that.'

'She was a touch taken aback. Bruce wasn't there, of course, and he wouldn't have it anyway. He's only just got over the shock of becoming a prospective father.'

Libby shook her head. 'I just hope it doesn't split them up. She'd be bound to descend on you like she did last time.'

'Don't worry,' said Fran grimly, pouring water into mugs. 'She won't get the chance.'

They carried their mugs through to the sitting room and sat down either side of the huge inglenook fireplace. Balzac promptly jumped on Libby's knee and nearly sent her tea flying.

'So what did Campbell have to say?' asked Fran. 'You still haven't told me.'

Libby told her everything Campbell had said. 'So now perhaps we ought to look it up backwards, if you know what I mean,' she finished. 'Although I really don't know why all this history didn't come up before when we were researching it.'

'What we still don't know,' said Fran, staring thoughtfully into the empty fireplace, 'is who owned it in the fifties.'

'No.' Libby frowned. 'And that's the most puzzling bit of all. We know it was a merchant's house, then a workhouse, then a TB sanatorium, but we don't know what happened after that, and who was excavating. Who dug up the body? And Campbell said it was someone who worked there who put around the story of the ghost.'

'But far more puzzling,' said Fran, 'is who is clearing the grave and laying flowers now?'

'Well, I said to Campbell, it surely wouldn't be a relative of the person who's buried there. It would be too long ago.'

'Fifties? A child? We're talking between forty and fifty years ago. It could easily be a relative. A younger sibling. An older one, even. It could even be a parent.'

'I suppose so, but not a parent. They'd be too old to clear the grave.'

'It still doesn't seem right to me.' Fran put her mug down on the hearth. 'Why, if there are graves from that long ago, is someone trying to scare us off?'

'Not just us,' said Libby, 'everybody. That music plays for the police, too.'

Chapter Thirteen

'ANDREW'S GONE THROUGH THE records he can find and apparently Ian's demanded Land Registry information,' said Fran on the phone the following morning.

'And?'

'I don't know. Andrew thinks he's got something, but he isn't sure what.'

'Can anybody look up previous ownership of houses?' Libby was tapping various combinations of words into her search engine.

'I think you have to pay,' said Fran. 'Anyway, Andrew said he'd phone later. He was going to see Rosie.'

'You're right. It does look as though you have to pay. Did you know that the Canterbury Land Registry office is in Nottingham?'

'How ridiculous. Well, I hope Ian has some joy with it. Although if he thinks that it's an old body I can't see why he's bothering.'

Libby sat for a while in front of the laptop, wondering how she could find out any more about White Lodge. As it was Saturday, she could reasonably expect no results from either Andrew or Ian until Monday and it irked her to sit and do nothing, even if there was nothing she was expected to do.

"Gone cold" was the term she had used to Ben the previous evening when telling him about the developments. He had been careful not to show how pleased he was about this, but she'd known, and been depressed.

This morning, however, he'd gone off with his cousins Peter and James to make a rare visit to his son who lived somewhere in the north. Ben's relationship with his children had been soured by the break-up of his marriage, and he rarely had the opportunity to see either of them, so despite the fact that it would mean a weekend on her own, Libby was pleased for him.

And, she reminded herself, it meant she could do exactly what she wanted until Sunday night. Harry had suggested she joined him at The Pink Geranium for Sunday lunch, but, other than that, she was free. So free, in fact, that she immediately decided to go and have another look at White Lodge. But first, she looked it up on the satellite mapping site to see if there was any other way in.

It was confusing, however. She could see the open road by which she and Fran had approached it, but the grounds around it looked heavily wooded and seemed to have no definitive boundary. There did appear to be a lane which led towards the back of the property, but it petered out as far as she could see. Still, she thought, it was worth a try.

The easiest way to approach the other side of the property was to go via Steeple Mount, a village which hadn't always had happy connotations for Libby, but she drove through happily enough, noting as she did so that the baker's shop had gone, and gave a quick glance upwards to the standing stone Grey Betty, keeping watch over the town. The road dipped down to become a cut between high, heavily treed banks, similar to many others in this part of Kent, although Libby knew that either side of the lane the fields spread out with hardly a tree in sight.

Then, she came to a crossroads. A few houses and a pub were gathered round it, and to her right what looked like a small estate of new houses. Hesitating, she looked round for clues. Nothing. As there was no one to be seen, she couldn't ask directions, but then she didn't know where she was aiming for herself. With a shrug, she put the car into gear and went straight on.

The lane began to climb a slight slope. On Libby's right were a few more cottages, on her left a terrace of them and what looked like a coach-house, with a carriage entrance. Then, on a rise to her left surrounded by even more trees, a church. She frowned. This was odd. She had assumed White Lodge was quite isolated, but creeping up behind it was all this civilization. Although to be fair, she told herself, she didn't know exactly how far away from White Lodge she was. And sure enough, as shown on her computer, the lane, by now thick with last year's fallen leaves and almost completely shaded from the sun by huge trees, petered out. Yards ahead of her an old gate hung half open on its hinges, and to her left, a bank of rubble and tree roots, behind which the forbidding grey face of a large, stone building.

Libby got out of the car. It looked as though where she had parked had once been some kind of drive or entrance, but now access to the building had effectively been silted up. Nevertheless, she climbed over the worst of the roots and scrambled to the top of the bank, where she peered past huge tree trunks to the building itself.

At this end there were no windows, but further along there were a few. Many were cracked or simply missing, and she could see nothing of what was inside except the flutter of a piece of rag at one of the upper casements. There was little clue as to what age the building was, other than iron building ties high up on the blank wall.

She contemplated climbing down the other side of the bank but the area between it and the building was so overgrown with brambles it was even worse than the gardens of White Lodge. She looked up at the grey wall in front of her. White Lodge. Was this in the grounds of White Lodge?

She climbed back down the bank, went round the car and to the end of the lane where the gate hung open. Peering to the left, she could see nothing but a line of trees, and, in front of her, a wide, open field, full of something golden and waving. Wheat, she supposed. Well, logically, it could be the back boundary of the grounds of White Lodge, and, she thought suddenly, this could in fact be one of the old workhouse buildings. She went back to it and shivered. Above the trees the sun was still shining, but here all was cool and ominously still.

'Can I help you?'

Libby almost screamed. When she turned round, so quickly she almost fell, she found herself being regarded politely by a dark-skinned man with a moustache and a very sharp suit.

'Oh, goodness!' she said. 'You startled me.'

'I'm sorry.' The man stepped forward a little. 'I wondered if you were lost?'

'Not exactly,' said Libby, feeling uncomfortable and wondering how much she should say. 'I was hoping to find – um – a back way to Cherry Ashton.'

'Ah.' The man smiled. 'This is Cherry Ashton.' He waved a hand behind him. 'Not very big, you see. Were you looking for someone in particular?'

Someone, he said, not something.

'Well, I was, actually.' Libby gave what she hoped was a disarming smile as her brain raced. 'The Cherry Ashton workhouse.'

He raised his brows. 'Really? But that has been gone since the beginning of the last century.'

Bum. Think again. 'Yes, I know, but I was hoping to find some remnants of it. You see,' she went on, gathering confidence, 'the main house is still standing, and it was turned into a sanatorium after the workhouse was demolished. I thought there must have been at least one other building in use as the sanatorium.' She gestured behind her. 'So I wondered if this was it?'

'Yes, we all know about the sanatorium.' He looked serious. 'But I'm afraid I don't know if that building was ever used. Here in the village we all assume it is just a derelict building.'

'And you don't know if it forms part of the White Lodge estate?' Might as well go the whole hog, now.

'I'm afraid not.' He nodded towards the solid looking undergrowth. 'As you can see, no one would be prepared to try and get near it.'

Libby clambered down to stand closer to him. 'Doesn't anyone know anything about it? In my village there's always someone who knows. Always a gossipy old lady who was born there.'

'Ah. Yes. There are people who remember the sanatorium. The Princess Beatrice.'

'But not this building.' Libby sighed. 'Oh, well. I expect we'll find out on the estate plans.'

'We?' The man raised an interrogative eyebrow. Libby cursed herself.

'For the sale,' she improvised hurriedly. 'White Lodge is being sold.'

'Ah, of course. Although who would want to buy it with that history?'

'What history? As a workhouse? Or a sanatorium? I understand several people died there. Children.'

He nodded. 'Many. There are those who say it is haunted.'

'Yes,' said Libby, 'but that's only a rumour. Nobody believes it really.'

'Really.' The man frowned. 'I thought many local people believed it.'

'You're obviously local. Do you believe it?'

The man smiled. 'Yes, I'm local. I live in Ashton Terrace, there.' He indicated the row of cottages. 'And I don't know if I believe it or not. I have long accepted it as fact.'

'Have you lived here long?' Libby asked before she could think better of it.

He laughed. 'Longer than you would think. I have restaurants. In Canterbury and Nethergate. My sons run them now.'

'Oh, goodness. The Golden Spice?'

'Yes. You know them?'

'My friends and I go to the Nethergate one regularly.' Libby held out her hand. 'I'm pleased to meet you.'

'Aakarsh Vindari.' He bowed over her hand.

'I'm Libby Sarjeant, Mr Vindari. And thank you for your help.'

Vindari shrugged. 'I think you knew everything I could tell you.'

'Well, it was nice to have it confirmed.' Libby smiled. 'And although I know of it, I've never been to Cherry Ashton before. I didn't know it was so small.'

'That is how we like it. Of course, just down the road we have the caravan park, but that keeps other people away.'

'Caravan Park?'

'They call it "The Roses".' There was an unmistakeable sneer in Vindari's voice.

'Oh, that! That's near here?'

'If you had turned right at the crossroads instead of coming straight on, you would have seen it.'

So, thought Libby, he knew which direction I came from. But then, it's so quiet here they probably all looked out of their windows when they saw an unfamiliar car.

'Well, perhaps I'm glad I didn't, then,' she said aloud. 'And now I'd better be going. Thank you again, Mr Vindari.'

'A pleasure, Mrs Sarjeant,' he said, bowing again. 'And please, next time you go into one of my restaurants, mention my name.'

‘Thank you,’ said Libby, resolving to go as soon as she possibly could.

He watched as she climbed into the car, turned it round and drove carefully back down the lane. When she got to the crossroads she wanted to turn left and go and have a look at “The Roses”, a holiday park much maligned in the area, but which she had never seen. With Aakarsh Vindari watching from the top of the lane, she didn’t dare. However, she did turn right, wondering if this road might bring her out on the main Creekmarsh road.

And that was odd, she thought. The map had indicated that the lane she followed and the Creekmarsh road both led to Cherry Ashton, but the Creekmarsh road didn’t. Unless there was yet another spur not marked on the map. However, when she finally emerged from the tunnel-like lane she found herself at a T-junction with the Creekmarsh road, and opposite her a small, old black-and-white sign pointing back the way she had come to Cherry Ashton. She must have missed it both times she had been here with Fran.

On impulse, she turned right and drove up to White Lodge, surprised to find police tape still across the gateway, although with no noticeable police presence. She parked the car on the verge opposite and crossed the road. Without going in through the gate and crossing the police tape, she walked along the boundary hedge until she came to the end. The high wall that surrounded the garden led away across an open field. Cautiously, Libby, with a glance over her shoulder to make sure she wasn’t observed, began to follow it.

Chapter Fourteen

AFTER A FEW HUNDRED yards, the wall turned slightly to the left and appeared to lead straight into a copse. Libby stopped. Could it be the woodland that surrounded the building at Cherry Ashton? She continued towards it, until she realised that around the edges was a barbed wire fence. Stepping slightly away from the wall into the field, she tried to peer past the wooded area to see if she could see the village, but she could see nothing except a slight rise topped by more trees.

Disappointed, she turned back the way she'd come. It certainly looked a possibility that the derelict building was part of the White Lodge estate, although what significance that had she had no idea. Except that maybe, somehow, it was connected to the music? Hidden away? But if so, she chided herself, it would need very sophisticated wiring in order to play music through speakers in the main house. And no one could be seen approaching from there, either.

She reached the edge of the wall and found Ian Connell leaning against it.

'Exploring?' he said.

Libby felt heat rising into her face once more. 'Yes.'

'And why, exactly?'

'Am I trespassing?'

'Don't avoid the question, Libby.'

'I was just interested. I wondered how far the

estate stretched.'

'Quite a way, according to the plans we've found.'

'Oh?' said Libby eagerly. 'You've found plans?'

'Yes.' Ian grinned at her, and taking her arm, led her back to her car. 'Andrew's been very helpful, and found two or three maps which show the position of the house and the other buildings.'

'And what about ownership?'

'Nothing after the sanatorium, but then, we shall hear about that on Monday. A Home Office order does wonders.'

'Why do you need that? I thought it wasn't a murder enquiry any longer?'

'We have to make sure the graves here are legal.' Libby thought Ian was being evasive.

'But they were buried years ago. Would it matter now?'

'There are all sorts of issues, Libby. Now get off home and stop –' he paused.

'Interfering, I know.' Libby unlocked the car. 'How did you know I was here?'

'I didn't until I arrived to check on something. Your car tends to be a giveaway.' He held the door for her to climb in. 'Go on. I'll see you soon.'

'Will you let us know anything you're able to?' Libby poked her head out of the window.

'As much as I can.' He patted her cheek. 'Now, go!'

OK, thought Libby, he's still working on it. That means there's still something to be found out. Which, of course, was obvious. Something or someone was playing the recordings of Debussy, which was suspicious, if not illegal.

She drove home slowly, past Creekmarsh and on a whim, turned off towards Heronsbourne. She hadn't seen George at The Red Lion for ages, and it was an outside chance that he might know something about Cherry Ashton and White Lodge. She parked in Pedlar's Row and looked over to March Cottage, former home of her friend Bella, and now let. There were unsuitable patterned net curtains at the window.

'Libby!' George put down his paper and came round the corner of the bar to greet her.

'Hello, George. Have you still got your excellent coffee machine?'

'Course I have. You drivin', then?'

Libby hoisted herself onto a bar stool. 'Yes. I've just been over to Cherry Ashton.'

George turned from inserting a cup into the coffee machine in surprise. 'What d'you want to go there for? There's nothing there!'

'No, I found that out. There's a pub, though.'

'Yeah, that's not bad.' George put a foaming cup in front of her. 'Does good food. Won't let people in from that holiday camp place, though.'

'Oh, "The Roses"? Why not? I heard someone say today it wasn't very good.'

'Oh, I don't know about that. I reckon it's as good as most places of that sort, probably better than most. Quite – whatd'youcallit – upmarket.'

'Is it? Wonder why the pub won't let them in, then?'

'Snobbery.' George resumed his own seat behind the bar. 'So what d'you go to Cherry Ashton for, then?'

'My friend Fran – you remember Fran?'

'Could 'ardly forget either of you, could I?'

Libby pulled a face. 'All right. Well, Fran and I have been looking into the old workhouse over there.'

'That's over on the marsh road, though,' said George. 'The main road.'

'I know White Lodge is, but presumably most of the workhouse buildings would have been down on the Cherry Ashton side if that's what the place was called.'

'Makes sense,' said George. 'No buildings left now, though, are there? Wasn't it turned into a hospital, anyway?'

'A sanatorium, yes. Do you remember it?'

'Not really. I wasn't living here then. Heard tell, of course. There was that ghost, wasn't there?'

Libby sighed. 'Everyone knows about the ghost.'

George shrugged. 'That's about it, then. Wasn't the police up there the other day?' He narrowed his eyes at her. 'Ah! That's what you was over there for.'

'Sort of,' said Libby, licking froth off her coffee.

'What's it all about, then?'

'They thought they'd found a body, but it turned out to be a patient from the hospital.'

'How could they tell that, then? And how come bodies were buried there and not in the churchyard?'

'Yes, it is odd, isn't it? Perhaps as it was all TB victims they didn't want to infect an ordinary graveyard.'

George snorted. 'Wouldn't matter none to they

residents, would it?'

Libby giggled. 'No.'

'How's that old cat, then? Your friend still got him?'

'Balzac? Yes, he's fine. Very friendly. Fran's married now, you know?'

'Is she now. That's nice. What about you?'

'No, I'm not. Still with my chap, though.'

'Chap! Don't hear that word much these days,' said George.

'Well, I don't know what else to call him. Not boyfriend – not at my age.'

George shrugged again and talk turned to mutual acquaintances. Half an hour later, Libby finished her coffee and went on her way, promising to bring Fran over some time soon.

So, no more information. Just that there was a snobbish pub in Cherry Ashton and that the holiday park was upmarket. Then she remembered, with slight surprise, that she hadn't mentioned her visit to Cherry Ashton and her meeting with the urbane Mr Vindari to Ian. Although what that would have added to his investigation was probably negligible. Still, she thought, perhaps it would be a good idea to go back to the satellite mapping website and go in a bit closer. She might be able to see the strange building. She put her foot down with new determination.

The weather had changed. Yesterday's perfect summer holiday had turned into a pre-cursor to autumn. The sun that had trickled through the leaves at Cherry Ashton had disappeared behind an ominous yellowish-grey blanket. As Libby drew up opposite number 17 Allhallow's Lane the first fat drop of rain hit the windscreen, and by the time she put the key in the lock her hair was damp. Sidney shot in between her legs seeking the shelter of the sofa cushions.

Libby put the kettle on and went to change into a dry top. After leaving tea to brew she woke up the laptop and found it still on the satellite mapping page. Positioning the cursor exactly over the point she wanted, she zoomed in as close as she could, and sat back with a satisfied 'Ah!'

There was the building, surrounded by trees, not only on the side where she had parked the car, but on all sides, right up to the little cemetery that surrounded the church one side and – incredibly – almost as far as White Lodge behind. She pulled out a little way and viewed the whole estate. Sure enough, although no boundary could be seen, it appeared that the building did belong to White Lodge. There was the barbed wire, of course, but that was outside the wall she'd walked along earlier.

Where this got her, she wasn't sure, and presumably, on reflection, Ian knew about this, as he'd been watching her. But had he, or his team, actually searched the whole of the grounds? Had they found that building? She got up and went to pour tea. Of course, Andrew had found documents, hadn't he? So presumably the buildings would be marked on deeds. She sighed. It didn't seem as though she was learning anything useful that wasn't already known. She picked up the phone.

'Harry, have you got room for me tonight instead of tomorrow?'

'I can find you a seat by the gents, I expect. Why?'

'I don't fancy sitting here all on my own all evening.'

'But you don't mind tomorrow lunchtime.'

'Well, no. I can do stuff tomorrow, and anyway, Ben'll be home in the evening.'

'My, my, life has changed.'

'What do you mean?' Libby was suspicious.

'Nothing, dear heart, nothing. Don't come too early tonight.'

'Eight-thirty? Nine?'

'Nine. See you then.'

Happier now she had something to do in the evening, Libby went back to the laptop with her tea and began another fruitless search for information about White Lodge, workhouses, sanatoria and ghosts.

Adam wasn't in The Pink Geranium when Libby arrived. A child masquerading as a waiter asked her nervously if she had booked and looked horrified when she told him she thought so. A stentorian bellow from the kitchen of "Friend" made it even worse, and Libby thought the boy would burst into tears.

'Don't worry,' she said, patting his shoulder. 'I'll just go and sit on the sofa until Harry tells me where I'm to sit. You just bring me a bottle of the house red and a glass.'

In fact it was Donna who arrived with the wine, rolling her eyes.

'Honestly,' she said, taking her time over pouring. 'Harry's not making it any easier for that poor boy. It's his first night.'

'Bit much, throwing him in the deep end on a Saturday night,' said Libby. 'Is he Adam's replacement?'

'Not replacement, exactly, but you know Harry's always said Adam can choose when he works? Well, we need someone here most of the time now we're getting busier. Adam will still work when he wants to. This Jacob's still at school, so can only work a few hours a week.'

Libby nodded. 'How's the fiancé?'

Donna grinned and waggled her left hand. 'Great, thanks. We're not going to hang about. Getting married in October.'

'Good stuff,' said Libby.

Jacob came over after a few minutes to tell her that Harry had told her to sit at the table in the window when its current occupants left. Libby thanked him nicely, by name and with a smile, and he went away looking marginally happier.

An hour later, after her quesadillas con hongos, Harry joined her with another bottle of wine and a glass.

'I haven't finished this bottle yet,' she said.

'But I'm going to drink that,' he said, pouring it into his glass. 'So, come on. What have you been up to? How's that investigation?'

Libby told him everything that had happened since she'd last seen him, including her inconclusive trip of this afternoon.

'Was he a sinister Indian gentleman straight out of Sherlock Holmes?' Harry twirled an imaginary moustache.

'No, he was the owner of the Golden Spice restaurants. Very nice.'

'Oh, we've been to the one in Canterbury. Yes. Very good.'

'He told me to mention his name if I went again.'

'In that case I'm coming with you. I could perhaps add a few veggie curries to the menu in here.'

'Anyway, I haven't got any further. Ideas?'

'Me?' Harry shook his head. 'All I can see is that your Rosie knew the house when she was little, associates it with someone playing music and dreamt about it. Why she should go to all the – the–'

'Palaver,' suggested Libby.

'Yeah, palaver of getting you two to investigate I can't think. Seems to me she's using you, but for some reason other than she's said. And it also looks to me as if Ian *has* found something that's worth investigating but hasn't told you.'

'Did you think she was that devious when you met her the other day?'

'No, I thought she was quite a nice attractive elderly lady. And she was flirting like mad with the professor bloke.'

'Was she? I thought it was the other way round. And I wouldn't call her elderly.'

'No, you wouldn't. She's not that much older than you.' Harry ducked as Libby aimed the menu at him. 'And she was definitely showing out.'

'Well, good luck to her,' said Libby. 'And I believe her – or now I do, anyway.'

'You didn't at first.' Harry opened the second bottle.

'No. I was very suspicious.'

'But, being the nosy cow you are, you couldn't help barging in.'

'If you want to put it like that. And Ian was interested, so it wasn't wasted.'

'Rosie could have told the police about the music the time she went there herself.'

'I know, but I think she thought they'd put her down as a mad old woman.'

'Hmmm.' Harry poured more wine. 'And she isn't?'

'Anyway, now I want to find out about that building. It must belong to White Lodge, and it's logical that as it's actually in Cherry Ashton it's part of the workhouse. And therefore, possibly part of the sanatorium.'

'And there will be murder victims buried inside, obviously.'

'Don't mock. I still can't get over that cleared grave. That must mean something.'

Harry sighed. 'Yes, it's a ghost playing the piano and leaving flowers. Or someone playing an elaborate practical joke. Have you thought about that?'

Chapter Fifteen

'NO.' LIBBY STARED AT Harry's sardonic expression. 'You mean Rosie, don't you?'

'Who's a novelist.' Harry leant back in his chair. 'I said. She's using you.'

'But now the police are involved. She'd have to back off. Or confess. And she hasn't.'

'She'd be too embarrassed. And I don't suppose she's done anything illegal.'

'What about the music? She'd need an awful lot of expertise to rig that, and she'd have had to break in, too.'

Harry sighed again. 'Wake up, Lib. Think of the most obvious explanation.'

'Which is?'

'She says she knew it as a child. Described it. When you find out it actually is how she said, she has to make up some cock and bull story. But suppose she did live there? Suppose she actually owns it? The agents have been told to keep the ownership quiet, and have they confirmed that she visited a year ago, or whenever it was?'

'Oh.' Libby was conscious of a sharp sense of disillusionment.

'Makes sense, doesn't it?'

'Unfortunately, yes.' Libby emptied her glass. 'But why hasn't Ian seen through her? He's the detective.'

Harry pushed the bottle towards her. 'I told you. He's actually found something but hasn't told you.

It may be that he's sussed Rosie.'

'Oh,' said Libby, even more gloomily. 'How dumb can you get.'

'Oh, much dumber than you. Look at Jacob.'

'Harry! That poor boy. It's his first night and you were shouting at him. You're not some foul-mouthed TV chef.'

Harry grinned. 'Rotten, wasn't I? It's OK, I apologised, he's coming back.'

'Good. Poor lad didn't know what to do.'

'So, what are you going to do about your investigation?' Harry waved a packet of cigarettes and gestured outside. Libby followed him into the back yard, where there were a few white cast iron tables and chairs for hardened smokers.

'I shan't do anything else, I suppose,' she said, bending forward to Harry's lighter. 'Unless anyone asks me.'

'But not Rosie.'

'No.' Libby shook her head. 'Not Rosie.'

'And will you tell Fran what I said?'

'Yes.' Libby sighed. 'What I don't understand is that Fran didn't see through it.'

'Look, I may not be right,' said Harry, beginning to look uncomfortable. 'I'm only saying what it looks like on the surface. But if I am right, why, Fran attends the woman's writing class, doesn't she? She wants to write like her. That would be bound to blind her to anything she didn't want to see.'

'Maybe,' said Libby doubtfully. 'But things come to her. She doesn't ask them to. And she can't block things on purpose, either.'

'Oh, well.' Harry shrugged. 'I expect the dashing

Inspector Connell will find out soon enough.'

'Dashing?'

Harry grinned. 'Well, he is. All that saturnine splendour. He's like a Jane Austen hero.'

'Is he?' Libby was surprised. 'What do you know about Jane Austen heroes?'

'I've seen them on TV, haven't I? He's just like that.'

'Yes, I suppose he is,' said Libby. 'Although he's mainly angry, which is a bit off-putting.'

'Go on.' Harry blew smoke at her. 'You fancy him a little bit.'

'Of course I don't,' said Libby carelessly. 'Anyway, he was after Fran, remember?'

'Course I bloody remember. She was living upstairs here, wasn't she?'

'So she was.' Libby giggled. 'With two men after her.'

'Lucky.' Harry stubbed out his cigarette. 'Well, that's me. The washing up calls.'

'It'll be done by now,' said Libby. 'Don't kid me.'

'I sent Jacob and the boy home, and Donna's going in a minute. I often do it on my own. Not so much washing up, that goes in the dishwasher, but there's the rest of the cleaning. Elf-an-safety. They'll close me down if they find a speck of dirt.'

'Would you like some help?"

'Don't be daft. Go and drink the rest of your wine. I'll be out in a while and I'll walk you home.'

Libby began to protest, but he pushed her before him into the restaurant, and she went back to the table to finish her wine. Most of the other customers had gone by now, and Donna came past buttoning a jacket. She waved and Libby lifted her glass. The remaining two customers stood up and stared at her as they left the restaurant. Libby looked the other way.

After a while, Harry came back with his jacket over his arm.

'There's no need to walk me home, you know.'

'It's late. Ben would have my guts for garters.'

'I always used to walk home on my own before I met Ben.'

'But you don't now. Come on. Pete's away with Ben, anyhow, so there's no one waiting for me.'

'That sounds vaguely illicit.'

Harry grinned down at her and tucked her hand through his arm. 'While the cat's away, eh? Well, you did tell me Ben was jealous of me.'

'Yes, odd that.'

'No, it isn't. You use me like a girlfriend and talk to me. Not the same way that you talk to him.'

'I do now,' said Libby. 'I think part of it was because he was always so against me doing things on my own, I didn't want to discuss them with him.'

'Not so much doing things on your own, as investigations on your own.'

'Yeah, I know.'

The village was quiet. A few cars swished down the high street, but all the lights were out in the shops and the pub. Somewhere on the other side of the road, the little river Wytch trickled along its deep gully towards the dewpond near Steeple Farm, after which it disappeared underground and eventually joined the creek near Creekmarsh. Libby and Harry turned the corner by the vicarage, where the great lilac tree overhung the wall.

'At the risk of sounding even more illicit,' said Libby, 'do you want a nightcap?'

'Thought you'd never ask.' In gentlemanly fashion, Harry took the key from Libby and opened the front door. Sidney glared from the third stair.

'Hello, walking stomach,' said Harry.

'Scotch? Or wine?' Libby turned on lights and went into the kitchen.

'Scotch, please.' Harry followed her. 'Still happy here in Bide-a-wee?'

Libby turned to him smiling. 'I love it. I can never thank you enough for finding it for me.'

'It seemed to suit. Pete and I looked at lots for you, but this one struck a chord. Still not going to Steeple Farm, then?'

'No.' Libby carried the bottle and glasses into the sitting room. 'It doesn't feel like home. And Ben's accepted that now.'

'I know. But I do wonder what will happen in the future.'

'What do you mean?' Libby handed over a glass and offered a jug of water.

'Steeple Farm is Pete's and James's when their mama dies, so that doesn't come into it, but what about the Manor?'

'Oh.' Libby shifted uncomfortably. 'I don't know. We've never discussed it.'

'Won't he expect you to go and live there when Greg and Het shuffle off?'

'I don't know. I don't want to think about it.' Libby took a healthy swallow of whisky and coughed.

'No. So what do you want to talk about? Grisly murder?'

'Don't be daft.' Libby added water to her whisky. 'There haven't been any, but ...'

'But what?' Harry heaved a theatrical sigh. 'Come on. You've got a theory.'

'Well, I just wondered ...' Libby thought for a moment. 'Suppose some of those bodies, even though they do belong to the sanatorium, shouldn't be there? Suppose there were mistakes in medication? Or people were used as guinea pigs?'

Harry stared at her. 'You know, you've got the most unpleasantly fertile imagination.'

'No, but it could be, couldn't it? After all, they haven't been buried in consecrated ground. I always thought that was illegal.'

'I don't think so. I think you have to get permission to bury someone in the garden, but I don't think it's illegal, exactly.' Harry shook his head. 'What a conversation.'

'Well, you must admit it's odd. Especially back in the fifties. I mean, most people had a normal funeral in those days, didn't they?'

'I suppose it's possible,' said Harry. 'But if the body Ian dug up had something wrong with it he'd have noticed, surely?'

'The cutter-up would, not Ian himself. And if something had gone wrong, I doubt if it would show after all this time. All they were looking for was a modern body, and it wasn't.'

'I assume you mean the pathologist?'

'Couldn't think of the word. Yes, him. Or her.'

‘So will you tell Ian your new theory?’

‘I don’t see how I can. Unless he gets in touch with me. With us.’

‘And you think he won’t?’

‘We-ell, he sort of said he would this afternoon. Just have to wait and see, I suppose.’

‘And you’re not exactly good at that, are you, Mrs S?’

‘No.’ Libby made a face. ‘Let’s talk about something else.’

Half an hour later after Harry had left, Libby turned on the laptop and typed “TB treatments” into the search engine. It soon became apparent that although TB was still around today, for some years it had not been considered fatal and, apart from the increasingly outdated “fresh air” treatment, was treated very successfully with antibiotics.

There were other stories, she found, similar to the one Cameron had told her, of people being virtually incarcerated in hospital for months. And descriptions of the operation to collapse a lung, and the more frightening descriptions of tuberculosis of other parts of the body. Tales of doctors who worked in these isolation sanatoria who had the disease themselves and had the shortest possible prognosis. After a while she switched off, thoroughly depressed at the thought that there were still millions of cases diagnosed every year, and frequently those cases were also HIV sufferers.

Nevertheless, it looked as though there were no recorded treatments of TB that could have been either unethical or illegal, so that particular theory bit the dust. Libby turned off the laptop.

On Sunday morning, feeling distinctly on edge, she forced herself to concentrate on the abandoned painting on the easel in the conservatory. Routine, that was the ticket. Forget all about weird buildings, ghostly music and exhumed bodies. Unfortunately, all that happened was that she began a new watercolour of a weird building, a ghostly piano and an exhumed body.

It was almost twelve o'clock when the phone rang.

'Libby?'

'Terry! what's happened? Is Jane OK?'

'It's a girl!' Terry Baker sounded exhausted.

'Oh, Terry!' Libby found herself unexpectedly close to tears. 'How big? When? Is Jane all right?'

'Six pounds eleven ounces, this morning at about nine. Jane's fine, but it was a long time.'

'When did you go in?'

'Actually, she went in on Friday afternoon on her own.'

'I knocked on Friday. Wish I'd known. Don't say she was in labour since then?'

'Not really. Her waters broke. So she called an ambulance. I met her there, but nothing happened until yesterday evening.'

'Oh, it's terrific, Terry. When will she be home? Oh, and what's her name?'

'Imogen, and they'll be home tomorrow. I'll get her to give you a ring.'

'You do that. Lovely name. And I'd go home and get some sleep if I were you. Have you phoned Fran?'

'No, she was next on the list. Will you do it?'

'Course I will. Give Jane and Imogen lots of love.'

Fran was at Guy's shop.

'Will we go and see them?' she asked.

'After Jane's rung us. They'll have enough to do getting themselves settled, and they've got to deal with Jane's ma. Do you think she'll mellow with a grandchild?'

'Goodness knows. I'm not sure I did.'

'You used to look after them in London, though,' said Libby.

'Of course, and I love them, but Lucy used to take advantage of me. She doesn't now, and Jane said she didn't want to rely on her mother, didn't she?'

'Have to wait and see, I suppose,' said Libby. 'Heard anything from Ian or Rosie?'

'No. Have you?'

'Well, in a way.'

'Oh? What have you been up to?'

'I went exploring.' Libby took a deep breath, feeling guilty. 'Yesterday. I went to Cherry Ashton.'

'To White Lodge?'

'Yes, but first I went to the village.' Libby recounted her adventures of the previous day, including meeting Mr Vindari and Ian. 'And I went to see George at The Red Lion on the way home.' She told him what George had said.

'None of that is any use, is it?' said Fran. 'And if Ian's still investigating he won't want us poking our noses in.'

'No,' said Libby slowly. 'And there's something else.'

'What?' Fran sounded resigned.

Reluctantly, Libby told her Harry's theory about Rosie. 'And I said if that was the case you'd have seen through her,' she concluded.

There was silence at the other end. 'Fran? You still there? Are you offended?'

'No, I'm not offended, I'm thinking. Is Ben still away?'

'He comes back this evening. I've put something in the slow cooker for him.'

'Are you going to Harry's for lunch?'

'No, I told you, I went last night instead.'

'Would you like to come here? Only for a snack. Or we could go to Mavis's.'

'You want a chat?' Libby grinned to herself. 'Yes, love to. What time?'

Having settled on half past one, Libby cleaned her brushes and left the conservatory to go and get changed. Despite herself, she felt happier, her interest in White Lodge rekindled, yet she knew it shouldn't be.

At half past one, parked behind Mavis's Blue Anchor cafe at the end of Harbour Street next to The Sloop inn, Libby wandered down to meet Fran, who appeared from her own front door.

'I've just left some sandwiches for Sophie and Guy,' she said. 'We'll have our roast this evening.'

Libby turned, and they made their way back to the Blue Anchor. Mavis appeared with a tin ashtray and nodded at them before returning inside the cafe. Bert and George weren't there this morning, both being out on their boats, the *Dolphin* and the *Sparkler*, taking holiday makers round Dragon

Island in the middle of the bay, or along the coast to the less populated beaches.

'So,' said Libby. 'You've had some thoughts?'

'Yes.' Fran stared out to sea. 'What you said about Rosie.'

'Well, it was Harry who said it, really,' said Libby hastily. 'It just made me think a bit.'

'Yes.' Fran turned to look at her. 'And I really wondered if I'd missed something. When you look at the facts it's quite hard to escape them, isn't it?'

'Yes,' said Libby, feeling uncomfortable, 'but don't forget we've already been back and challenged her about it once. And she admitted it.'

'She admitted everything we challenged her with,' said Fran. 'What if we went back and challenged her again?'

Libby frowned. 'But I really don't know why she's done it, if she has. And if she has, why? And would we be in danger?'

'No idea. But I think we ought to.' Fran's mouth set in a hard line.

'This has upset you, hasn't it?'

'Bloody right it has. I don't like being taken for an idiot. And even if she doesn't own it, she's used us to a degree anyway.' Fran looked at Libby. 'And what about Andrew?'

'What about him?'

'I wonder if she really didn't know him? Or if he's been in on the scheme from the beginning?'

'Oh, surely not,' said Libby. 'And we don't know that there is a scheme, anyway. Or if there is, what it's for.'

'I wonder,' said Fran slowly, 'if it really is what

you said at first? She's using us to plot one of her novels?'

'Bit bloody manipulative if so,' said Libby, smiling up at Mavis who slammed a menu in front of her. 'Just a bacon sandwich, please, Mavis.'

'It was manipulative even if all she's done is what she admitted to the second time we went to see her.' Fran frowned. 'Sorry, Mavis. Ham sandwich, please.'

'Why don't we just ignore what Rosie's said or done,' suggested Libby, 'and take it from there? Ian's interested in something, after all, and whoever's doing it, someone's using that music to scare people off.'

'And yet it's such a crude method of doing it,' said Fran. 'More suited to the fifties and sixties than the high tech noughties.'

'I see what you mean. Yes, almost like the Victorians' fake séances.' Libby sighed. 'Oh, bum. I wasn't going to get involved any more.'

Fran laughed. 'You can't help it. And this is a proper mystery. With no nasty murders getting in the way.'

Chapter Sixteen

'WHY DON'T WE,' SAID Fran, after Mavis had cleared away their plates, 'go and have another look at your weird building this afternoon?'

'I thought you were helping in the shop?'

'Guy and Sophie can cope on their own. I only get in the way, half the time. What do you say?'

'I'm up for it,' said Libby, 'but why do you want to go?'

'To get a feel of the place. It sounds – fascinating. I'll take my camera. My phone isn't good enough for photos.'

'Oh, I didn't think of photos,' said Libby. 'Mind you, my phone camera isn't much cop, either.'

Fran went to tell Guy she was going to play hookey and collect her camera, while Libby sat in her car studying a map. It looked, she realised, as though the road to Cherry Ashton she'd followed yesterday petered out, as indeed it did, but just beyond it was another road which at one time would have joined it.

'Look,' she said as Fran got into the car. 'We could go that way and walk through, I'm sure of it. If Mr Vindari sees me drive up again he'll be after me like a ferret down a rabbit hole.'

'I thought you said he was nice. Why do you want to avoid him?'

'He was nice,' said Libby, driving down Harbour Street. 'I just don't want him thinking I'm a nosy mare, and I don't want him to think I'm poking my nose in.'

'Same thing,' said Fran. 'And you are.'

They drove from Nethergate towards Creekmarsh, then on past White Lodge, where blue-and-white tape still fluttered. About half a mile further on Libby took a turning to the right, which plunged between high banks topped with wide fields. It seemed to be almost turning back on itself and they'd travelled several hundred yards when Libby slowed down.

'Look,' she said.

On their right was what had obviously once been a lane, across which, in the distance, was an old wooden gate.

'That's it,' said Libby. 'When I looked yesterday, all I could see was this field here,' she waved a hand to the cornfield on their left, 'and this road must have been hidden because it was so low. That's the lane to Cherry Ashton. I wonder why it was closed off?'

'Are we getting out?' asked Fran. 'If so, you'll have to pull over into that gateway or nothing will get past.'

Libby parked as close to the gate as she could, and they crossed the road to the end of the lane.

'It's like looking into a tunnel,' said Fran. 'And look, under the leaves you can just see a faint white line. It was a proper road at one time.'

'It still is further down,' said Libby. 'It's odd though. Let's have a look down this side. See if we can see anything.'

The trees stretched away slightly to their right, now, and also ahead, following what Libby supposed to be the other side of the White Lodge estate.

'Although you don't know that,' said Fran. 'You couldn't even link it up yesterday from the other end. For all we know we could be miles away and this could be a totally different wood.'

Libby scrambled over some brambles and swore. 'If I keep ruining jeans like this I shall put in a claim.'

'No one's asking us to do this,' said Fran. 'It's self-inflicted. And better jeans than bare legs.' She rubbed at a large scratch on her left shin.

'Why you wear skirts I don't know,' said Libby. 'Look. There's the same thin wire fence along this side of the woodland that I saw yesterday near White Lodge.'

'That doesn't prove anything,' said Fran. 'And it doesn't actually look navigable along there. Let's go back. I want to see the building.'

They retraced their steps and began to walk down the lane through last year's rotting leaves. Libby managed to pull the gate a little further open and they squeezed through.

'There,' she said, and Fran stopped dead.

Libby watched for a moment, unwilling to break in on whatever her friend had seen or sensed, then walked slowly towards the bank she had negotiated yesterday. After a minute or two, Fran scrambled up beside her and pointed her camera.

'What is it?' asked Libby. 'Did you see something?'

'Not see, exactly,' said Fran in a strange voice. 'Felt. I couldn't get my breath.'

Libby looked at her sharply. 'TB sufferers couldn't breathe. Their lungs were collapsed on purpose.'

'Yes.' Fran nodded slowly. 'It was frightening.'

'Is that what was happening?'

Fran shook her head. 'I don't really know, but I think so.'

'So this is part of the hospital? Or the workhouse? Or both?'

'The hospital, certainly,' said Fran, her voice sounding more normal now. 'Possibly the workhouse. The building's more that age.'

'We ought to tell Ian.' Libby peered down the other side of the bank.

'Why?'

'He ought to know.'

'We don't even know what he's found to investigate,' said Fran. 'It might not be relevant at all.'

'It might. I still think we ought to tell him.' She stepped experimentally on to the other side of the bank. 'Fancy trying to get a bit nearer?'

Fran put a steadying hand on her shoulder. 'Go on, then. Careful.'

Helping each other, they managed to scramble over and through the vegetation to the bottom of the bank, where they stood staring up at the blank grey face of the building. Libby shivered.

Fran set off round the side, Libby following. The trees still pressed in closely on either side until they rounded the front.

'Someone's been here,' said Libby.

'Oh, yes.' Fran moved slowly across the roughly

cleared area towards the only door, scarred metal and heavily padlocked. Two broken windows on the ground floor level looked into blackness, and from one of the two higher up a scrap of cloth fluttered forlornly, exactly the same as the one on the other side.

'Well, now we will have to tell Ian,' said Fran giving a crooked smile.

'I thought you said this might not be connected to White Lodge?'

'Oh, I think so.' Fran scraped at the cleared ground with her foot. 'This is recent. Like the grave was.'

'But Ian said the body wasn't recent.'

'He didn't say the grave wasn't.'

'How could that be?' Libby frowned at her friend. 'New grave and old body?'

Fran shook her head. 'I don't know.'

'Oh, bloody hell,' said Libby. 'Do you think we should try and get through those trees and see if we get to White Lodge?'

'I don't fancy it. It looks impregnable. The only reason we managed to get here is that some of that undergrowth at the front had been hacked back.'

'Had it?' said Libby in surprise. 'It didn't look like it.'

Fran nodded. 'You could see cut marks. This is very like the sort of thing I used to do for Goodall and Smythe, and believe me, I got used to nosing things out even if they were down to earth physical. The smell in that shed, for instance.' She wrinkled her nose.

'What was that? You've never told me much

about what you did then.'

'You've never asked.' Fran smiled and looked round at the trees. 'Come on, let's go, and I'll tell you in the car.'

After Fran had taken more photographs, they fought their way back to the overgrown bank, Libby looking all the while for signs of recent use of a saw. As far as she could there weren't any.

'Yes, there are, look,' said Fran, reading her mind. 'There.' She pulled at a section of bramble, and sure enough Libby could see where branches from the trees behind had been cut off.

'So someone's using this as a way in there? But for what?'

'Presumably the same reason they're trying to keep people away from White Lodge.'

'But in that case why aren't they doing the same thing here?' Libby lost her footing and slid down the bank into the lane.

Fran joined her and looked down the lane towards the cottages. She stepped back and looked at what could be seen of the church. 'I should think that's the reason. There will be people up and down this lane every day, not only people who live here, but churchgoers.'

'All the more reason to keep them away.'

'No, playing Debussy every five minutes would attract attention here, exactly the reverse effect of the other side.'

'Oh, I see.' Libby cast one more look at the grey building and turned back towards the road and the car. 'Come on, this place is spooking me out.'

'Where does this road lead to?' asked Fran as

Libby pulled away.

'I think it must join up with the road to Steeple Mount. But come on, tell me about the shed.'

Fran sighed. 'Goodall and Smythe were selling this rather grand house in Kensington. The lower ground floor had been let as a separate flat, but no one was there and the prospective buyers wanted to turn it back into one house. She was very nervy and didn't like the idea of the basement, so I was sent to have a look round.' Fran sighed again and shook her head. 'Honestly, I think I was a mug. Goodall and Smythe didn't really believe in what I did, I was a "service" to make purchasers feel more secure.'

'So come on, what happened?'

'There really was something nasty in the woodshed. I don't talk about it because it was horrific, but it was nothing to do with my having a "moment", it was to do with the ghastly smell.'

'And?' prompted Libby after a moment. 'Was it a body?'

'Yes. Of the former tenant.' Fran shuddered. 'Not that you could tell.'

'Blimey! You poor thing. No wonder you gave up on it all. Was he murdered?'

'Yes. It was in the papers. The bloke who was selling the house killed him and went abroad. He must have known it would be discovered as soon as someone went to view, but I think he'd gone to ground, somewhere like Brazil.'

'So you'd already been involved in murder before you met me?'

Fran laughed. 'There's no need to sound so affronted! And I certainly wouldn't recommend finding a partially decomposed body.'

'I wonder.' Libby frowned over the steering wheel.

'Wonder what? Decomposed bodies. At White Lodge?'

'Or that barn. Looks as though it was a barn once, doesn't it?'

'Why should there be decomposed bodies there?'

'I don't know. But the whole thing's weird. We must tell Ian.'

'And he'll tell us off again,' said Fran.

'It was your idea to come back today,' said Libby. 'I shall say I was misled.' She slowed at a road junction. 'Oh, look. It doesn't go to Steeple Mount, it goes to Steeple Cross.'

'In that case can we go back? It's completely the wrong direction.'

'It's all right,' said Libby. 'Look, if we go right we go back to Heronsbourne. That's a coincidence, isn't it? Me having gone there yesterday.'

'Yes, but we're not stopping for a drink today,' said Fran. 'I need to get back and get the dinner on.'

'So,' said Libby a little later, 'you think it was definitely part of the TB hospital?'

'I felt as though I couldn't breathe. There was this awful pain. There was something wrong, I'm sure.'

'Are we going to tell Rosie? Or are we not friends with her any more?'

'I think we might tell Andrew. Ask if there's any evidence of that barn in the old documentation. If there's anything wrong with Rosie's story Ian'll find out.'

'All right.' It was Libby's turn to sigh. 'Isn't it funny how whenever we get involved with one of these investigations there comes a point where we say we'll stop and back out.'

'And we never do,' said Fran wryly.

Libby dropped Fran at Coastguard Cottage and drove slowly back to Steeple Martin. Fran had promised to call Ian and leave a message rather than disturb his Sunday, although, as she said, policeman often don't get Sundays. Libby was to contain her soul in patience once more and wait until she heard from either Ian or Fran.

'Can't I even ask Andrew about the plans and stuff?' she'd asked, but Fran had been adamant. And, as Fran was usually the sensible one, she had to agree. When she reached home, she tried to put the whole thing out of her mind and concentrate on looking forward to Ben's return.

Chapter Seventeen

WHEN MONDAY AFTERNOON WAS almost over and Libby still hadn't heard anything from Ian or Fran, she broke and rang Fran.

'No, I haven't heard either,' she said, 'but I was going to ring you because I've just heard from Andrew.'

'Oh, great! What's happened? Has he found something?'

'Well, yes, but it's all rather odd. He's been helping Rosie and he says it's her story, so would we like to go either to her cottage or his flat and hear all about it. He says she's a bit upset.'

'So, another false confession, do you think?'

'I think we should reserve judgement. He said to go this evening, but I said it was too short notice. Tomorrow?'

'Yes, as early as possible. You don't think we ought not give her the opportunity to sleep on it and change her mind?'

'I think Andrew will keep her to the sticking point.'

'There's definitely romance in the air there, isn't there? Harry must have been right about her flirting with him.'

'Not necessarily,' said Fran. 'You must admit Harry can be a bit of a bitch sometimes.'

'True. He means well, though.'

'Sometimes,' said Fran. 'Right, what shall I say to Andrew? Ten o'clock?'

After several more phone calls it was arranged that Fran and Libby should meet at Rosie's cottage the following morning at ten thirty.

'Andrew said he didn't want to give her the opportunity not to turn up,' said Fran, 'so he's a bit dubious about her, too.'

'Perhaps he's an all right bloke, then,' said Libby. 'And not in on the scam.'

'Oh, shut up about the scam,' said Fran. 'You're not in a Mafia movie.'

Fran's car was already parked when Libby arrived at the cottage. It was a grey, drizzly day, and the lupins, foxgloves and hollyhocks drooped and dripped either side of the path, drained of colour. Andrew opened the door.

'Libby, come in.' He stood aside for her to enter, smiling. 'Forgive me for playing the host, but Rosie's a little fragile at the moment.'

Fragile? wondered Libby. What does that mean?

Fran was sitting on a comfortable-looking sofa in front of the french windows, while Rosie sat in what was obviously a favourite armchair beside the fireplace. She looked washed out, and years older than the last time Libby had seen her.

Andrew brought in a tray with coffee percolator, mugs and milk and set it on a large square footstool.

'Thank you, Andrew,' said Rosie. 'I'm sorry to be such a sad case, ladies, but I'm a bit overcome by all this.'

'By all what?' said Libby.

'You know Rosie came with me last week to Maidstone to carry on with the research?' said Andrew, handing round mugs of coffee. 'Well, we looked in the archaeology society's library and the Maidstone archives. And eventually, we tracked down some evidence.'

'I wouldn't have known how to go about it,' said Rosie, 'but Andrew did. He found some documents relating to the workhouse, and eventually the title being transferred to the owners of the Princess Beatrice sanatorium.'

'I expect Inspector Connell would have been able to find that too, eventually,' said Andrew.

'Yes, he was going to get in touch with the records office yesterday morning,' said Libby. 'So who bought it?'

'No one we'd ever heard of,' said Rosie, 'but then Andrew followed a trail to some other documents.' She shrugged and spread her hands. 'It was incomprehensible to me.'

'I found some references to piano concerts given to raise funds for the sanatorium.' Andrew paused as both Libby and Fran drew in sharp breaths. 'Yes, that's what I thought. Well, if Inspector Connell's been to records, he'll know this already. He obviously hasn't told you?'

'We haven't heard from him,' said Fran. 'He doesn't tell us everything.'

'No, of course not,' Andrew smiled again. 'Sorry. Well, what we found out was that the man who bought White Lodge after it was closed as the Princess Beatrice Sanatorium was Paul Findon.'

Fran and Libby looked at each other.

'Who?' said Libby.

'Paul Findon.' Rosie cleared her throat. 'You two are probably too young to remember him, but he was a concert pianist and the greatest exponent of Debussy's work of his generation.'

'No!' said Libby.

'Heavens,' said Fran.

'It doesn't stop there,' said Andrew.

'It wouldn't,' said Libby. 'Rosie remembers the music and the interior of White Lodge as it was years ago. There's obviously a connection.'

'Quite.' Andrew raised his eyebrows at her. 'So we looked him up online, found his birth and death dates and looked him up in the historical records.' He looked across at Rosie.

'And he's my uncle,' she said.

After a short shocked silence Libby said 'And you didn't know?'

Rosie shook her head.

'It's been a bit of a shock,' Andrew continued for her, 'and we've no firm knowledge because of course Rosie's parents are dead and Paul Findon had no children and doesn't appear to have married.'

'No other relatives?' asked Fran. 'Cousins?'

'He was my mother's only brother,' said Rosie. 'So strange to think that all these years I didn't know. And yet I must have, once. I must have visited him at White Lodge.'

'There was a huge resistance in you,' said Fran. 'You really didn't want to go back, did you? That's why you asked us and didn't tell us the whole story at once.'

Libby looked at her in surprise.

'I didn't understand it, though,' said Rosie. 'I had to know, yet I didn't want to. I suppose that makes me sound even madder.'

'No.' Fran shook her head. 'Simply that there's a reason for it. Something must have happened that you've blocked out.'

'The ghost,' said Libby eagerly. 'Could that be it?'

Rosie shook her head. 'I don't know. I don't think so.'

'I wonder why he bought it?' mused Libby.

'I think we know,' said Andrew, 'although it's a rather strange reason. In his Wiki entry it says he was in hospital for several years with tuberculosis.'

'More coincidences,' said Libby.

'Not at all,' said Fran. 'Simply cause and effect. He was in hospital here, wasn't he?'

'Yes,' said Rosie. 'That's why he gave concerts in aid of it.'

'So he was in the sanatorium, grew up to be a pianist, gave concerts to raise money for it, bought the house when it closed as a sanatorium, and meanwhile his sister had married and had Rosie, who has a buried memory of the house and Debussy. It's all perfectly logical.'

Rosie smiled at her in relief. 'Put like that it seems so much better,' she said.

'I suppose so,' said Libby grudgingly.

'All we had to do was unravel it,' said Fran, 'which Andrew has done.'

He inclined his head. 'I merely knew where to go and what to look for,' he said.

'But it doesn't take us any closer to the original body that was dug up, the ghost story, or why the music is played now,' said Libby.

'No, and I'm sorry about that.' Rosie sighed.

'But at least we know why it's Debussy. Maybe your Inspector won't have to carry on looking now.'

'Have you told him all this?' asked Fran.

'No, but I suppose we should.' Rosie looked at Andrew.

'I'll tell him.' He patted her hand and Libby resisted the urge to look at Fran. 'He still wants me to get in a buildings expert, so I expect he'll speak to me.'

'I'm sure he will.' Fran smiled her serene, Madonna-like smile. 'I'm glad you're happier, Rosie.'

The subject was subtly changed and though Libby was dying to chew over all these new discoveries with Fran, she was forced to sit through another half an hour of conversation and cold coffee before she could decently make her excuses.

'What did you really think of that?' she said, when they got to the end of the path.

'What do you mean?' Fran looked surprised.

'All that about cause and effect.'

'I meant what I said.' Fran frowned. 'It was obvious.'

'Was it?'

Fran sighed. 'Oh, come on, Libby, stop looking for more mysteries. Of course it was true. It was obvious, as I've said. No coincidences.'

Libby looked at her narrowly. 'Are you sure?'

'Yes, I'm sure. You know. Absolutely sure.'

Libby sighed. 'I suppose it did make sense. Wish we knew about the body and the music, though.'

'What I want to know,' said Fran, opening her car door, 'is if the Debussy was played before Rosie went to visit a year ago, or whenever it was. Or was it dug out just for her?'

'She said that the estate agent who accompanied her was already scared, so something else must have been happening before then.'

Fran nodded. 'Let's go home and think about it. I'll call you later.'

Libby looked up Paul Findon when she got home. Apart from his Wikipedia entry, which was extensive, there were many recordings available, surprisingly, most of them digitised from the originals, most of which dated from the ten years after the end of the last war. She clicked on the listening sample for *Clair de Lune* and decided it didn't sound any different from any recording she'd heard. Then she went back to his biography, to find out who his parents were and where he came from. Presumably Rosie would know this, as his parents would be her grandparents, but Libby wanted to see for herself.

However the biography merely said "born in London" with no mention of parents. There was no mention of anything strange or mysterious in the biography, merely the fact that he'd been in a sanatorium with tuberculosis as a child. Then she realised she hadn't looked up the Princess Beatrice and typed it into the search engine.

The entry wasn't long in Wikipedia, and there seemed to be very little other mention of it anywhere else. There was certainly nothing about buried children or ghosts.

The phone rang.

'I've just thought,' said Fran.

'What?'

'You know those windows at the barn? We couldn't see into them, could we?'

'We couldn't get close enough, but it looked dark inside.'

'Suppose those windows had been deliberately blacked out from the inside. You couldn't tell from a distance.'

'No. But why?'

'Did you watch the local news last week?'

'Eh? Some days. Why? What's that got to do with anything?'

'The police found a cannabis factory.'

'They're always doing that. Little terraced houses with the windows – ah.'

'Exactly. It would be a perfect place. Out of the way, no one goes near it.'

'It would, but what would that have to do with White Lodge and the music? Or the bodies, come to that.'

'Probably nothing, but we ought to tell Ian.'

'Would he let us know if he was going to investigate the barn place?'

'I doubt it,' said Fran. 'He might tell us afterwards.'

'Should we go back?'

'No, of course not. We couldn't get into the woods on Sunday, so why would we today?'

'I suppose so.' Libby blew out a sigh. 'How frustrating.'

'Just be patient,' said Fran. 'I'm sure we'll find out eventually.'

The next phone call was from Jane, saying thank

you for the flowers Libby had found time to send on Monday.

'So when can we come and see you? Are you home yet?'

'Oh, yes, we came home yesterday.'

'Don't they throw you out quickly these days? I was in for a week with mine.'

'Oh, how could you bear it?' said Jane. 'All I wanted to do was get home.'

'I wanted someone there to tell me how to do it all first. And to let me sleep when I wanted.'

'Oh, Terry's been terrific. He's doing everything except the feeding.' Jane giggled. 'And he can't do that.'

'Fran and I will come one day this week, if that's all right? What time would be best? Not afternoon, you need to sleep then!'

'Oh, anytime. Be lovely to see you both.'

'OK, we'll ring before we come just to make sure.'

Rather than annoy Fran by ringing her again, Libby sent a text message, then, determined to take her mind off everything else, she cleaned the bathroom.

It was while she was dishing up a rather strange version of chilli and rice that the phone rang again.

'Ian's going to look at the barn. I don't think he was that thrilled about us having been exploring, but he agreed it was worth looking into.'

'And no news on the other end of things?'

'None. And I don't see what we can do about it.'

'Tell you what we could do. We could go and see Jane tomorrow morning and go and have lunch at The Golden Spice.'

'The–? Oh, yes. You met the owner. Why would we do that?'

'Because we want to see the baby?'

'I meant have lunch at an Indian restaurant.'

'Because he said to mention his name.'

'And you think we'll get a discount?'

'No, of course not,' said Libby, who had.

'We'll go and see Jane,' said Fran, and rang off.

'If you're going to an Indian restaurant, why can't I come?' said Ben, who had finished dishing up and was now tucking in.

'You can,' said Libby. 'Fran doesn't want to go, so perhaps you and I should go one evening. There's one in Canterbury, too.'

'Be nice to get away somewhere, just the two of us.' Ben reached over and patted her hand. She smiled at him.

'It would. And not just for an evening, either.'

'Are you actually suggesting we go away for a dirty weekend?' Ben raised his eyebrows in mock horror. 'To somewhere nobody knows us?'

'Well,' said Libby, forking up rice, 'we do always seem to go to places where we know the owners or the other customers. Which reminds me, we haven't been to the pub for ages.'

Ben laughed. 'Which I take it means you'd like to go this evening? OK, as long as we go to that restaurant tomorrow.'

Peter joined them at the pub, and demanded an update on the progress of the investigation, only parts of which he'd heard from Harry. Libby told him the whole story from the beginning.

‘So Harry was wrong?’ he said when she’d finished. ‘She wasn’t just using you?’

‘In a way she was, but not in the way he thought. And she’s genuinely shocked about Paul Findon.’

‘You know,’ said Peter slowly, leaning back on his settle and stretching long legs out sideways, ‘he could still be partly right.’

‘How do you mean?’

‘Maybe she does own it.’

Libby stared at him.

‘He’s right,’ said Ben. ‘Suppose he left it to her?’

‘She’d have known before this,’ said Libby. ‘He died when she was a child.’

‘I was thinking more of her mother. If, when he died, he left it to his sister, which would be logical if he had no wife or children, when she died it would presumably go to her child or children. Didn’t you say the agents said it was a complicated probate sale?’

Libby groaned. ‘Oh, not that again. Remember the trouble Fran had over her legacy?’

‘And she didn’t know about it, either,’ said Peter.

‘She didn’t know she was entitled to it, you mean?

‘Well, it only came to light after her old auntie died, didn’t it. Strange that this has only just emerged. I wonder when Rosie’s mother died?’

‘You’re getting as bad as she is,’ said Ben. ‘Another pint?’

‘He’s right, though,’ Libby said later, as they walked home. ‘But surely she’d have known if it belonged to her mother?’

‘Well, that’s something else to ask her, isn’t it?

She'll be sorry she asked you in at this rate.' Ben tucked his arm through hers. 'Now where are we going for this dirty weekend?'

Chapter Eighteen

LIBBY PARKED AS NEAR to Coastguard Cottage as she could the following morning.

'So what do you think of Pete's idea?' she asked when Fran had been told of last night's conversation.

'It's a possibility, but why wouldn't her mother have known she owned it?'

'I thought about it this morning. It's like those programmes on TV, where companies search for missing heirs. Lots of people don't know they're legatees.'

'But they do that just after someone's died, surely? Not years later? Anyway, no one appears to be looking for Rosie. The agents were very shifty about who owned the property.'

'Well, whoever it is, they must have the deeds and be able to prove title.' Libby looked sideways at her friend. 'Remember all your trouble with your legacy?'

Fran shuddered. 'Don't remind me.'

'Let's have a look online after we've seen Jane. I expect we'll find out how to trace missing heirs.'

Terry let them into Peel House and led them to the front room, where Jane sat, looking slightly smug, a Moses basket by her side.

'Meet Imogen,' she said.

Libby and Fran duly cooed over the grumpy pink face, almost hidden under a beautiful light, lacy shawl.

'That's gorgeous,' said Libby. 'Was it a present?'

'Yes,' said Jane, 'my mother knitted it. I'm still faintly surprised.'

'My, my! Coming round, is she?'

'She's actually being quite helpful and sensitive. Staying out of the way but there if we need her.' Jane shook her head. 'Can't quite believe it.'

'She's all right,' said Terry, a man of few words. 'Tea?'

The conversation turned naturally to Jane's labour and Imogen's birth, and when Terry reappeared with mugs, he rolled his eyes and disappeared again.

'So how are you getting on with your investigation?' asked Jane.

Libby and Fran told her.

'And we've you to thank for the children,' said Libby. 'Sorry if it upsets you.'

Jane made an involuntary movement towards the Moses basket.

'But after you mentioned it, we managed to find out about it, and we've found so much since,' said Fran gently. 'And the children don't come into it.'

'Good.' Jane smiled her relief.

'One thing, though,' said Libby, 'you remember you looked to see how back your archives went for me last year?'

'Yes?'

'Well, I thought, what about Colindale? Does it still exist?'

'Colindale?' asked Fran.

'The Colindale newspaper library. Part of the

British Library. They have copies of everything back to about 1700, don't they, Jane?'

Jane nodded. 'Although it's being digitised, and it was going to be moved to a storage facility somewhere in Yorkshire, I think, but that was under the last government. I think you can order digitised copies at the Library proper.'

'But you have to be a member, don't you?'

'You have to have a pass to use the reading rooms,' said Jane, 'but there's a lot you can do online.'

'But what for?' asked Fran.

'Don't they have to post details of people who died intestate?'

Jane shook her head. 'Not any more. They do in cases of bankruptcy still, but I think it's probably only the national broadsheets that print intestacy notices, if even they do.'

'Oh, I see what you're getting at,' said Fran. 'To see if someone other than Rosie's mother claimed the estate?'

'What?' Jane looked puzzled, and Libby explained. 'Of course, he might have actually left it to Rosie's mother, but in that case, why was Rosie never told? And why isn't Rosie the owner now?'

'She might be,' said Jane.

'Harry thought that, too, but I swear she was shocked to find out about Paul Findon.'

Fran nodded. 'She was, that was genuine. No, I think we'll have to try and find a way to get hold of his will. If there isn't one, then he died intestate.'

'But Ian should have found out by now who owns the building,' said Libby. 'He was going to the records office on Monday.'

'So we've been talking about heirs and intestacy for nothing?' Fran threw back her head and laughed, stopping suddenly with her hand over her mouth and an anxious look at the Moses basket. Jane peered in, but smiled and shook her head.

'A slight twitch,' she said, 'nothing more. So what will you do now?'

'Oh, nothing, I suppose,' said Libby. 'I think I just come up with these ideas to keep myself busy. I'd forgotten about Ian asking for the records.'

'Even if we find out who owns the property now, it would be interesting to know who it went to when Findon died,' said Fran. 'We could still try and find that out.'

Libby cheered up. 'You never know, Rosie could have a claim on the estate.'

'After all this time? I doubt it,' said Jane.

'Well, it must happen,' said Libby, 'because I remember a case in the paper where someone had claimed an estate and the solicitors made them take out this special insurance in case someone closer to the deceased turned up, and they did. The – oh, I don't know – brother or something had emigrated to Australia and knew nothing about it. Must happen all the time.'

'Keep me posted,' said Jane. 'It sounds fascinating.'

Libby and Fran left shortly after that.

'Shall we go to the cafe on Marine Parade?' said Libby. 'I never go there these days.'

'What for? Do you want an ice cream? I've got to get back to the shop. Guy's going out buying at lunchtime, so I couldn't have gone to the Golden Spice with you, anyway.'

'It's all right, Ben and I are going tonight.' Libby sighed. 'OK, no ice cream, but if I come back to the shop with you, will you try and get hold of Ian about the owner?'

'No, I won't Libby. Poor bloke's already had us pestering him –'

'Giving him information,' corrected Libby.

'I know, but I still think we ought to let him tell us in his own time.' Fran smiled at her friend. 'You can come and keep me company, though. Sophie's gone off somewhere with Adam, so I'll be on my own.'

'Funny about those two, isn't it?' said Libby. 'My son and your daughter.'

'She's not my daughter,' said Fran.

'Step-daughter, then. Still funny.'

Libby went home when Guy got back to the shop and called Ben to remind him they were going out that night.

'I know. I've even booked a table.'

'Really? I say, do you remember where we went on our first date? That Thai restaurant in Canterbury.'

'I do. I even remember what you wore,' said Ben.

'You old romantic, you,' said Libby.

They reached the Golden Spice just before eight o'clock and were shown to their table by a beautifully suited young man with a heavy moustache.

'Are you one of Mr Vindari's sons?' asked

Libby, as he held her chair for her.

'Libby!' hissed Ben, but the young man stepped aside and smiled widely, white teeth gleaming in the forest of black.

'I am.' He bowed at Libby, then at Ben. 'You know my father?'

'Not know him, really,' said Libby. 'I've met him, though. He told me to mention his name when I came here.'

'But of course,' said the young man. 'In that case you must have a drink as my guest. What would you like?'

'There, see?' whispered Libby, when the young man had departed barwards. 'Free drink!'

'You are shameless,' said Ben, as another young man of solemn aspect presented them with menus.

The food was wonderful. As she finished off the last of the sauce with a piece of naan, Libby leant back and sighed.

'Whoof. That was without doubt the best Indian meal I have ever eaten. I shall never go anywhere else.'

'Thank you.'

The younger Mr Vindari had silently appeared at their table.

'Oh!' Libby sat up and felt heat creeping up her neck.

'It was delightful to hear such a spontaneous compliment,' he said. 'Please, may I tempt you to a dessert?'

Libby shook her head.

'I think we're just too full,' said Ben. 'It really was delicious.'

Mr Vindari bowed. 'I am delighted. I shall tell my father – but I am sorry, I don't know your names?'

'I'm Libby Sarjeant.' Libby held out her hand. 'And this is Ben Wilde.'

Mr Vindari shook hands with both of them. 'May I ask where you met my father?'

'Um,' said Libby, feeling the heat creep back up. 'At Cherry Ashton.'

'Oh?' Mr Vindari looked inquiring, but Libby chose to ignore it, flicking a pleading glance at Ben, who, without a beat, said 'Perhaps we could have the bill?'

'Of course.' Mr Vindari flicked a finger and the solemn young waiter appeared magically with a leather bill folder.

Ben looked briefly at the bill and placed his credit card in the folder, which was immediately whisked away. When the payment procedure had been concluded, Mr Vindari and his acolyte returned to see them off the premises with much bowing and promises to return.

'Why were you so anxious to get away all of a sudden?' said Ben as they walked back to the car park.

'I didn't want to explain that I'd been poking around a derelict building and he'd come to see if I was trespassing,' said Libby. 'How embarrassing.'

'I didn't think you could be embarrassed by something like that,' said Ben. 'You do things like that all the time.'

'I don't trespass.'

'You poke about. You nearly got yourself into

trouble at Creekmarsh that way, didn't you?'

'All right, all right.' Libby squeezed his arm. 'That was a lovely dinner, thank you.'

'It was, wasn't it? Shall we try the Nethergate one next time? Perhaps Fran and Guy could join us. And Harry, he said he'd like to.'

'Oh, I see,' said Libby, as he held the car door open for her. 'Had enough of me on my own, now, have you?'

Ben laughed. 'I've got you on your own now, haven't I?' He slid in beside her and patted her knee.

The answerphone button winked that there was a message when they got in. Libby pressed play while Ben fetched them both a nightcap.

'Libby, it's Fran. I've just had a rather surprising message from Ian. If you get in before ten, give me a ring, otherwise I'll speak to you tomorrow. Your mobile's switched off, by the way.'

'Oh, damn, it's half past ten,' said Libby. 'I didn't realise we'd spent that much time over dinner.'

'Relax,' said Ben, guiding her to the sofa. 'If it was urgent she'd have told you to ring whatever time you got in. A message from Ian doesn't mean life and death.'

'No,' agreed Libby reluctantly, 'but now I'm seething with curiosity.'

Ben sighed. 'End of quiet evening, then.'

'Oh, sorry, Ben.' Libby turned to him, put down her glass and wound her arms round his neck. 'I shall stop seething and start soothing.'

'So I should think,' said Ben.

The following morning he had to prevent Libby

from calling Fran almost the minute she woke up.

'Wait until I've gone up to the Manor,' he said. 'That'll be a more respectable hour. And you could wait until Guy's gone off to open the shop, too.'

'That's not until ten!' wailed Libby. 'I can't wait that long.'

Ben laughed and ruffled her hair. 'Well, at least wait until I've gone. And stop trying to shoo me out the door!'

At last, after shutting the door on him at ten past nine, Libby was free to make her phone call, which maddeningly, wasn't answered. She then tried Fran's mobile, which also went to voice mail. Beginning to get worried, she rang the number of the shop.

'Sophie? I can't raise Guy or Fran. Do you know where they are?'

'Yes, Libby, I'm here,' said Guy's voice. 'I've started opening at nine thirty during the summer. Did you try Fran's mobile?'

'Yes.'

'She'll have it switched off then while she's driving.'

'Oh, where to?' said Libby. 'She wanted to talk to me this morning.'

'Exactly,' said Guy. 'She's on her way to you.'

Libby leapt upstairs, had the quickest shower ever and threw on some clothes. She'd just thrust her feet into sandals when she heard the front door.

'What is it? What's so urgent?' She opened the door and stood back for Fran.

'All right, all right, let me get inside.' Fran went straight into the kitchen.

‘Tea?’

‘Yes, please.’ Fran sat down at the table. ‘You obviously got my message?’

‘I did. Ben and I got back from the Golden Spice too late to ring you, so I rang this morning. Guy said you were on your way here.’

‘Ian called yesterday.’

‘You said it was a rather surprising message.’

‘It was – and it wasn’t.’ Fran grinned at Libby’s cross expression. ‘It’s all right, I’ll explain.’

Libby pushed a mug across the table and sat down on the opposite side. ‘You’d better.’

‘Ian had someone look into the ownership of White Lodge.’

‘Yes, we knew that.’

‘And it was left to Rosie’s mother.’

‘*What*?’ Libby almost dropped her mug.

‘Apparently, it’s never been transferred into Rosie’s name, so it looks as though we were right and she doesn’t know.’

‘So he’s going to tell her?’

‘Today, apparently. There’s another thing, though. Someone leased the property through Riley’s, only it was Riley and Naughton in those days.’

‘Riley’s? Who are handling it now?’ Libby frowned. ‘And what happened to the tenant?’

‘Left after six months. After which it was just – left.’

‘How did Ian find that out? Through Riley’s?’

‘No, the solicitor who drew up Findon’s will. Not the man himself, but his firm, they drew up the lease because Rosie’s mum wanted nothing to do with it.'

'And she just ignored it for the rest of her life? And told Rosie nothing?'

'Looks like it. But there must have been a reason.'

'The same reason that Rosie can't remember any of it now. Must have been a trauma.' Libby stood up and went to the window. 'What does Ian think now?'

'He's wondering how Findon died.'

Libby turned back. 'That occurred to me, too.'

Fran put her head on one side. 'Did it, now? And were you thinking perhaps that was the cause of the trauma?'

Libby looked at her friend suspiciously. 'Yes, why?'

'Because it's almost too obvious to be true.'

'Well, that doesn't make it less true. It fits.'

Fran nodded. 'Too neatly, perhaps?'

'Does it matter? Ian will look into it and find out the truth, even if Rosie doesn't remember it. Although what it's got to do with what's happening now, I don't know.'

'If Findon's death wasn't an accident, there was a reason for his death. Perhaps that's why people are being scared off the site?'

'What after all this time?' Libby snorted with disbelief. 'No, it strikes me it was particularly to scare off Rosie.'

'So that she doesn't stake her claim?'

'Makes sense, doesn't it? Mind you, I can't see how the deeds have remained in her mother's name. I would have thought there would be some kind of automatic notification to the records office.'

'Considering that official bodies send communications and bills to dead people for years, I don't know why you would think that,' said Fran.

'True.' Libby sat down again. 'So what now?'

'I don't think there's anything we can do. But I did remember something. When we first looked up the estate agents' details it said there was a barn, didn't it?'

'So it did! I'd forgotten that.' Libby got up and went to fetch the laptop. 'Hope they haven't taken it down.' She clicked through a few links. 'Yes, here we are – seven bedrooms, cellar, walled garden, barn. I wonder why they've left it here?'

'It isn't the agents' own site, is it?' Fran pulled the laptop towards her. 'Simply a link from a property site. But cellar. We haven't seen that.'

'And I don't particularly want to,' said Libby with a shudder. 'I'm not a fan of cellars.'

'That could be where the music's playing from.'

'I expect Ian's found it now, anyway,' said Libby.

'I expect he has. He didn't say much at all in his message.'

'But you came dashing over here to tell me.' Libby rested her chin on her hands. 'Come on, you're brewing something. What is it?'

'There's a local Records office at Dover. I bet that's where the documents about White Lodge are.'

'Dover? When we've been haring off to Maidstone?'

'We haven't, Andrew has. But it's Dover where most of the stuff is. I can't think why there wasn't some kind of link to it when we were looking before.'

'Can we go and look?'

'It's only open Tuesday, Wednesday and Thursday, but I think we can go. It's in the Dover library.'

'It's Thursday today,' said Libby standing up again. 'What are we waiting for?'

'I thought you'd say that.' Fran stood up. 'That's why I came here, it saves time.'

'Why didn't you say straight away? Honestly!' Libby locked the back door into the conservatory and went to find her basket.

Chapter Nineteen

LIBBY HADN'T KNOWN QUITE what to expect at a Records Office, but it appeared to be quite straightforward. On request, documents were produced for White Lodge, the Princess Beatrice Sanatorium and the Cherry Ashton Workhouse.

'There,' said Fran. 'If only we'd come here first.'

'We didn't know we were looking for a workhouse or a sanatorium at first,' said Libby.

'If we'd come looking for White Lodge we might have found these.' Fran spread the fragile documents out on the desk before them.

Unfortunately, there was little that appeared to be of use. In the workhouse papers there were some lists of items bought for a couple of years prior to its closure and some unintelligible legal documents pertaining to its adaptation as a workhouse. There was a leaflet promoting the Princess Beatrice Sanatorium as using "the most advanced techniques for the treatment of consumption", but the best thing Libby turned up was a reference to the "isolation unit", "at a distance from the main house and wards".

'Bet that's the barn,' she said. Fran nodded absently.

They leafed through the papers for a while, unsure of what they were looking for, until Libby sat back.

'The only thing I can see is that it all looks perfectly normal.'

Fran looked up. 'There is one thing here, though.' She pushed a newspaper clipping across the desk. 'It's a report on the death of one of the TB patients.'

Libby squinted at it. 'What's the date?'

'1948, I think.' Fran leaned over to look. 'The trouble is that the patient seems to have died of some kind of poisoning.'

Libby pulled the cutting towards her. 'It doesn't say she was actually poisoned, though.'

'No, it's worded as if it was a miscalculation.'

'Well, it probably was,' said Libby.

'Weren't you suspicious of the treatment of the patients the other day? Suspecting that some of them could have died through mistreatment?'

'Oh-oh.' Libby frowned down at the cutting. 'Do you think that's what this is?'

'It might explain the burials.'

'But this was reported. There was a post-mortem. Would have been buried somewhere else.' Libby sat up again. 'Hey, I've just thought. What if those bodies weren't reported?'

'Ian would have come across some evidence of that when he got the forensics on the one they dug up.'

'Why? He was only looking for a date, not who it was.'

'Right.' Fran pulled the large black ledger which contained patients' details towards her and began to flick the pages. 'No good,' she said eventually. 'The entries in here stop well before the War. They must have been recorded in some other way.'

'Or not at all.' Libby was looking excited. 'Bet

you that's it! They were trying things out on the patients. There must be evidence somewhere.' She pulled a stack of Princess Beatrice documents towards her.

But there was nothing. Fran asked for permission to photocopy two or three documents she thought might be relevant and once that was done, they left.

'So how do we find out?' Libby squinted in the sunshine.

'If patients were guinea pigs? No idea.' As they reached the car Fran unlocked it and gave Libby the documents to hold, as there was no back seat to dump them on.

'And didn't we assume that some of the graves were really old? From when the Princess Beatrice first opened? They wouldn't be guinea pigs, would they?' Libby struggled with her seatbelt.

'They probably were,' said Fran with amusement. 'After all, they were trying out TB treatments then.'

'Hmm.' Libby stared unseeingly through the window. 'Would Ian ask for another exhumation?'

Fran chuckled. 'I can't see it. He might let us go and find the cellar, though.'

'I'm not sure about that. I told you, not a big fan of cellars.'

'We could at least find out where it is. Where are we going now?'

Libby looked at her in surprise. 'I don't know. I thought you were taking me home.'

'I can, of course, but I thought perhaps we could go and see Rosie. If Ian's already been, of course.'

Libby laughed. 'That's not like you. It's usually

me who wants to gatecrash somebody.'

'I want to see an unvarnished reaction. Even when we saw her the day she told us about Paul Findon she'd had a night to think about it. And with any luck Andrew won't be with her.'

'Oho! Suspicious of him, are you?'

'No, simply that he's come over all protective, hasn't he? From not knowing her at all to Keeper at the Gate.'

'Mmm. He obviously fancies her.'

'They must both be in their sixties, though!' Fran sounded horrified.

'Fran! I'm surprised at you.' Libby frowned at her. 'We're both in our fifties and in comparatively new relationships. And look how your kids disapproved.'

Fran sighed. 'You're right. It's not like me to be so narrow-minded.'

Libby raised an eyebrow but forbore to comment.

Fran parked up against the hedge again and Libby clambered out complaining.

'Look.' Fran pointed up the lane.

'Ian's car.' Libby squinted at it. 'Do we go in? Or do we wait?'

The appearance of Ian at the garden gate made the question unnecessary. He frowned when he saw them, but waited for them to approach.

'I might have known you wouldn't be able to resist it,' he said.

'Resist what?' Libby tried to look innocent.

'Finding out how Rosie took the news.' He looked from one to the other. 'Well, go on then. Go and ask her. But be gentle. She's in shock.'

'Did she phone Andrew?' Libby asked.

'Professor Wylie? Not as far as I know. Why?'

'We just wondered.' Libby looked at the closed front door. 'Do you think she'll send us away?'

'I can't tell you that.' Ian looked at the documents Libby was carrying. 'Anything you want to tell me?'

'Only some old Princess Beatrice documents we found at the Dover records office,' said Fran. 'I'll call you about them later. They aren't very interesting.'

Ian narrowed his eyes at her. 'Really. Why do I find that hard to believe?'

'They aren't. There aren't even patient records after the end of the forties.'

'Right.' He still didn't look convinced. 'Well, give me a ring if there's anything you think I ought to know.' He nodded at them and walked off to his car.

'He's not happy, is he?' said Libby watching his upright back.

'He often isn't. I suspect being a policeman isn't the happiest of jobs.' Fran pushed open the gate and went up the front path. 'Come on, I don't want to be chucked out on my own.'

But Rosie stepped aside to let them in as soon as she opened the door, not saying a word.

'As though she expected us,' whispered Libby after they'd gone into the sitting room and Rosie had disappeared into the kitchen.

'She probably did,' said Fran, perching on the edge of one of the sofas.

Rosie returned and sat down. 'Kettle's on,' she said.

Libby watched as she pleated and repleated the fabric of the long top she was wearing. She was pale, un-made-up and her long hair was loose. That, thought Libby, is not the result of Ian coming to tell her about the will. Something else had already happened.

'Rosie,' she began gently, 'what's happened?'

Rosie sent her a quick look. 'Don't you know?'

Libby frowned and shook her head.

'But I saw you talking to Ian. He must have told you.'

'Oh, the will? Yes, we know about that. It was why we were coming to see you.' Libby leant forward. 'I didn't mean that, though. Something else has happened, hasn't it?'

Fran was looking startled. 'Libby,' she said warningly, but Rosie interrupted.

'It's all right.' She stood up. 'I'll get the tea – or did you want coffee?'

They both murmured agreement to tea and she went back to the kitchen.

'What's the matter with you?' hissed Fran. 'The poor woman's in no state to be harried.'

'I'm surprised at you,' said Libby. 'It's usually you who spots these things. She wouldn't be in that state just because of Ian's visit. She was in a state before he arrived.'

'How–?' began Fran, but Rosie reappeared with the tray and cut her off. She sat down and handed out thick mugs, quite unlike the previous dainty china.

'Sorry,' she said, 'can't be bothered today.'

'That's fine,' said Libby. 'More what we're used to.' She waggled her eyebrows furiously at Fran.

'How are you, Rosie?' Fran's voice was soothing. 'I suppose this shock on top of the others is all a bit much.'

Rosie shook her head. 'It's not that.' She looked up at them, her eyes tragic. 'Look, I don't go in for confidences and I don't have any real close friends here any more.'

'What about Andrew?' said Libby.

Rosie suddenly leant forward and put her head in her hands. 'That's the trouble,' she muttered.

Libby and Fran exchanged glances.

'Andrew is?' Fran prompted, after the silence had stretched into at least a minute.

Rosie sat up. 'Yes.' She cleared her throat and picked up her mug. 'I've made a fool of myself.'

Libby was forced to clamp her jaw shut to stop it falling open.

'We all do that sometimes,' said Fran. 'We get over it.'

'I know we do.' Rosie put her mug down. 'But this is different.'

'If you want to talk about it we're fairly safe,' said Libby.

'I'm sure you are.' Rosie smiled at her, a little shakily. 'That's why I started by saying I don't normally share confidences, but this time I might. I was brought up not to talk about – well – private things, and I don't. But –' She stopped.

'Shall we talk about what Ian came to tell you, instead?' asked Fran, after a moment.

'Yes.' Rosie turned to her gratefully.

'After finding you were Findon's niece this must have been a double whammy,' said Libby.

'Not as much as you'd think,' said Rosie, leaning back in her chair and beginning to recover her composure. 'I suppose getting used to the whole Paul Findon thing had made me realise that my mother must have kept it from me for some reason. It almost came as a relief. At least I know why I remember the house and why Debussy has always been a favourite.' She sighed. 'But I don't want to keep it. I shall have to get in touch with the agents, although I think I need to put it in the hands of someone else. They haven't exactly done well with it, have they? And I suppose I'll have to find out who's trying to sell it.' She smiled at the other two. 'And thank you for helping. I never would have found out without you.'

'It wasn't us,' said Libby, 'it was Andrew.'

Rosie closed her eyes briefly. 'Yes, it was, but we wouldn't have called him in if you hadn't suggested it.'

There was a short, uncomfortable silence.

'Well, anyway,' said Libby eventually, 'we've found out that the barn at the back of the estate was the isolation unit.'

'Barn? What barn?'

'Oh, you don't know, do you?' Libby shook her head. 'My fault. Well, here's what happened.'

She proceeded to tell Rosie everything that had happened since the last weekend, including her meal at the Golden Spice and this morning's visit to the Dover Records Office.

'There still wasn't much there,' she finished, 'but at least we know now that the barn is part of the estate and what it was years ago.'

'And did you say cellar?' Rosie shivered. 'I hate cellars. I have a real phobia about them.'

'I don't think even Ian's found a cellar in the building,' said Fran soothingly.

'So what's your theory now?' Rosie asked.

'I think they were experimenting on the patients,' said Libby. 'The post-mortem report on one of the patients in the newspaper was that she had been poisoned.'

'Poisoned?' gasped Rosie. 'No! When was that?'

'1948 wasn't it?' Libby looked across at Fran. 'Near the end of its life as a sanatorium.'

'Perhaps that's why.' Rosie stared down at her mug. 'And then Paul bought it. Do you think he knew?'

'We don't know that there was anything to know,' said Fran. 'This is just speculation.'

'It's plausible.' Rosie looked up. 'And would explain the graves. I'm still puzzled as to why they're there rather than in a churchyard. It looks as though someone was trying to cover those deaths up.'

'That's what I thought,' said Libby enthusiastically. 'I think Ian should dig the lot up and find out if they've been poisoned. That sort of evidence sticks around in the bones, doesn't it?'

'But why would he need to do that?' Rosie frowned.

'To find out why someone's been trying to scare you off,' said Libby.

Chapter Twenty

'IT'S OBVIOUS NOW THAT'S what the music has all been about. But there's some connection with the estate agents, too,' Libby went on.

'Yes, that's why I need to find out who's trying to sell it. Your Ian told me.' Rosie gave a shaky laugh. 'I don't know what to call him, now. You always say Ian, and I have to say Inspector. He's a bit scary, isn't he?'

Fran smiled. 'He can be. But he's a real charmer underneath that dark exterior.'

'Oh, I can see that,' said Rosie, with an answering smile. 'All pent-up passion underneath his saturnine mien.'

'Gosh, that's the novelist in you,' said Libby.

'If I wrote like that I'd be dropped like a hot potato,' said Rosie with another, more natural, laugh.

'So does he still want to get to the bottom of the music?' said Libby. 'He hasn't told us much.'

'I expect he will,' said Rosie. 'He seems to keep you informed.'

'Not always, but I suppose we put him on to this, so he might,' said Fran.

'You said you had a phobia about cellars,' Libby mused, her eyes on a corner of the ceiling.

'Yes?' Rosie looked surprised.

'Do you suppose the cellar at White Lodge had anything to do with it?'

Fran and Rosie looked at each other. Fran raised

her eyebrows and shook her head.

'You said Ian hadn't found a cellar,' said Rosie slowly.

'That doesn't mean it isn't there to be found,' said Libby. 'It's in the records.'

With another quick look at Rosie, Fran said, 'I should think it's been blocked up by now.'

'Was there anything in those records to say there had been an earlier building on the site?' asked Rosie after a moment.

'Yes, there was, wasn't there Libby? Didn't it say fourteenth century?'

'Yes, it was burnt down, or something. Didn't we already know that?'

'Yes,' said Rosie, 'but I don't think we knew what period it had been.'

'Oh, and we know the sixteenth-century building was timber-framed, and then tile-hung in the seventeenth, and then Lutyens had a go in the early twentieth, so that must have been when it turned into the Princess Beatrice,' said Libby. 'The Poor Board, or whoever they were, wouldn't have paid out for a Lutyens re-design.'

'So it's had a very chequered history,' said Rosie. 'No wonder there are stories of hauntings.'

'We still don't really know anything about that,' said Fran. 'It's all hearsay. And it must have been around the time you were visiting.'

Rosie frowned. 'I know. It's so frustrating. I still feel that the house is friendly and warm, so I must have got on well with my uncle, yet the minute I try and get further than that I get this feeling of dread and my stomach turns to water.'

'Well,' said Libby robustly, 'we shall have to find out why. Ian's looking into it, so he's bound to turn up something. Meanwhile, at least part of the mystery is solved.'

'Yes.' Rosie looked uncertain and Libby suddenly didn't want to hear any more. She stood up.

'Come on, Fran,' she said, 'I think we ought to leave Rosie to come to terms with everything on her own.'

'Right.' Fran stood up with a curious frown. 'You'll be all right, Rosie?'

Rosie also stood. 'Yes, of course.' She leant forward and kissed them both on the cheek. 'Thanks for being such a support and not judging me too harshly.'

'I –' began Libby, then shut her mouth with a snap. Don't ask any more questions, she told herself severely.

'That was unlike you,' said Fran as they reached the car. 'She still hadn't told us what she wanted to tell us in the beginning.'

Libby made a face. 'I didn't want to hear.'

'Really?' Fran's eyebrows disappeared into her hairline. 'Even more unlike you.'

Libby sighed gustily and fastened her seatbelt. 'I had a feeling it would be highly unsavoury and I wouldn't know how to react.'

'I don't see how sleeping with someone can be called unsavoury,' said Fran, putting the car into gear.

'See, you knew what she was going to say, too,' said Libby. 'And you were the one who was horrified about people in their sixties doing it.'

Fran laughed. 'I didn't say it was unsavoury.'

'No, but she was upset about it. That means she *did* think it was. Unsavoury, I mean. Or at least a mistake. She said she'd made a fool of herself.'

'She could have meant that she made a pass at Andrew. That could be all it is.'

'Maybe.' Libby looked doubtful. 'Harry said she was the one doing the flirting.'

'No use speculating now. She didn't tell us and that's all there is to it. And she'll be very glad she didn't, she would have been even more embarrassed and probably not been able to look us in the face.'

'Ian didn't tell us if he'd had a look at the barn,' said Libby, changing the subject. 'Do you think he will?'

'Have a look or tell us? I don't know, and you're not to pester him. I told him I'd call him about the things we found at Dover, so he might tell me then, but until then I think we should leave things alone.'

By the time Fran dropped Libby at home it was lunchtime. On a whim, she decided to go up and see Ben at the Manor. There was no point in taking him anything for lunch, as Hetty always fed him, a fact reflected in his expanding waistline.

'Want a spot of lunch, girl?' Hetty appeared as Libby pushed open the heavy oak door. 'Got a pasty in the oven.'

'Love some, thanks, Het,' said Libby after a second's hesitation. 'Ben in the office?'

'He's over in the orchard. Be in in a minute. Come into the kitchen.'

So Libby sat at the long table and watched while

Hetty bustled about the kitchen.

'How's Greg?' she asked.

'So-so. Up and down.' Hetty gave a brief smile over her shoulder. 'The original creaking gate is my Greg.'

Greg had been in a prison camp during the war and his health had suffered badly. Occasionally there were episodes where the whole family were convinced he wouldn't last another day, but somehow he had always rallied.

'So, tenants coming into Steeple Farm?' Hetty said.

'Yes. Peter's pleased.'

'You decided not to go, then.'

Libby sighed. 'That's right.'

Hetty turned round and grinned, her face collapsing into a thousand wrinkles. 'Don't blame you. Never liked it.'

'Really?'

'No. Neither did Milly when she first went there. That's why she changed it all. She should've been in one o' them executive 'omes.'

'Yes.' Libby nodded. 'I thought that when I first went there. And I didn't like the eyebrows.'

'Eyebrows?'

'The windows in the thatch. Like eyes.'

Hetty nodded. 'Yeah. No wonder she went a bit peculiar.'

Libby thought there was far more to it than a weird house, but didn't say so. 'Anyway, I'm happy in my cottage,' she said. 'And I think Ben is, too.' She waited for Hetty to agree, but she didn't.

Instead, she turned back to the sink and said,

'And what about living here?'

Libby's heart thumped madly and she felt dizzy. Tempted to ask if Hetty had been talking to Harry, she merely coughed and made an indeterminate sound. Hetty looked round. 'Thought so,' she said.

'Hello! What are you doing here?'

Libby turned at the sound of Ben's voice with relief. 'I came to see you, of course.'

'Not like you.' He came over and kissed her cheek. 'Are you going to feed her, Mum?'

'Course. Pasties OK?'

'Lovely.' Ben rubbed his hands and Libby made a face at him.

'No wonder you're putting on weight.'

He patted his waistline. 'Two women's wonderful cooking.'

'And your own,' said Libby, with a glance at Hetty, who didn't react. Ben raised his eyebrows. Libby smiled.

The pasties were enormous and filling. For once Hetty allowed Libby to wash the "pots" after they'd loaded the dishwasher, while she went to put her feet up in the sitting room with Greg.

'So, what was the atmosphere I sensed when I came in?' said Ben, taking a tea towel from the rack over the Aga.

Libby sighed. 'I really don't want to tell you, but I suppose I'll have to. Hetty was asking me about living here.'

'She's asked before,' said Ben mildly.

'I know. But that was about coming to live here now. I think what she meant was – well – um – later.'

‘Ah.’ Ben slowly dried a baking sheet. Libby turned round to face him.

‘It’s not something I want to think about, or even talk about, but I suppose at some point we ought to. Your parents are getting on. Hetty’s nearly eighty and Greg’s – what? Early eighties?’

‘Mum’s seventy-seven and Dad’s eighty-one.’ Ben let out a gusty sigh. ‘Yes, I suppose you’re right. One or other of them’s going to get left on their own eventually and will expect to stay here. We can’t sell it while they’re still alive.’

‘*Sell* it?’

‘Well, we won’t want to live here, will we?’ Ben said reasonably.

‘Good lord.’ Libby shook her head. ‘But you won’t want to sell it. It’s been in your family for – how long, exactly?’

‘Oh, I don’t know. Not that long, only a couple of generations. My great-grandfather, I think. And it isn’t entailed.’

‘I know, but –’ Libby shrugged. ‘It just doesn’t seem right.’

‘Look.’ Ben put down the tea towel and the baking sheet and took her by the shoulders. ‘You don’t want to live anywhere but the cottage, and there’s enough room for us, so that’s where we’ll stay. When Millie dies Pete and James will sell Steeple Farm and when my parents die I’ll sell the Manor. It’s the way of things.’

‘What about Susan?’

‘My sister hasn’t any interest in the Manor. She comes in for something in the wills, obviously, but the Manor comes to me in time-honoured tradition.’

'Not even halves with you?'

Ben shook his head. 'She didn't want it.'

Libby turned back to the sink. 'What about turning it into something?'

'Not an old people's home, surely?' Ben sounded horrified.

'No! I was thinking more of a – oh, I don't know – a cultural centre.'

'A what?' Now he was laughing.

'No – listen. One of those places where they have creative holidays, you know, painting courses and creative writing courses. And provide accommodation.' Libby turned back, a look of excitement on her face.

'Are there such places?'

'Oh, yes. When we get home I'll show you. It's a brilliant idea.'

'But, Libby, they're not dead yet,' he said gently.

'Oh, bother.' Her face fell. 'How bloody insensitive.'

'No, it's a great idea, and if you're still painting and your Rosie's still teaching creative writing when the time comes we'll have the creative core, won't we?' He pulled her to him. 'And I tell you what, I bet neither Mum nor Dad will want to stay here on their own anyway. I bet they'll want to go into one of those units with Flo and Lenny.'

'Het might, but Greg wouldn't.'

'He wouldn't have much choice,' said Ben, 'if we aren't going to move in to look after him.'

'Oh, that makes us sound mean,' said Libby, pulling away.

'No it doesn't. He wouldn't want that, anyway.'

Libby sighed. 'It's all very difficult. You'll have to talk to them about it. Het's obviously thinking about it or she wouldn't have mentioned it to me.'

Ben nodded. 'I'll do it this afternoon. You go home and prepare a light but sustaining snack for supper.'

Libby groaned. 'Don't talk about food.'

'That's why I said light.' Ben dropped a kiss on her cheek. 'Go and say your goodbyes and I'll see you later.'

Libby walked slowly down the Manor drive wondering what it would be like when Ben's parents were no longer there. They had been a part of her life as long as Ben had and the thought was incredibly depressing.

By the time she turned into Allhallow's Lane her mobile was ringing.

'Where are you?' said Fran.

'Walking home from the Manor. Why? What's so urgent?'

'Ian called. He wants to see us.'

'Wants to –? Why?'

'About the barn. He wouldn't talk over the phone.'

Libby's stomach took a dive. 'Bloody hell.'

'That's what I thought. But at least he said he'll come to us, we don't have to go to the station.'

'Where? Are we to be interrogated separately on our own turf?'

'No,' said Fran, and Libby looked up.

Detective Inspector Connell was leaning on the bonnet of his car with a thoughtful look on his face.

Chapter Twenty-one

'HE'S HERE,' LIBBY SAID into the phone.

'I'm on my way,' said Fran. 'I'm on hands-free.'

'Hands –? Oh, the mobile. In the car. OK, see you in a bit.' Libby put the phone in her pocket and stopped in front of Ian. 'Hello.'

'Libby.' Ian stood up and looked down his nose at her.

'OK.' She sighed and fished for her key. 'What have we done now?'

'I'll tell you when Fran arrives,' said Ian, following her into the house and tripping over Sidney. 'Blasted cat.'

'Well, she won't be long.' Libby went through to the kitchen to put on the kettle.

'Was that her on the phone? From her car?' Ian followed her.

'Yes, but on the hands-free.' Libby turned to face him. 'You know how law-abiding Fran is.'

Ian made no comment, merely folded his arms and leant against the door jamb. Libby sighed and took the teapot down from above the Rayburn.

'Hello?' Fran called from the front door. 'You left it open.'

'That was Ian.' Libby looked at him accusingly. 'Hardly security-conscious was it?' She pushed past him into the sitting room. 'Sit down, Fran. I'm making tea.'

Ian came in and took a chair by the table in the window. 'Do I get a cup, Libby?'

Libby sniffed and returned to the kitchen, where she loaded a tray with mugs, milk in a jug and a sugar bowl. She poured the boiling water into the teapot and carried the tray into the sitting room.

'Right,' she said, depositing it on the table. 'While we wait for it to draw, you can tell us what we've done.' She sat down on the sofa.

Ian looked amused. 'I love the way you assume I only want to talk to you because you've done something wrong.'

'Well, it's usually that or you're warning us off,' said Libby.

'What about when I invited you over to the White Lodge with Professor Wylie?'

'You wanted information,' said Fran. 'Is that what you want now?'

'In a way.' Ian gestured to the teapot. 'Is that ready yet?'

Libby grudgingly got up and poured three mugs of tea.

'Thank you.' Ian sipped gratefully. 'Haven't had a chance to catch my breath today.'

Fran and Libby exchanged surprised glances. This wasn't like Ian.

'Nice to know you come here to relax,' said Libby. She turned to Fran confidentially. 'He fell asleep in that chair once last winter, Fran. Poor old soul.'

Ian put down his mug. 'It's not actually funny, Libby.' He looked from one to the other. 'Which of you is going to tell me what happened when you went back to the barn?'

'You know what happened.' Fran frowned at

him. 'I told you.'

'That you thought it might be a cannabis factory, yes. What made you think that?'

'You don't mean to say it *was*?' gasped Libby.

Ian looked at her. 'I said, what made you think it was?'

'It wasn't me, it was Fran. She remembered a report on the local news.'

'All right, Fran, what made you think it was?'

'I thought the windows might have been blacked out. We couldn't actually get close enough to see, and there aren't many windows anyway. And it looked as though someone had hacked through the undergrowth but tried to cover it up.' Fran looked nervous. 'I'm sorry, have I wasted your time?'

Ian sighed. 'Not exactly. Was that all you noticed?' He turned to Libby. 'And you saw nothing else when you went on Saturday?'

Libby shook her head.

'I suppose,' Ian went on, 'I should have had you both down to the station for questioning, and I have no doubt whatsoever that I shall get hauled over the coals for not doing so, but I know you both so –' he paused. 'We did go in. At least myself and DS Maiden did.'

He was quiet for so long, staring into his mug, that Libby began to get worried.

'Ian,' she said, 'please. You've got something to tell us. Put us out of our misery.'

He looked up. 'You were right.'

'Cannabis?' they said together.

'No. Murder.'

Libby drew in a sharp breath but Fran just stared.

'Not TB victims?' she said in a shaky voice.

'No, Fran, I'm afraid not. But victims plural, I'm afraid, yes.'

'In the barn?' whispered Libby through a throat that felt as if it had closed right up.

'Yes. It looks as if it's quite organised. Almost a little cemetery.'

'But how?' said Fran, who was looking anguished. 'Why didn't I know?'

'You can't know every time, Fran,' said Ian. 'And you and Libby put us on to the whole thing in the first place, so don't feel guilty.'

'It was Rosie who started it,' said Libby. 'Have you told her yet?'

'No. After I told her this morning she owned the property I thought she ought to have a break. I shall have to tell her of course. I was wondering –' he looked from Libby to Fran.

'If one of us would come with you?' supplied Libby. 'Well, of course.' She looked at Fran. 'You don't think we ought to see if Andrew could be there?'

'After this morning?' Fran raised one eyebrow. 'Don't be daft.'

'What's this?' Ian snapped. 'Have they had a row?'

'Er – we're not sure,' said Libby, 'but it's possible. I think it should be one of us, anyway.'

'Or both,' said Fran.

'When?' said Libby.

'Before she gets to hear about it from the radio or TV,' said Ian. 'SOC's in there now, with Maiden in charge. We only went out there after I saw you this morning, so the machine's only had a couple of hours to get going, but that much activity isn't going to go unnoticed, especially in a place like that.'

'Did Mr Vindari come out to find out what you were doing?' asked Libby.

'No one did,' said Ian. 'It's a weekday afternoon, so unlikely there are many people around. House to house is getting going of course, but I don't suppose we'll get much response until later.'

'I thought it looked the sort of place where there would be mostly retired people,' said Libby.

'Well, no one had been raised when I left there. My DCI wanted me to interview you as quickly as possible, which I've done, and now perhaps we ought to go and see Rosie.'

'Now?' said Fran doubtfully.

'Yes,' said Ian firmly. 'If you don't want to come I'll raise a policewoman, but I thought she might prefer you.'

'OK.' Libby finished her tea. 'Can I call Ben in case I'm back late?'

'You won't be late,' said Ian. 'We won't be long.'

'What about the estate agents?' asked Fran. 'They must be mixed up in it somehow.'

'Looks like it, doesn't it?' Ian stood up. 'Do you want to call Guy? I'll take you both in my car and bring you back here if you like.'

'I'll take my own and go home afterwards,' said Fran, 'but I expect Lib would like a lift.'

'A lift?' Libby came back from the kitchen where she'd called Ben on her mobile. 'Yes, please.'

'Did you tell him what was going on?' asked Ian

as he shepherded Libby to his car.

'Briefly. He just sighed.'

'Poor Ben.' Ian smiled as he put the car into gear.

'He is not.' Libby was indignant. 'He's very understanding.'

'He'd have to be,' said Ian.

'So what exactly did you find when you went to the barn?' Libby asked after a few minutes. 'Graves?'

'Yes. Fairly shallow and very obvious.' Ian was frowning.

'Could you – I mean – were they –'

'They all appear to be female, if that's what you're asking, but I was only there at the start of the examination of the site, so I could be wrong. They will, however, be very difficult to identify.

'Oh,' said Libby, feeling sick.

'Have you warned Rosie we're coming?' she asked presently. 'She might be out.'

'I said I wanted to drop in late afternoon. I think she assumed it was still about the ownership of the house.'

'Well, it is, in a way,' said Libby. 'But at least you can be sure she has nothing to do with it.'

Ian didn't reply.

'Oh, come on, you can't think she did! She didn't even know she'd been there as a child.'

'That's what she says, and she's very convincing.' Ian paused while he took a sharp bend. 'But to a jaundiced eye it could look as if she got you and Fran involved deliberately to give weight to the fact that she'd never been there before and knew nothing about the sanatorium, her uncle or the barn.'

'Harry said that. Well, not about her uncle and the barn, but he thought she was using us and that Fran couldn't see it because she wanted to be like her. As a writer, I mean.' Libby fidgeted with the strap of her bag.

'And what did you say to that?'

'Oh, I agreed it looked like that, but then there was all the business of finding the records and Paul Findon and I sort of believed her again. And she was in a shocking state when we arrived this morning.'

'Yes.' Ian shot a quick look at her. 'She was in a state before I got there, too. Is this something to do with Andrew? You said they'd had a row.'

'I don't know, really,' said Libby uncomfortably. 'We just guessed. But I'm sure she didn't know about owning the place. And she said she wants to sell it, but the agents will have to be looked into, won't they? There's definitely something been going on there.'

Ian looked amused. 'I should say there has.'

They had arrived at Rosie's cottage. It was raining again, and as Libby struggled out of the passenger door of Ian's car, the hawthorn hedge enveloped her in a wet embrace. Fran, pulling up behind, and Ian stood together under Fran's umbrella watching her.

'Don't help, will you?' she said grumpily.

Rosie's eyes widened in surprise when she opened the door and saw Libby and Fran with Ian.

'Has something else happened?' Her voice faltered slightly, and Fran moved forward to take her hand and lead her into the sitting room. Talbot the cat, spread out on a windowsill, pricked one ear and opened an eye.

They all took seats around her and Ian leant forward.

'I'm afraid something else has happened, Mrs George,' he said. 'We had reason to investigate the barn on your property and – well – I'm afraid we found something.'

'Not more graves?' Rosie whispered, colour fading from her face to leave it almost grey.

'I'm afraid so.'

Libby and Fran edged closer to Rosie and Fran took her hand. Libby was pretty sure this wasn't an act. Rosie was genuinely shocked, as she had been earlier in the day. She hoped Ian was wrong about her.

'So that barn was an isolation unit?' She turned to Fran. 'That's what you thought, wasn't it?'

If that's an act, it's a good one, thought Libby.

'I'm afraid these aren't old graves, Mrs George.' Ian cleared his throat and sat up straight. 'We think they're murder victims.'

Rosie's mouth opened but no words came out.

'Would you like some tea?' asked Libby, hoping Rosie wasn't going to faint or throw up. 'I could find my way around the kitchen.'

Ian looked up quickly and nodded. Libby stood up and went out of the room. Talbot followed.

'OK, chum, where's the kitchen?' Libby asked him. Talbot obligingly wound round her legs and trotted ahead of her into the kitchen, where he stood hopefully by a shiny chrome bowl.

‘I’ll see to you in a minute,’ said Libby, ‘after I’ve sorted the grown-ups out.’ She filled the electric kettle, found mugs on a shelf and tea in a caddy. So far, so good. The teapot was harder to locate and she was just bending down to look in a cupboard beside the cooker, when she heard a movement behind her.

‘So, what have you done to upset her now?’ said Andrew.

Chapter Twenty-two

LIBBY STOOD UP AND banged her head on the worktop.

'Not half as much as you've just done to upset me,' she said, rubbing her head and trying to stop her eyes watering. 'What do you want and how did you get in here?'

Andrew looked surprised. 'Through the back door,' he said. 'I always do.'

'Always? But you've only known her a few days.' Libby spooned tea into the teapot.

'Well, all right, since I've known her.' Libby noticed his cheeks were faintly pink underneath his beard and moustache.

'Yes, I gather you've got quite close,' she said. 'But if you don't mind, the police brought Fran and me here, so I don't think they'd necessarily be happy if you barged in.'

'The police?' Andrew looked wary. 'Why?'

'It's not up to me to tell you,' said Libby, now enjoying herself. 'And I think it would be better if you went home. Rosie can call you if she wants to after we've gone.'

Andrew's face took on a stubborn look. 'I'm staying.'

'Fine, but not in here. If you want to wait it'll have to be in the garden.' Libby watched him as he folded his arms and took up a stance, reminding her of Adam and Dominic as small boys, refusing to tell which was the culprit. She sighed in exasperation.

'Look Andrew. When did you last see Rosie? Last night?'

'Er – yes,' he said, going slightly pinker and losing some of his rigidity.

'And has she called you today?'

'No.'

'Well, we've already seen her once today and so has DI Connell. And if she'd wanted to see *you*, I'm sure she would have called. So if I were you, I'd go home and wait.'

'Will you let her know I called?' he said after a moment.

'Yes.' Libby put the mugs on a tray, reflecting that this was the second time within an hour she'd done exactly the same thing.

'All right.' Andrew turned to the back door, then turned back. 'I'm sorry she's upset,' he said, and left.

How did you know she was upset? mused Libby as she avoided Talbot looking reproachful by his bowl and left the kitchen.

'Did I hear you talking to someone?' said Rosie as soon as she entered the sitting room.

Libby nodded. 'Andrew. I sent him away. I said you'd call him if you wanted to see him.'

Rosie positively sagged with relief. Ian frowned.

'Has Professor Wylie been bothering you?' he said.

Rosie's colour changed from white to bright red and back again. 'No, not at all,' she croaked. 'He's been most helpful.'

Libby handed Fran a mug and made a face. 'I'm sure,' she said.

Rosie sipped her tea and her colour returned to normal. 'So who are these bodies?' she said eventually.

'We don't know,' said Ian, 'but you'll understand I have to question you as you now appear to be the owner of the White Lodge estate.'

'But I didn't know I was until this morning,' said Rosie. 'And I don't want it now. The Lord knows I don't earn a fortune from my books, but I've got enough to live comfortably.'

'I know that, Mrs George,' said Ian, 'but nevertheless, we'll have to go back over everything you've told us, and see if you can remember anything else at all. We're particularly interested,' he looked quickly at Libby, 'in the estate agents, Riley's.'

'Yes,' said Rosie slowly, 'you would be. How odd that I should have gone there as a prospective purchaser of my own house.' She shook her head.

'When you were taken to see it,' Ian went on, 'you said a woman escorted you. And she seemed nervous right from the start.'

Rosie nodded. 'Plain scared by the end. And that's another thing that's funny. Do you know, they never got in touch with me afterwards. You know, like estate agents normally do when you've viewed a property. They phone up later that day, or the next day, to find out what you thought and if you'd be likely to make an offer.'

'That's right,' said Libby, 'and they always say things like "There's been a lot of interest in this property, it won't stay on the market long," or "There's a couple going for a second viewing this very afternoon." They did that to me with number seventeen.'

'Yes, all right, thank you, Libby,' said Ian. 'So did you call them, Ro – I mean Mrs George?'

'Oh, please call me Rosie,' said Rosie tiredly. 'And no, I didn't. I thought it was odd, but I had no intention of buying the place, and they'd already told me it was a complicated probate sale.'

'That's what they told me,' said Libby and Ian sent her a dirty look. She sat back in her chair and glowered at him.

'I assume the original Riley is no longer with us,' said Ian. 'Anybody know?'

'No idea. The original Naughton is obviously long gone. You know, from when they leased the house. You knew about that, Rosie?' said Fran.

'I think one of you has told me,' said Rosie. 'The tenants left, didn't they?'

'That was because of a haunting, too,' said Libby. 'But it can't be the same reason if these new bodies are – well – new.'

'I didn't say they were new, Libby,' said Ian sounding somewhat testy. 'Just more recent. Within a year or so.'

'Oh.' Libby contemplated her mug. 'That's quite new compared to the others, though. And another funny thing.' She looked up at the other three. 'What about those flowers?'

'Flowers?' said Rosie.

'On the grave we thought was new but wasn't,' said Libby. 'In the garden.'

'Actually, there's some news on that, too,' said Ian. 'It appears we were half right about that. It was a new grave after all – but it was a reburial.'

'A *re*-burial?' repeated Fran. 'Why on earth would they do that?'

'Whoever "they" are,' said Libby.

'And that's what we need to find out,' said Ian. 'There can't be two sets of people hiding something on that estate. We're going to have to take it apart.' He looked apologetically at Rosie. 'I'm sorry. We'll put things back as far as we can, but I'm afraid you won't be able to sell it quite yet.'

'I don't suppose I'll ever be able to sell it,' said Rosie. 'Not when people know its history.'

'Oh, you'd be surprised,' said Ian.

'I could always knock it down, I suppose.'

'No you couldn't,' said Libby. 'It's listed. You could sell it to the nation, perhaps. Or English Heritage or someone.'

'You know,' she said to Ian as they left Rosie's cottage and walked to the car, 'there's got to be a logical chain of events to all this. One thing that leads to another until we end up here. With bodies all over the place, old and new, and manufactured hauntings.'

'Well, of course there is,' said Ian, unlocking the car. 'There always is, although there's usually somewhere in the middle where things take a turn in another direction or someone new enters the picture. Often that's the piece we miss.'

'Hmm.' Libby buckled her seat belt. 'A bit like last winter when we ended up with one person linking two old cases and we all thought it was a coincidence.'

'It was a coincidence in that the people looking

into it,' he swivelled his eyes to Libby and waggled his eyebrows, 'came from the right place. Colin could have asked any of his other friends for help.'

'There'd still have been a murder, though,' said Libby. 'That didn't happen because of us.'

'No,' said Ian. 'Although one day someone might murder *you*.'

'Ian!'

He laughed. 'You must admit some people have had an urge to hit you with a blunt instrument.'

'Yes, all right.' Libby sunk down in her seat. 'Only don't bring that up if you see Ben. He'll only get all protective again.'

'As I said before,' said Ian. 'Poor Ben.'

Ian did, in fact, come in briefly to apologise to Ben for hi-jacking Libby. Ben seemed amused, especially as Libby was uncharacteristically quiet.

'So what's the matter?' he asked, closing the door behind Ian.

'What do you mean? Nothing's the matter.' Libby sat on the sofa and closed her eyes.

'There, you see? You don't collapse on the sofa with your eyes closed normally.'

Libby's eyes snapped open. 'I'm a bit tired. And it's quite wearing being a family liaison officer.'

'Eh?'

Libby sat up straight. 'Pour me a drink and I'll tell you all about it.'

Ben listened carefully while Libby recounted the afternoon's events.

'And on top of Hetty's pasties, it's had the effect of making me very, very tired,' she finished, swallowing the remains of her glass of wine.

‘I can see that it would,’ said Ben. ‘What happens now?’

‘Nothing, as far as Fran and I are concerned. I suppose we keep in touch with Rosie – that’s us being liaison again – but whether Ian will keep us informed of the progress of the investigation, I’ve no idea.’

‘I’m sure he will,’ soothed Ben. ‘After all, it was you two who brought him in. He wouldn’t know anything about it otherwise.’

‘He said that,’ said Libby. ‘Fran was feeling guilty that she hadn’t found the bodies.’

‘Sensed them, you mean?’

‘Yes. But she did feel as though she couldn’t breathe when we went to see the barn. I just thought it was TB.’

‘I’m glad I know you well enough to interpret,’ said Ben, getting up to fetch the wine bottle. ‘I assume you mean TB victims from the sanatorium?’

‘Yes. But obviously not.’ She sat forward. ‘I’m still worried about that re-burial. And the flowers.’

‘Yes, that is odd.’ Ben frowned. ‘I mean, the reburial had been long enough ago for grass to grow over it, hadn’t it?’

‘I think Ian said within a year, or something. But the flowers were only laid between our visit on Friday and Ian’s first visit.’

‘So someone who did the re-burial or knows who it is laid the flowers. And that was a female, too, wasn’t it?’

Libby nodded. ‘It’s all so odd. I do believe Rosie now, you know. And I’m pretty sure something happened with Andrew and she can’t come to terms with it. Or she regrets it.'

'Ah, the older woman syndrome!' said Ben. 'I've seen that before.'

'If you're referring to me,' said Libby with dignity, 'I am not as old as Rosie, and I did *not* regret anything.'

'You had a bit of trouble with the idea of a relationship though, didn't you?'

'Well, yes, but I think it's more than that with Rosie.' Libby sighed. 'Still, I don't really want to know the details. I told you Andrew came walking into the kitchen uninvited, didn't I?'

'No, you didn't. When? This afternoon?'

Libby nodded. 'And asked what I was doing to upset her. That made me think, actually. Why did he think she was upset? Presumably because she'd told him she was at some point during the day. And, I would think, because of her reaction when I told her I'd seen him off, she's already told him she didn't want to see him.'

'And she said she'd made a fool of herself.'

'Yes. So perhaps he seduced her and then she regretted it. Very easy to do.'

'But not when you're in your mid-sixties.'

'No. Fran was a bit horrified at first, until I reminded her that she was practically a newly-wed herself in her mid-fifties.'

Ben didn't reply, but gave her a slightly twisted smile and Libby cursed herself. The thorny marriage question had been decently buried for some time now, and she had to go and bring it up. She put down her glass and stood up.

'Come on, old-timer,' she said. 'Let's see how

easy it is to seduce people in their mid-fifties.'

'Which one of us,' said Ben, standing up and taking her hand, 'is doing the seducing?'

Libby smiled and led the way to the stairs.

Chapter Twenty-three

THE PHONE WOKE LIBBY far too early.

'Libby? It's Rosie. I didn't wake you, did I?'

'No,' croaked Libby. 'Course not.'

'Only I want to go and see the barn. I don't know how to get there. Would you take me?'

Libby struggled to sit up.

'Um – yes.' She cleared her throat, and Ben opened his eyes. 'When did you want to go?' Ben groaned and turned over.

'Well – sometime today,' said Rosie. 'If it's not too much trouble,' she added hastily.

'Can I ring you back?' asked Libby, glancing at the clock. 'It's only twenty to eight.'

'Oh, God, I'm sorry. Of course.'

'Did you call Fran?'

'No. I don't know why, I just thought –'

'That I'd be more likely to say yes.'

There was a small chuckle. 'Yes, I suppose so. I'll wait for your call.'

'What was that about?' Ben heaved himself onto one elbow. Libby told him.

'Will you go?'

'I can't think of an excuse not to. Unless I say Ian won't let us near the site.'

'Well, he probably won't,' said Ben, and swung his legs out of bed. 'I'm going to make tea. Do you want it up here?'

'No,' sighed Libby. 'I'm awake now. I'll come down.'

'So what are you going to do?' Ben said ten minutes later, as they sat at the kitchen table.

'Phone Fran.'

'Not Ian?'

'I think it might not be the right thing to do,' said Libby. 'If Rosie wants to, fine. I shall tell her I don't think Ian would allow it, then she can take it from there.'

'Sensible.' Ben stood up. 'Well, as I'm up early, I might as well go up to the office early. Then I might be back early.' He leered at her. 'I might get a repeat performance.'

'Don't push your luck.' Libby grinned up at him.

Deciding that it was too early to ring Fran, Libby rang Rosie back instead.

'Look, Rosie, Ian's not going to want to you poking around the murder site. In fact, you won't be allowed to. There will be police on site. You'd never get past them.'

'I know that. I just want to see where it is.'

'I suppose I could take you to Cherry Ashton,' said Libby doubtfully. 'There's a pub there. We could have lunch.'

'Oh, yes,' said Rosie, sounding more cheerful. 'I'd like that. Will you ask Fran?'

'If you like. Then she could pick you up. She's nearer you than I am.'

Libby looked at the clock and called Fran.

'I know it's a bit much,' she said, 'and we'll have seen more than enough of each other, but I don't know that I could cope with Rosie on her own, and she's your friend more than mine, anyway.'

'Hardly a friend,' said Fran. 'She's my writing

tutor. But OK. I'll give her a ring and tell her what time I'll pick her up.'

'If we're going to that pub for lunch, make it about midday. We can meet there.'

'What's it called?'

'I can't remember, but it's on the crossroads. If you go to Heronsbourne, take the road towards Steeple Mount and Steeple Cross, you'll find a turning to your left to Cherry Ashton. Then there's a crossroads with a pub on the corner. That's it.'

'Twelve o'clock then,' said Fran, and rang off.

Libby showered and dressed, rang Ben to tell him what was happening and to ask if he wanted to go The Pink Geranium for dinner.

'Again?' he said.

Libby sighed. 'All right, the pub, then.'

'What you mean is, you don't want to cook tonight.'

'I could get fish and chips in Nethergate.'

'You'll be nowhere near Nethergate and they'd be cold before you got home,' said Ben. 'We'll go to Harry's.'

The pub turned out to be called The Ashton Arms, and had an improbable looking coat of arms painted on its swinging inn sign. Libby parked behind the pub, reflecting on how few swinging signs there were left. Something to do with health and safety, obviously.

Rosie and Fran appeared to be the only customers, sitting in a window seat with cups before them.

'We decided on coffee rather than alcohol,' said Fran. 'Do you want one?'

'Depends,' said Libby. 'Not if we're going up to have a look before we eat.'

'Oh, yes, let's,' said Rosie and drank the remainder of her coffee in a hurry.

'Wait for me,' said Fran. 'I'm not going to give myself indigestion for anyone.'

Libby sat down and inspected the rather gloomy interior. It looked more like a town pub than one in a fairly isolated village. There was a lot of dark wood and red leatherette (Libby had a suspicion it might be Rexine), and a highly polished bar, behind which rows of optics were reflected in a mirror.

'George at The Red Lion said they did good food here,' she said. 'I can't even see a barman, let alone a menu.'

'There is one. Well, a bar-woman, actually. Very central casting,' said Rosie. 'A lot of blonde hair and a cantilevered bust.'

Libby giggled. 'Can't wait.'

'Come on, then,' said Fran, putting her cup down. 'Let's go if we're going.'

They walked up the lane leading to the barn. Ahead, they could see the blue-and-white police tape fluttering, and two large white vans parked at the side of the road.

'See? I said we'd never get near it,' said Libby.

'Near enough,' muttered Rosie.

Libby sighed and turned her attention to the cottages that lined the lane on the left-hand side. It was in one of these that Mr Vindari lived, although they looked rather small for someone like him, there was a coach house and carriage arch that looked as though it led to a courtyard and possibly a big house, and here was the church.

'It's really quite nice,' said Rosie. 'I wonder what's down there?' She pointed to the archway.

'I don't know. I think this terrace is called Ashton Terrace.' Libby peered at an overgrown sign near the carriage arch. 'I think that says Ashton Court.'

'I suppose all these people will have been questioned,' said Fran. 'Ian will have set up a house-to-house as soon as the bodies were discovered.'

Rosie shuddered and Fran looked at her apologetically. 'Sorry,' she said, 'but you wanted to come.'

'I know,' said Rosie.

They were much nearer now, and sure enough, there were two large uniformed policemen in yellow high-visibility jackets standing either side of the bank Libby and Fran had climbed a few days ago. They bent basilisk stares on the three women, who stopped.

'I don't think we'd better go any further,' muttered Libby. 'Can you see the barn, Rosie?'

Rosie nodded, her face white. 'What do you suppose they're doing inside?' she whispered.

'Taking soil samples and everything else they can take samples of, I expect,' said Libby, guessing that the bodies had probably been removed by now. 'Shall we go?'

'Ah, Mrs Sarjeant, isn't it?'

Mr Vindari had come up silently behind them. He looked older, thought Libby. Probably the knowledge that you'd lived almost next door to a murderer's graveyard would do that to a person. Also, he wasn't smiling.

'I imagine this has something to do with you?' he said, holding Libby's gaze.

'What do you mean?' said Libby.

'The police coming here and disturbing us.' He sounded angry now.

'It's nothing at all to do with Mrs Sarjeant,' said Rosie in a clear voice, stepping forward and confronting him. 'This happens to be my property.'

That's torn it, thought Libby.

'Your property?' Mr Vindari looked shocked. 'But – I thought –' He turned back to Libby. 'So you did know. You said the property was to be sold. But not this property surely? You said the White Lodge estate.'

'If you remember, I said we were trying to find out if this was part of the White Lodge estate. It is.'

'And it is to be sold?' He turned back to Rosie.

'When the police have finished with it,' said Rosie. 'I'm sorry if you've been put to any inconvenience by the police presence, but it really isn't my fault, you know. Or Mrs Sarjeant's.'

'No, no, of course not.' Mr Vindari was recovering some of his urbanity. 'But why did the police come looking after Mrs Sarjeant's visit?'

'I'm afraid that's not up to us to tell,' said Fran. 'Did the police tell you anything when they came to question you?'

'Question *me*?' He looked outraged.

'In the house-to-house enquiries,' said Fran.

'Oh. Oh, I see.' Mr Vindari took a step back. 'No, I haven't seen them yet. My wife answered their questions when they first came to the door. I was out.'

'They'll be back,' said Libby cheerfully. 'Don't worry about it, Mr Vindari. They go over and over things time and time again. Now we're going to try the food at your village pub.'

He bowed. 'I believe it is rather good, for pub food.'

'Not as good as yours,' said Libby. 'We went to your Canterbury restaurant the other night. Your son was most hospitable.'

The dark face was split by a startling white smile. 'I'm delighted. I hope you will come again.'

'Oh, yes,' said Fran. 'We shall go to the Nethergate one over the weekend. We've been there before.'

'I am pleased.' He bowed again. 'And I apologise about my – er – my,' he looked from side to side as if searching for inspiration. 'My *attitude*,' he concluded triumphantly.

'Please don't,' said Rosie. 'Murder always upsets people.'

'Murder?' Mr Vindari looked as though he had been turned to stone.

'Well, of course,' said Libby. 'Why else would there be all those police up there?'

'I – we – thought it was perhaps –' he looked round again and lowered his voice, 'drugs.'

Fran smiled. 'So did we,' she said.

'Oh?' Mr Vindari looked as if he would start asking more questions, and Libby decided it was time to make a move.

'Sorry to disturb you again, Mr Vindari,' she

said, 'but we must be off if we're to have lunch and get back in time. Lovely village you live in, by the way.'

'In time for what?' asked Fran as Libby hurried back down the lane.

'I don't know, anything. He was just about to start asking how we knew as much as we did and I didn't want to get involved. Is he still watching us?'

'No one's going to turn round and look,' said Rosie. 'Either he's watching us, or he's trying to see into the barn.'

'Do you suppose there'll be anyone in the pub who knows anything about the investigation? Or the barn?' asked Libby.

'I doubt it. It'll just be a load of speculation,' said Fran.

But, when Libby asked the cantilevered barmaid about the police presence up the road, she was surprised to be answered by a voice from the other end of the bar.

'They've been digging inside it.'

'Oh?' The three women turned to face the voice. It belonged to a large man sitting on a bar stool. He wore a long green caped wax coat, and before him on the bar lay a hat of the same material. His white hair was brushed back from a high forehead and a small, neat moustache and beard surrounded a small mouth.

'I can see from the top floor of my place,' he went on.

'The Colonel lives at Ashton Court, see,' said the barmaid, placing three more coffee cups on the bar with a menu.

'Oh, for God's sake, Bren, stop calling me the colonel,' he said. 'But yes, I live at Ashton Court.' He looked from one to another of them. 'You don't exactly look like tourists. You're not press, are you?'

Rosie opened her mouth and Fran and Libby spoke together.

'Of course not!'

'We were out for a walk.'

'A drive,' corrected Libby. 'I'm afraid we were just nosy.'

She smiled and shepherded the other two back to the table in the window.

'Why wouldn't you let me say anything?' asked Rosie.

'Because we don't really want anyone round here knowing you own the place,' said Fran in a low voice.

'In case someone round here is at the bottom of these murders,' said Libby. 'You shouldn't have told Mr Vindari.'

'But he seemed nice, I thought. Just upset by the police activity.'

'I'm sure, but we ought to keep it quiet as far as we can,' said Libby.

'But I don't see why?' said Rosie.

'Because,' said Libby wearily, 'you could be in danger.'

Chapter Twenty-four

'DANGER?' ROSIE GAPED.

'Cor, for a novelist you're not good at picking your way through plots, are you?' said Libby. 'Someone has been using the barn for dastardly doings. We don't know who, but you're in their way.'

'Not now, I'm not,' said Rosie. 'The police know all about it.'

'But eventually the police will go away. And you'll still be the owner. And then whoever it is – or was – will want to find out what's been going on.'

'Unless they've been caught,' said Rosie.

Libby sighed. 'OK, fine. I can see all sorts of pitfalls, but if you don't care, go ahead.'

'One of the things that strikes me,' said Fran, putting down the menu, 'is the Paul Findon connection. I can't see whoever's behind this whole thing – and I doubt very much if it's just one person – believing that you don't know more than you really do. And that could be dangerous.'

'But why?'

'Suppose there's something hidden there? That you might know about? Or something about Findon himself?'

'I told you, I don't remember him at all. Only Debussy.'

Libby shook her head. 'All right. Have it your way. I'd keep quiet if it was me, and I think Ian might say the same. What are you going to have? I think the sausage pie looks good.'

When the other two had chosen, Libby went to the bar to place the order.

'So why are you really here?'

Libby looked up, startled. The colonel was regarding her from over the top of a pint glass.

'We told you. Just being nosy.'

'Has it been on the news then? Or in the papers? I haven't seen it.' The colonel put down his glass. 'And you'd hardly happen upon Cherry Ashton by accident, as it's a dead end.'

Libby put her head on one side. 'At least our nosiness isn't rude,' she said. 'Unlike yours.' She smiled and turned away. 'Excuse me.'

'What was all that about?' asked Fran when she returned to her seat. Libby told them.

'Sorry, but he got under my skin a bit. What's it to him what we're doing here?'

'Perhaps he's one of the villains,' giggled Rosie, 'wanting to know how much we know!'

Fran and Libby looked at her in surprise. 'You've cheered up,' said Fran.

'I think it's hysteria,' said Rosie. 'I seem to have entered some kind of fairground crazy house where nothing's as it seems. And to think all that was worrying me a couple of weeks ago were dreams about a house.'

'Well, it's a good job you did call us in, isn't it? Those victims would never have been found otherwise.' Libby took a sip of coffee and made a face. 'Latte this is not.'

'You don't drink lattes,' said Fran.

'I don't drink crap instant, either,' said Libby,

pushing the cup away from her.

'To return to the colonel,' said Fran, 'I can't see him as a villain. And he volunteered the fact that he could see the barn from the top floor of his house. He wouldn't have done that if he had anything to conceal, would he?'

'I think he looks rather nice, actually,' said Rosie, peering over Libby's shoulder. 'And lonely.'

'You think everyone looks nice,' said Libby. 'Ian, Mr Vindari, Andrew – sorry.'

'Don't be.' Rosie sighed. 'I'm getting over it now.'

'Getting over what?' Libby mouthed at Fran, who shook her head.

The barmaid arrived with their plates and the appreciation of food took first place in their conversation for a while.

'The colonel's gone,' said Rosie suddenly.

'Have you been watching him?' asked Fran with amusement.

'No, I just noticed. Pity.' Rosie returned her attention to her plate. Libby raised her eyebrows at Fran.

'So what do we do now?' said Libby, when they had all cleaned their plates. 'I must say, that was very good. George was right.'

'Can we go back up the lane?' asked Rosie. 'Have another look?'

'I don't think that's wise,' said Fran.

'And bump into Aakarsh Vindari again? Or get questioned by the cops?' Libby shook her head. 'Definitely not a good idea.'

'Oh.' Rosie thought for a moment. 'Do you think

if I got in touch with your Ian he might let me in?'

'Probably not. They don't let people back into their homes after murders are discovered, do they?' said Libby.

'Especially not if they're the murderer,' said Fran.

'Oh, well.' Rosie shrugged. 'At least I've seen the village. Can we go back another way?'

'You mean can we go past White Lodge?' said Fran. 'Yes, but you won't be able to get in there either. I'd forget about it for now. Try ringing Ian, and if he has time he might update you. That's about all you can hope for at the moment.'

Libby was somehow unsurprised to find the colonel sitting outside the pub when they left, nursing a pint and smoking a pipe.

'Sorry if I appeared – ah – intrusive,' he said, waving it at Libby. 'So few strangers around here it's a novelty.'

'I thought the place was popular with diners,' said Fran.

'At weekends, yes, but not during the week. And we're too far off the tourist trail to get holiday makers from Nethergate.'

'But apparently the landlord doesn't allow people from the holiday camp? Yet it's quite respectable?' said Libby.

He grinned. 'And have the place overrun with children wanting games machines or an outside play area? No. That's not what the regulars want.'

'Ye-es,' agreed Libby reluctantly, although she had a sneaking sympathy with this view, having never really got used to the idea of pubs with children in.

'Anyway, thanks for coming.' He stood and knocked his pipe out on a low stone wall.

'Thanks –?' echoed Rosie.

'Sorry, yes. I'm the landlord. I thought you realised.' He beamed at them all.

'But the lady said you lived at Ashton Court,' said Rosie.

'I do. Brenda – that's the lady behind the bar – is my manager and lives in the flat above the pub.' He held out a hand. 'Hugh Weston.'

Rosie took it, introduced herself and Libby and Fran.

'Welcome any time. And,' he said twinkling at them from under bushy brows, 'if you want to come and look at the old barn from my upstairs windows, you're welcome to that, too.'

The three of them laughed and with many goodbyes, began to move off towards the cars.

'What do you suppose he meant by that?' hissed Rosie, as soon as she thought they were out of earshot.

'I think he was simply poking fun at our supposed nosiness,' said Fran. 'Now, come on. I've got to get back home.'

Libby drove home slowly, wondering what was likely to happen next. Nothing, she supposed, unless Ian saw fit to tell her and Fran what was going on, or, if he told Rosie, she kept them in the picture. It was infuriating not to know any more: if there was a cellar; the source of the music; how the barn had come to be used as a burial ground for a serial killer, if that's what it was; why there had been a re-burial in the garden of White Lodge and how it hadn't come out that Rosie was the owner for such a long time.

'Ian called,' said Fran later on the phone.

'What did he say?'

'His very words were, "I hear you were poking around at Cherry Ashton again today." I couldn't very well deny it.'

'How did he know? Those policemen didn't know who we were.'

'If they said three middle-aged women were hanging around, he wouldn't have much trouble making a guess.'

'More likely to have said three old birds,' said Libby, 'but you're right. Unless Mr Vindari informed on us.'

'Why would he do that? Anyway, he said he hadn't spoken to the police yet.'

'But they might have resumed house-to-house enquiries and cornered him.'

'Come to that it could have been the colonel or Brenda for the same reason. Three old birds nosing around this afternoon.'

'Yes, it could,' said Libby, sighing. 'So, did he tell you anything else?'

'He just said enquiries were progressing when I asked. He did say, though, that he would tell us more when he could.'

'I could invite him to dinner?' suggested Libby hopefully.

'He'd probably not be able to get away,' said Fran, 'and anyway, as you're a witness you'd be off limits.'

‘That’s never stopped him in the past,’ said Libby. ‘And he took you out when you were involved in a case.’

‘That,’ said Fran loftily, ‘was entirely different. I was an *expert* witness.’

‘I’m still going to ask him.’

‘And he’ll see right through you,’ said Fran, laughing. ‘If he says yes, can we come too?’

‘Of course. I wouldn’t dream of keeping him to myself,’ Libby lied.

‘Oh, really? But you won’t ask Andrew and Rosie again, will you?’

‘Definitely not. Anyway, I don’t suppose there is an Andrew and Rosie now. I can see there being a Rosie and Hugh, though, can’t you?’

‘She is a bit of flirt, isn’t she?’ said Fran. ‘But there’s more than likely a Mrs Colonel, wouldn’t you say?’

‘I expect so, although I don’t think that would stop Rosie from trying. What’s the betting that she goes back to the pub on her own?’

‘I’m sure of it,’ said Fran. ‘And now I must get on with cooking supper. Adam’s coming, did you know?’

‘No, he doesn’t keep me up to date with his day to day activities,’ said Libby, feeling a tiny bit jealous. ‘Give him my love.’

‘I will,’ said Fran and rang off. Libby sat for a minute looking at the phone and wondering if she should ask Adam and Sophie to supper one night. The she shrugged and dialled Ian’s mobile number. He answered almost immediately to her surprise.

‘What is it, Libby?’

'Oh, I didn't expect you to answer. I was going to leave a message.'

'Well, I did. What is it?'

'I was merely going to ask you to dinner one evening. Don't get shirty.'

'Oh. Sorry.' His voice softened. 'Even if it is a blatant attempt to get something out of me.'

Libby sighed. 'Fran said you'd say that.'

He laughed. 'Of course I would. However, I'd love to come to dinner. When?'

'I don't suppose you'd be free tomorrow night?'

'Saturday? I am, as it happens, unless something breaks on this case, which looks unlikely at the moment.'

'Oh, lovely. Shall I get in some non-alcoholic wine or something?'

'Are Fran and Guy coming?'

'Yes.'

'Then I shall offer to share a taxi and we can all have a drink.'

'Excellent idea,' said Libby. 'Eight o'clock?'

She rang off and called Fran immediately to tell her she was invited for tomorrow.

'He agreed?' said Fran in surprise.

'He certainly did, even though he said he knew I wanted to get something out of him.'

'Told you so.'

'I know, I know, but he's still coming, and he's going to suggest the three of you share a taxi so you can all have a drink.'

'Goodness me! He must really want to let his hair down.'

'I can't imagine that, somehow,' said Libby,

'although I suppose you've seen him like that.'

'*Will* you stop going on about that?' said Fran. 'It was over ages ago. In fact it never really got started.'

'If you say so,' said Libby. 'Anyway, he's coming. So now I'd better start thinking about what to cook. And I haven't even started on tonight's dinner yet.'

'Oh, dear. The Pink Geranium again?'

'I daren't,' Libby giggled. 'It'll have to be something from the freezer. And don't forget to think up some really good questions for Ian tomorrow night. I have the feeling he won't mind answering them, or he wouldn't have agreed to come, would he?'

Chapter Twenty-five

AFTER A MAMMOTH EFFORT, Libby was actually ready before eight o'clock on Saturday evening. The cold starter and the dessert were in the fridge, all the main course dishes in the warming oven, the table was laid and the glasses polished. Libby descended the stairs and was handed a scotch by Ben.

'Well done,' he said. 'Now sit and relax for a few minutes.'

Ten minutes later, and the guests arrived. Libby was pleased to see Ian looked relaxed and cheerful, although Fran didn't.

'What's the matter?' she whispered, bearing her friend into the kitchen on the excuse of checking the food.

'Being in a taxi with those two,' said Fran.

'But Guy's not jealous, you said. And Ian's a perfect gentleman.'

'I know, but it's your fault, bringing it all up again. I felt so awkward.'

Libby frowned at her. 'Sure it was just you feeling awkward, and not one of your moments?'

'Oh, no.' Fran sighed. 'It was just me. And they chatted away about all sorts of things. Football, cricket, the government …'

'Well, just you relax, now, and forget all about it. And I promise not to tease you any more. Here.' Libby fetched a bottle of Sancerre from the fridge. 'You like this, don't you?'

'I do, indeed!' Fran leant forward and kissed her

friend's cheek. 'Thank you. And did I ever say thank you for introducing me to my husband?'

'Gosh, no! You never did!' Libby laughed. 'Go on. Ben's got the bottle opener in there.'

When everyone had been served with drinks, Ian looked across at Libby and grinned.

'Go on then, Mrs Sarjeant. Start the catechism.'

Libby coloured. 'I don't know what you mean.'

Everyone laughed.

'All right then, I'll start without you,' said Ian. 'Where were you up to?'

'We came with you on Thursday to tell Rosie about the bodies in the barn,' said Fran.

'And you said they were all female as far as you could tell,' said Libby.

'And then you two and Rosie all turned up in Cherry Ashton yesterday lunchtime.'

Libby and Fran looked at each other.

'We discussed that,' said Fran. 'Was it the policemen who told you?'

'They told Maiden, who was also informed by a couple of the constables who were resuming house-to-house enquiries yesterday afternoon. He told me.'

'Right,' said Libby. 'So it was Mr Vindari?'

'And Colonel Weston at Ashton Court.'

'Who?' said Ben and Guy together.

Fran explained.

'I think Rosie took rather a shine to him,' said Libby.

'According to one of the constables, Weston was trying to find out who you all were. I think he assumes you've got something to do with us. That or the media. Incidentally, you didn't tell any of your pals about this, did you?'

'If you mean Jane or Campbell, no, we didn't,' said Fran.

'But Campbell already knew about the bodies at White Lodge,' said Libby. 'He told me that last week.'

'I didn't think you had, but nevertheless, the Kent and Coast van turned up in the village late yesterday afternoon, complete with your friend Campbell. And then of course, it was on the local news, but we managed to fob them off by telling them it was all part of the same investigation.'

'Well, it is,' said Libby.

'In a way,' said Ian, 'but the forensics on the bodies so far are completely different. The bodies in the barn are far more recent. And they're all murder victims.'

No one said anything for a moment, until Ben stood up. 'Refill?' he asked.

After the glasses were refreshed, Ian took a healthy sip of his gin and tonic and continued.

'The bodies at White Lodge are all young victims of TB who had been poisoned, but the pathologist doesn't think it was deliberate. She thinks it was someone trying an experimental treatment who got the dosage wrong.'

'That's what I said,' said Libby in triumph.

'But,' said Ian, fixing her with a look, 'not an experimental treatment for TB.'

'Eh?' They all stared at him.

'Apparently, the compound was being investigated back in the early fifties but was never used because it was thought to be too dangerous. So someone was testing it on those poor kids and killing them. That's why they were buried in the garden.'

'Then why mark their graves with stones?' asked Ben.

Ian shook his head. 'They were misleading. We discovered a chapel just beyond the garden, and most of those gravestones belong to that. We managed to get a conservator to clean some of them up and the dates are mostly mid-eighteen-hundreds. The bodies are nineteen-fifties. Mostly girls between eleven and fifteen, as far as the pathologist can make out.'

'What about the re-burial?' asked Fran. 'And the flowers?'

'We don't know.'

'So how did the pathologist find out that it was poison? None of the organs would have been there after all this time,' said Ben.

'It's very complicated, but the compound was of arsenic and something else. Arsenic apparently stays in bones and even back in the thirties tests were being done on bones over nine years old finding quite high concentrations. There was hair present in most of the burials, too. The only reason we looked for it was that report of so called "accidental" poisoning in the newspaper clipping.'

'So what about the bodies in the barn?' asked Guy after a moment.

Ian looked round at them all. 'Are you sure you want to hear about this? Wouldn't you rather wait until after dinner? I don't want to spoil your appetites.'

'Oh, glory, is it that gruesome?' said Libby.
'No, but it's murder. Always unpleasant.'
'All right, we'll wait,' said Libby. 'Anyway, I don't want the food to spoil.'
At the end of the meal, Libby took the cheese board into the sitting room, Ben topped up glasses and they all prompted Ian to continue with his story.
'We haven't had time to do full post-mortems on the bodies yet, nor get back toxicology results,' he said, leaning back in his armchair. 'It's not quite as quick as it is on television. But they are all female.'
'And were they poisoned?' asked Libby.
'He just said they've got no results yet, Lib,' said Ben kindly.
'Oh.' Libby's colour crept up her neck.
'It's a serial killer, then?' said Guy.
'We can't be certain. The women were certainly all attacked physically, and as far as we can tell none of them are more than a couple of years old. The bodies, I mean. The ages of the women are merely speculative so far, but in the region of late teens and early twenties.'
'So not the same as the previous victims?' said Fran.
'As far as we can see, again, there's no connection at all.'
'Then it's a coincidence?' said Libby. 'That's pretty remarkable.'
'As we're working completely in the dark there's nothing to link them, but it does seem odd.'
'Have you looked at Paul Findon?' said Fran.
'Why in particular?'
'Weren't you going to look into how he died?'

'We did. There was an inquest, and a report in the local paper. I expect it made the national press at the time, as he was still reasonably famous.'

'Well, how, then?' said Libby.

'Oh, he died after a fall. Hit his head apparently. His sister found him.'

'Well, that's suspicious for a start! And that sister was Rosie's mum.'

'The inquest found nothing suspicious, and the police did investigate – again because he was quite a famous local personality.'

'Was Rosie mentioned?' asked Fran. Ian turned to her in surprise. 'No, of course not. Why should she be? She was a child and probably wasn't even there.'

'No, that's not right,' said Libby. 'If her mother was there, she would have been, too.'

'I think you ought to look into it,' said Fran.

Everyone became fractionally more alert.

'Do you?' said Ian. 'From what angle?'

'Where did he fall in particular. Was it in the cellar?'

'Cellar? What cellar?'

'Haven't you found it yet? It was in the estate agent's details.'

'I haven't seen them,' said Ian. Libby got up and fetched her laptop.

'There,' she said, bringing up the familiar site. 'It isn't on their current site, you can only get them by going through this old link.'

Ian felt in his pocket and brought out a pen drive. 'May I?' he said holding it up. Libby nodded. They all waited while Ian copied the link and then watched in silence as he read through the details.

'This is very useful,' he said as he took out the pen drive and gave the laptop back to Libby. 'For a start there are actually details of the barn and it mentions the cellar and where the door is, yet we haven't found it yet.'

'Which means in the last two or three years it's been blocked up,' said Libby.

'Um – I suppose you wouldn't like me to have a look, would you?' asked Ben diffidently.

'Of course!' said Ian. 'Why didn't I think of that before? You're an architect.'

'A retired architect, but yes, I am.' Ben smiled round at them all. 'I should quite like to be involved if I'd be any use.'

'I don't know why I didn't think of it, either,' grumbled Libby. 'Or why you didn't mention it earlier.'

'Well, you had the prof, and it didn't seem as though I would be much use. And he did say he could put you on to a specialist. But if this is a case of looking for hidden rooms I'd probably be as good a bet as anyone.'

'It's got everything, this case, hasn't it?' said Guy. 'Secret rooms, spooky music, disinterred bodies, hidden family history – you name it.'

'I'd just as soon it didn't,' said Ian, 'but I suppose I ought to thank you two for bringing it to our attention. Although there's nothing much we can do about the bodies of the TB victims, hopefully we'll be able to find the modern murderers.'

'Modern murderers?' said Libby. 'Not a serial killer, then?'

'We think so.' Ian was cautious.

'But you're not going to tell us why,' said Ben.

'I can't really,' said Ian. 'I've told you more than I should already. As usual.'

'But you said you wouldn't know about it without us,' said Libby.

'Although it was pure – wrong – guesswork about the barn,' said Ian.

'Oh, yes,' said Libby, and subsided.

'When could you come and look at the house, Ben?' asked Ian.

'When you like. Monday?'

'Can I come with him?' asked Libby.

Ian sighed. 'Yes, I suppose so.' He looked over at Fran. 'And you'll want to come, won't you?'

Fran grinned at him. 'If Libby's going I'm not going to be left out.'

'And meanwhile,' said Ian, 'I promise I'll see if I can't find out more about Findon's death.'

'And perhaps his life,' said Fran.

Chapter Twenty-six

IAN WAS AT THE door of White Lodge to meet them on Monday morning. The weather had become summer-like again, and Libby was almost pleased to step inside the cool, dark hall.

'Shall I leave you to it?' said Ian. 'I've got to go out and see what's happening outside anyway. We're cutting a path through to the barn.'

'Does Rosie know?' asked Libby.

'Of course, we had to ask her permission. There's actually already a track there, but it's completely overgrown.'

'No traces of anyone having used it recently?'

'We are looking, Libby. We had actually thought of that.' Ian turned to Ben. 'OK, then? All the doors are unlocked, and there'll always be someone in the garden who can fetch me if you need me.'

'Well,' said Ben, after Ian had left through the back door. 'You two had better show me around. Are we likely to hear this music?'

'Yes, if we go upstairs,' said Fran, 'but I thought you wanted to find the cellar?'

'That's what I'm here for. Libby, have you got those details?'

Libby had printed the old details from the estate agent's website and fished them out of her basket. 'It says door to cellar in hall.' She looked round. 'But I can't see it.'

'It's a bit of a rambler, this house,' said Ben. 'This probably isn't the only hall. This part is the later addition, I think. We need the earlier house.'

'Through there, then,' said Fran, pointing to the left. 'That corridor leads to the rooms beyond the piano room.'

'Oh, yes, the piano room. I'd better have a look at that.' Ben led the way into the room.

'It feels friendly, doesn't it?' said Libby. 'It felt spooky upstairs, and in the garden after we'd heard the music, but I don't think it *is* an unfriendly house.'

'I agree,' said Fran. 'I really like this room. I can just see drifting white curtains at these long windows.'

'And a big log fire in the winter,' said Libby going to the Adam-style fireplace. 'This isn't original, though, is it? This room's been upgraded.'

'It's a complete mish-mash,' said Ben, frowning. 'The Georgian owners obviously gave the interior a complete makeover. And I imagine upstairs there are even more desecrations from when it was turned into a workhouse.'

'Not too many,' said Libby. 'Don't forget this was the master's house. The actual workhouse buildings were outside and were demolished.'

'Except for the barn.' Fran turned round in a full circle and then stopped. 'I've had an idea.'

'What?' said Ben and Libby together.

'Do you remember when we were at Creekmarsh? We went round the outside to try and find traces of the cellars?'

'So why aren't we doing that here?' Ben patted her on the shoulder. 'Brilliant, Fran. Might not be quite so easy as this is older and I think there's more subsidence.'

'There was subsidence at Creekmarsh,' said Libby. 'All we need to find is the top of a lintel, isn't it? Then work out where it is on the inside.'

'All? There's a lot of outside to this place,' said Ben. 'Come on.'

It wasn't easy to get all the way round the outside. The side of the house that led to the wall and the garden gate was part of the newer house and contained nothing suspicious, the garden where the bodies had been exhumed was almost impossible to traverse, but by dint of keeping close to the wall past the piano room windows in single file, they reached the hedge which divided the garden and managed to squeeze through.

'I've never been this side before,' said Libby.

'It looks as though this was the formal garden,' said Fran. 'Look, there are lupins and delphiniums over there.'

Ben was grubbing around the bottom of the wall. 'Look,' he called over his shoulder. Fran and Libby bent down.

'There,' he said. 'I think that's a lintel.'

It was a bleached beam at a forty-five degree angle, disappearing into the ground. Further along, there was another, which Libby pointed out.

'Cellars? Or actually the original ground floor of the house?' she asked. 'If it's subsidence, that's what it could be.'

Ben nodded, fished a tape measure out of his back pocket and started taking measurements. Libby and Fran took turns to hold the end, while he wandered up and down muttering and making notes.

Finally he stood back and peered up at the walls.

'I think I know where it is,' he said. 'Now we've just got to get inside.'

The started round the other side of the house into more unkempt gardens.

'Did you notice there was no music in the garden?' said Libby.

'Of course not. The garden gate has been taken off. There's nothing to trigger it,' said Fran.

'What I want to know,' said Ben, as he poked along at the bottom of the wall, 'is why they haven't traced that music. There's got to be a wiring system.'

'Perhaps they have,' said Libby. 'You could ask.'

They came up against a wall that blocked their way to the front of the house.

'Come on then,' said Ben. 'Back the other way.'

'We can go in the back door if it's unlocked,' said Fran, 'or through the french windows into the piano room.'

Back in the garden where white-coated figures still worked, Libby called out to the nearest.

'Do you know if the wiring's been traced from the gatepost?'

Three of the figures turned round. The first pulled her mask down. 'Don't know anything about it. What wiring?'

'Wrong sort of investigators,' said Ben as they entered the passage from the back door. 'I expect they're soil samplers or something.'

'We'll ask Ian,' said Libby. 'Come on, let's find this cellar.'

But they couldn't.

'Do you remember,' said Libby eventually, as, hot and dusty, they reconvened in the hall of the older part of the house, 'at Creekmarsh it was inside a cupboard.'

'I've looked,' said Ben. 'There's only one place where it can be.'

'Where?' said Fran and Libby together.

'Under the staircase at the other end of the building. There's no under-stairs cupboard, and although it looks genuine, I guarantee that the wall is recent.'

'What do we do? The listing people won't let you knock that wall down, will they?' said Fran.

'I'll tell Ian,' said Ben. 'I'm sure he can get round it. Shame I can't get a sample of the brick work or plaster to date it.'

'Shall I go round to the outside and see if it's the right place?' said Libby.

'It's more or less the right place. And you could be right. It isn't so much a cellar as an original floor.' Ben led them to the staircase in question. 'It looks like a return, doesn't it?'

Fran and Libby looked.

'If you say so,' said Libby. Ben sighed.

'Let's see if we can find Ian,' suggested Fran. 'He'll know what to do.'

But Ben was suddenly on his knees again.

'What is it?' asked Libby, crouching down beside him.

He waved her away. 'Get out of my light,' he muttered, and began feeling his way along the wall until he came to the outer one. 'There!' he said triumphantly, and stood up.

'What?'

'Wiring. Not sure if it's going or coming, but that should be enough to allow us – or the police – to knock through.'

'We've found the music?' said Libby.

'I think so. Come on, we really must find Ian now.'

One of the white suits confirmed that Ian was still somewhere in the wood, and Fran called his mobile.

'He's coming straight back,' she said switching it off.

When Ian arrived, Ben took him to see the half covered lintel, then into the house to where the wiring confirmed the presence of the hidden cellar. Fran and Libby inspected the sagging door frame in the garden wall.

'No wiring, but it was here.' Fran ran her finger down a newish looking scrape in the old wood. 'How on earth did they manage to come in and dismantle it with all this police activity going on?'

'There was no police activity last weekend,' said Libby. 'Only Ian on Saturday afternoon, and I don't think he was here for long.'

Ian and Ben appeared round the side of the house. Ian was talking into his mobile and scowling.

'He's got to get an expert to look at it to see if it's genuine. My word isn't good enough apparently,' said Ben. 'Back to the Archaeological Society.'

'Andrew said he knew a buildings person,' said Libby, 'but it might not be tactful to mention it if he and Rosie have had a falling out.'

'We'll let Ian sort it out,' said Ben. 'I've done my bit.'

'And we've found where the wiring was here,' said Fran, pointing to the door frame.

'So have we.' Ian came up putting his mobile in his pocket. 'And the speakers.'

'Oh,' said Libby and Fran, defeated.

'Very cunningly concealed. It was a real specialist job. Now we can see the other end, thanks to Ben, and I expect we'll find the equipment in the blocked up cellar.'

'But if it's blocked up, how are they getting to it?' asked Libby. 'They can't leave it unattended – or can they? It might go wrong.'

'Well, it certainly will now we've disconnected everything this end,' said Ian. 'We'll have to find the hidden speakers on the staircase next, but if we can get the buildings archaeologist down here, that'll help.' He turned to the white coats who had carried on with their careful scraping and sample taking and didn't appear to be listening. 'Have we got a dendrochronologist on the team?'

'In the lab,' said one.

'Not on site?'

They all looked up at him blankly and shook their heads. Ian muttered under his breath.

'Shall we leave you to it?' asked Libby. 'You've got enough on your plate without us cluttering up the place.'

'Thanks, Libby.' Ian held out his hand to Ben. 'And thanks, Ben. Will you be able to give a proper statement about this?'

Ben nodded. 'I'll do a report and email it to you. What's your address?'

Ian wrote his email address on an official card.

'Why isn't it on there already?' asked Libby, peering over Ben's shoulder.

'I'd be inundated,' said Ian. 'The only numbers there are the police station switchboard and my dedicated mobile.'

'Different from the one we use?'

'Definitely.' Ian gave them all a grin. 'Now I'd better make some more phone calls.'

'Whatever did we do before mobile phones?' mused Libby as they went back to their cars.

'Led a different lifestyle,' said Ben. 'Shall we go and persuade Guy to come out for lunch at The Sloop?'

'Good idea,' said Fran. 'You suggest it, though. He's more likely to agree.'

Guy agreed, and half an hour later the four of them were sitting outside The Sloop, the pub at the end of the hard in Nethergate, next to Mavis's Blue Anchor café.

'Difficult to believe all that horror going on at White Lodge while you're sitting here,' said Libby, squinting out over the sea, where ripples sparkled like sequins in the sunlight.

'I've been thinking about that,' said Guy.

'And?' prompted Fran after a moment.

'You said the bodies were quite recent?'

'The ones in the barn, yes,' said Libby.

'It may be nothing, but you remember Rachanda, Sophie's friend?'

'Nice girl, yes. What's happened to her?'

‘Not to her, but her sister Rachita. She’s been missing for three weeks, apparently.’ Guy sipped his beer and shook his head.

‘When did you find this out?’ asked Libby. ‘It hasn’t been on the local news or in the papers, has it?’

‘No, but I’m not really sure why. Sophie went to see Rachanda yesterday, but the family’s closed ranks and she wasn’t allowed in. Rachanda managed to call her late last night.’

‘The police must think it’s racially motivated, then?’ said Ben. ‘Otherwise they’d have been appealing all over the press.’

Libby looked across at Fran. ‘Are you thinking what I’m thinking?’

Chapter Twenty-seven

'ACTUALLY, THAT'S EXACTLY WHAT I was thinking,' said Guy. 'It just seems like too much of a coincidence.'

'I suppose they *have* told the police?' said Libby. 'You said they'd closed ranks. They're not trying to deal with it themselves, are they?'

'I don't know. Sophie said Rachanda was speaking in a whisper and couldn't tell her much, except that she was frightened.'

'Frightened?' Fran looked alarmed.

'About Rachita, I expect she meant,' said Libby.

'Rachita, how old is she?' asked Ben.

'About seventeen, I think,' said Guy. 'Younger than Rachanda, who's the same age as Sophie. She wanted to go to university, too, but wasn't allowed to by the family.'

'So it's entirely possible that Rachita's run away if she's being controlled in the same way,' said Libby. 'That's probably why they haven't told the police.'

'We don't know that,' said Fran. 'They may have told the police.'

'In which case, wouldn't Ian have been checking to see that none of his bodies is Rachita? He'll be checking missing persons, won't he?' asked Guy.

'Oh, yes, or the team will. Poor old Ian. This is turning into a hell of a case, isn't it?' Libby sighed.

'There's a link, somewhere.' Fran was frowning. 'I know there is. The TB bodies and now these.

Must be a link.'

'I don't see how,' said Libby. 'The TB bodies were fifty odd years ago, and these are new. Recent, anyway.'

'It's to do with Paul Findon,' said Fran.

'And the estate agents, I reckon,' said Libby. 'I never trusted them.'

'Riley's in particular, or all estate agents?' said Ben, amused.

'Most of them. And I do object to the practice they have of employing beardless boys, who then pretend to know all there is about houses, bylaws and all the other things you need to know when buying a house.'

'It doesn't inspire confidence,' agreed Fran. 'Goodall and Smythe never employed anyone under thirty-five. They knew about gravitas.'

'Back to the subject under discussion,' said Guy, 'what about this Rachita. Could she be – heaven forbid – one of Ian's bodies?'

'We need to know more about it.' Libby was decisive. 'We can't just barge in.'

Her nearest and dearest hooted with laughter.

'No, what I mean is,' said Libby, waiting patiently until their mirth had subsided, 'we can't go and ask Rachanda's family, and we can't really suggest Ian does, either. We need to know if she's been reported to the police first.'

'I'm sure it would have been in the local papers and probably on local TV. A missing seventeen-year-old girl is news,' said Ben. 'And if she really is missing, and not being hidden away, the police need to be told.'

'Can you imagine the scene, though?' said Libby. 'Police go knocking on the door and say they understand someone's missing. Family say, of course not, who told you? A friend of your daughter's. And who told her? Your daughter. Family, laughing hysterically, and you believed her? Exit police, tail between legs.'

They were all silent, considering this scenario.

'Was Rachita at school?' asked Fran.

'Just about to go into the upper sixth form,' said Guy, 'so Sophie says. But on holiday at the moment, of course.'

'Did she work?'

'I think the family have a couple of shops. She may have worked in one of them.' Guy shrugged. 'I don't really know.'

'Oh, how are we going to do this?' Libby banged a fist on the table. 'How frustrating.'

'It may be unconnected, Lib,' said Fran. 'We're only speculating on a coincidence.'

'But you don't think it's unconnected, do you?' said Libby, with a shrewd look at her friend's face. Fran looked discomfited, and shook her head.

'In that case, we have to do something. This has landed in our laps. We can't just ignore it.' Libby looked round the table. 'I think we have to tell Ian.'

Everyone groaned.

'Guy – you tell him,' said Libby. 'You're the one that got the first info from Sophie and he'd take it better from you than from Fran or me.'

Guy looked at his wife. 'Do you think so?'

She sighed and nodded.

'He's likely to ignore his personal mobile at the

moment,' said Ben, 'but I've got his card, haven't I? We can ring his other mobile. Then he'll know it's important.'

'Genius!' said Libby, as Ben fished Ian's card out of his pocket. He handed it to Guy, who took it and walked away from the table. 'Not having you lot listen in,' he said, with a grin.

'Are we going to order food?' asked Libby, watching Guy's back.

'Sandwich?' suggested Ben, taking a menu from another table.

'He's got through,' said Fran. 'He's talking.'

A minute later, Guy switched off his phone and came back to the table.

'He's interested,' he said, sitting down and handing Ben the card. He looked round at them all. 'He actually said, "Ah. That fits." I said does it, and he said he'd tell us later and could Sophie give him Rachanda's address. He won't bring Sophie into it.'

They looked at each other.

'Good job we told him, then,' said Libby. 'He wasn't mad, then?'

'Not at all. I think it was a good idea to use his police mobile, and that it was me who told him – thanks, Libby.'

Libby nodded. 'And now you'd better get the address from Sophie.'

'Can she close the shop for a bit?' asked Fran. 'She could come here.'

'OK,' said Guy, picking up his mobile. 'I'm not a slave driver!'

Sophie joined them five minutes later and they ordered sandwiches and fresh drinks. He called Ian and dictated the address and phone number Sophie had given, then switched off.

'How long have you known Rachanda, Sophie?' asked Libby.

'Years,' said Sophie. 'We were at school together. We were put in the same form when we were about twelve, and as we were both new we sort of stuck together. We used to walk home together and go and get sweets in her uncle's shop. And I used to get asked to eat with them sometimes, remember, Dad?'

'Yes, you always made me jealous,' said Guy.

'So they were nice people?' persisted Libby.

'Oh, yes, lovely. Rachanda's mum didn't say much, but smiled a lot, and grandma could talk for England, but not in English. Or India – or wherever. Her dad and the uncles were a jolly lot, too. There were cousins, as well. I don't think they all lived in the same house, but fairly close to each other.'

'But they wouldn't let Rachanda go to university?' said Fran.

'No.' Sophie shrugged. 'You know what they're like. Woman's place is in the home, and all that.'

'But there are loads and loads of Asian women doctors and lawyers,' said Libby. 'How did they get away with it?'

'I don't know,' said Sophie. 'That's exactly what Rach told them, but it didn't make any difference.'

'And what about Rachita? Does she want to go to university?' said Libby.

'Oh, yes. And she told Rach what she thought of her for not standing up to the family.'

'So do you think she might have run away?'

asked Ben.

'I don't think she'd do that until she'd got her A levels,' said Sophie. 'Then she could hide until it was time to take up her uni place. And she would never tell them where she'd been offered a place, either. So, no, I don't think she's run away.'

'And what about boys?' asked Fran. 'Boyfriends?'

'Oh, they're both set up to marry some distant cousins or something,' said Sophie. 'Rach doesn't seem to mind, but Rachita hated it. I don't know if she's been seeing anyone, though. She would keep it very quiet.'

'Do you think they've told the police?' asked Libby. 'Ian hadn't heard about it, and it would have been reported to his division.'

'I don't know. Rach was a bit funny about it. She said she was frightened but I'm not sure of what. Perhaps it's a kidnapping and they've been told not to involve the police? That's what it would be on the telly.'

'She's right.' Libby looked round at the others. 'But would she be worth much?'

'Libby!' said four voices together.

'What I meant was, would the family be able to raise enough to make a ransom worthwhile?'

'Oh, I see.' Sophie shook her head. 'They all seemed very comfortably off, but you can't really tell, can you? It wasn't as if they had really flash houses, or anything. And they worked like slaves. The shops were open all hours.'

'They sound like most of the Asian families I know. Ali and Ahmed in the village are the same,' said Libby.

'What about your Mr Vindari?' said Ben. 'He looks a bit flasher.'

'He's only got the two restaurants,' said Libby, 'and he seems to live in a small cottage. I wouldn't have said he was particularly rich.'

'When Ian said "that fits" what do you think he meant?' asked Fran.

'No idea,' said Guy, 'but I gather we're all thinking along the same lines, aren't we?'

They all nodded gloomily.

'I feel really bad about it,' said Libby. 'Ali and Ahmed are friends, and Mr Vindari was really nice. And Ben and I got free drinks in his restaurant. It seems so wrong to start suspecting their community.'

'No different from suspecting anybody else,' said Ben. 'When a murderer comes from a poor background we don't say, "that is damaging to the whole poverty-stricken community", or if he's rich, "that's an insult to all fat cats", do we?'

'It does get said,' said Fran. 'There are always media pundits who will make a point of the background or community, whatever it is.'

'Maybe it isn't what we're suspecting,' said Guy. 'And maybe Rachita's just bunked off for the summer before settling down to her A levels. And perhaps Rachanda's frightened of what her family are going to say when she comes back. The most almighty row, I should think.'

The sandwiches arrived.

They ate in silence, then Sophie said she would go back to the shop and Guy reluctantly said he would follow her.

'Are you going to hang around?' he asked Libby and Ben as he stood up to go.

'Don't know,' said Libby. 'Why?'

'Just wondered,' he said looking at Fran, who grinned.

'He wants to ask you to stay to supper, but he has to ask me first! Would you like to stay?'

'Love to,' said Libby.

'If it's not too much trouble,' said Ben.

'I'll see you later then,' said Guy, and with a wave set off down Harbour Street after Sophie.

'What shall we do this afternoon, then?' asked Libby. 'Will you have to go shopping, Fran? Shall I come with you?'

'I suppose I will,' said Fran. 'You can come if you like. What will you do, Ben?'

'I might go and visit the new baby,' he said.

'Oh, well,' said Libby, 'we can all do that. If Fran and I do a really quick shop, we can all go up to Peel House afterwards.'

'If that won't be too much for her?' said Fran. 'Or you two could go and I could go back and start preparing food.'

'Oh no, you must come too,' said Libby. 'I'll ring Jane and ask.'

Finally, all three went shopping in the little supermarket halfway up the high street.

'Look,' said Libby as they came out, 'Riley's is closed.'

'So it is,' said Fran. Ben crossed the road to read the notice in the window.

"Due to unforeseen circumstances this office will

remain closed until further notice. We apologise for any inconvenience," he quoted when he came back.

'That'll be Ian pursuing his enquiries,' said Libby. 'We said he should look into Riley's. After all they had a connection with Paul Findon and Rosie's mother and they're still handling the sale – supposedly. They're bound to be worth investigating.'

'I'm sorry for the employees,' said Fran, as they started down the hill. 'They may well be out of a job.'

'Serve 'em right,' said Libby.

'No, I don't think they knew anything about – well – about whatever it is. Otherwise that first man wouldn't have told you it was a difficult place, nor given you the keys to go yourself. He probably got the sack for that.'

'Oh, dear! Do you really think so? I feel awful, now.'

'Well, you didn't know, did you?' said Fran. 'Are we going to take this shopping home before we go to see Jane?'

'Is there anything that will spoil? If not, I can't see the point in going all the way back to Coastguard Cottage and then retracing our steps here again,' said Ben. 'We can carry it between us.'

'And to get the stuff back gives us an excuse not to stay too long,' said Libby, 'in case we begin to feel baby overload.'

'Or the boot's on the other foot,' said Ben.

Chapter Twenty-eight

IMOGEN HAVING BEEN DULY appreciated, and Jane given an update on the White Lodge investigation, leaving out Rachita's disappearance, Fran, Libby and Ben went back down to Coastguard Cottage. Fran made tea, then she and Libby returned to the kitchen, where Libby got under her feet, under the impression that she was helping, and Ben sat reading a paper in the window seat with Balzac on his lap.

Sophie had been invited to supper as well, but she said Adam was coming over and they were having a take-away.

'She said they might pop in after they've eaten,' said Guy when he arrived after closing the shop.

'I think you see more of my son than I do these days,' said Libby.

'Not much,' said Fran, accepting a glass of white wine from her husband. 'They tend to stay closeted in the flat. Young lurve, eh?'

'Hmm.' Libby sipped her own glass of red. 'Young lust, more likely.'

'Libby!' Ben said, appalled, but Fran and Guy laughed.

Conscious of the fact that Ben wouldn't be able to drink more than one glass of wine, Fran served up early, and they were just finishing their fruit and cheese at half past seven when there was a knock on the door.

'Ian!' Guy held the door open and Ian stepped

inside.

'I'm sorry,' he said. 'I should have rung, but I was actually looking for Sophie.'

'She's in the flat.' Fran stood up. 'You sit down and have a cup of coffee and we'll ask her to come over here. I don't suppose you've eaten, have you?'

'Well, no,' said Ian, sitting on the chair that Guy pulled up to the table for him, 'but I don't want to interrupt.'

'Help yourself to cheese,' said Fran handing him a plate. 'I'll get you a cup.'

When Ian had been supplied with food and drink and Sophie had been summoned, he looked round the assembled company and laughed.

'Here we are again,' he said, 'and I suppose you're going to ask me more questions.'

'Only if you're allowed to answer them,' said Libby, looking hopeful.

'We won't know that until you ask them, will we?' said Ian, cutting himself a piece of brie.

'Why don't you just tell us anything you can,' suggested Guy, 'especially, of course, what it was about Sophie's information that you said fitted.'

Ian paused to eat his brie and cut a slice of apple.

'Well,' he continued, 'as I'm sure you've guessed, our bodies in the barn are all from the Asian community.'

There was a collective sigh.

'That's why I said it isn't a serial killer. It's more likely to be a burial place for honour killings, and I'm sure that's the conclusion you've come to.'

'Only today,' said Libby. 'It was Sophie telling us about Rachita. We thought she might have run away because of a boyfriend or something.'

'We don't know of course – ah – is that Sophie?'

Sophie, looking nervous, came in followed by Adam, who came and gave his mother a quick kiss before sitting next to his beloved on the sofa.

'I was just explaining, Sophie – you don't mind me calling you Sophie, do you?' Sophie shook her head. 'I was explaining that the bodies buried in the barn are all Asian girls. So after you gave me their address, I went to call on Rachita's family.' He sighed. 'Who were furious and exceedingly unhelpful.'

'Oh, dear,' said Sophie. 'I hope Rach isn't in trouble.'

'I never mentioned you, or her,' said Ian. 'I merely said that we were concerned about the whereabouts of many Asian girls who hadn't been seen in the community recently.' He sighed again. 'Her father hit the roof. You know – nosy neighbours, racial prejudice, police brutality – you name it, he said it. Then mother interrupted and said Rachita had gone to stay with an aunt in London for the summer as she was bored down here, and would be back at the beginning of term. Even told me the address of the aunt.'

They all looked at each other.

'So that's the end of that,' said Libby. 'Complete red herring.'

'No,' said Ian.

'No?' echoed several voices.

'We rang the local nick in London, who confirmed that there was such an address, a large block of council flats, apparently and they actually had a patrol car there at that very moment.'

'Sounds like a TV programme,' muttered Ben.

'Quite. So, they asked the two guys to check out the address. I got the report back about ten minutes later. The woman who answered the door very obviously didn't know what they were talking about and assumed at first that Rachita – who is her niece, by the way – was missing. Then she realised and tried to cover up. While they were still with her, her phone rang, but she wouldn't answer it, so they concluded that it was someone this end trying to warn her.'

'So she's not there?' said Fran.

'No. So they are actually trying to cover up the fact that she's missing.'

'Oh, God.' Sophie put her head in her hands.

'It doesn't necessarily mean that she's one of our bodies,' said Ian. 'She may have run away. But we need to find out.' Ian leant forward and touched Sophie's arm. 'That's why we need your help.'

Sophie looked horrified. 'How can I help? They won't let me into the house.'

'But you can call Rachanda, can't you?'

'Her phone goes straight to voicemail,' said Sophie. 'I've tried.'

Ian sat back, looking annoyed. 'What we really need is a DNA sample.'

'Could you go and say you've checked in London and she's not there? And you need a DNA sample to try and trace her? They might genuinely believe she's at her auntie's.' Libby looked hopeful, but doubtful.

'They would accuse us of interfering again and

we'd probably end up with a complaint.' Ian sighed. 'Do you know when Rachanda last saw her, Sophie?'

Sophie shook her head. 'She just said three weeks.'

'Do they all go out to work?' asked Ian.

'No. Rach's mother and grandmother stay at home. Rach works for one of the uncles in the office, bookkeeping and stuff, I think.'

'What about her father? He was at home yesterday afternoon.'

'He's usually at the shop. Rachita helped him there sometimes.'

'Was that the shop you used to go to on the way home from school?' asked Fran.

'No, that was an uncle's. Rach's dad's shop is just round the corner from their house. *On* the corner, actually.'

Ian stood up impatiently. 'Nothing we can do, then. The most recent death, as far as the pathologist can tell us, was roughly two weeks ago. The others are more difficult, but nothing over a couple of years according to remaining clothing.'

'No identifying wallets or anything?' asked Libby.

'Nothing. Labels in the clothes, such as they are, are all high street.'

'No saris?' said Sophie.

'No.' Ian frowned. 'Why?'

'Because both Rach and her sister wore saris. Even to school.'

'But if she was running away, or seeing a boyfriend she wouldn't,' said Fran. 'And that's another thing. If she really is missing, what will her family say when the school asks where she is at the beginning of term?'

'And we're nearly at the end of August already,' said Guy, 'so that won't be long.'

'I suppose we can't do anything about it.' Ian sat down again. 'We can't identify any of them, so the experts are going to go into all the more esoteric dating techniques which I don't understand. That will take weeks, so we may as well seal the place up and get on with everything else.'

'Have they taken all the soil samples and that sort of thing at the barn?' asked Libby.

'They're still there, but it's winding down now. They're trying to establish the route taken to get in there, as there should be traces from the most recent body, but no luck so far.'

'There were when Libby and I went there,' said Fran. 'We could see where there'd been fairly fresh cuts. On the undergrowth on the bank.'

'Really?' Ian frowned. 'Then why haven't we found them?'

'Someone covered them up?' said Guy.

'You can't cover that sort of thing,' said Ben. 'The actual plant – what was it, Fran? Hawthorn? Something like that?'

'It had whippy green stems. Like thin willow.'

'They could have uprooted the whole thing and covered up the traces in the ground. But that would mean someone was watching all the time.'

'Colonel Weston,' said Libby and Fran together.

'What?' Ian looked startled.

'He lives in Ashton Court,' said Fran.

‘Yes, I know who he is,’ said Ian, ‘but what about him?’

‘He said he could see the barn and everything from the top floor of his house,’ said Libby. ‘He even asked us to go and have a look.’

‘Did he now?’ said Ian. ‘Could it have been to warn you?’

‘I don’t know,’ said Libby. ‘I didn’t think so at the time, although he was bloody nosy when we first went into the pub.’

‘Probably thinks of himself as the local squire,’ said Ben.

‘Maybe, but he also owns the pub. Although a lot of landowners owned the whole village, didn’t they, so I suppose that’s not all that odd.’

‘Perhaps we ought to go back and have a word with Colonel Weston,’ said Ian.

‘Or it could have been Mr Vindari,’ said Libby. ‘He saw me when I first went there, and when wc went with Rosie. He obviously watches what’s going on.’

Ian sighed. ‘They’ll all have to be talked to again,’ he said and stood up. ‘Thanks for the coffee and cheese, Fran.’ He turned to Sophie. ‘And thanks for coming down, Sophie. I’ll try not to involve you any more.’

‘Well,’ said Libby, when he’d gone. ‘He’s never normally that forthcoming, is he?’

‘He is when he’s stumped,’ said Fran. ‘It does look bad for Rachita, Sophie.’

‘I know.’ Sophie shook her head. ‘I can’t bear it. How do you two cope when you’re involved in these awful cases?’

'It's not so hard for us,' said Libby. 'It's not usually people we know.'

'You knew a lot of people over at Creekmarsh,' Adam reminded her.

'Yes, but we didn't know the victims, did we?' said Fran.

'No, but –' began Adam grudgingly. His mother interrupted.

'It doesn't matter, Ad. It's just very hard for Sophie because her friend's family are involved. Maybe not in this *case*, but certainly something, or they'd have admitted they didn't know where Rachita is.'

'You don't think it's an honour killing, do you?' asked Sophie in a small voice.

'I'm sure it isn't.' Guy went and sat on the arm of the sofa, his arm round his daughter's shoulders. 'I think she's run away and they're ashamed to admit it. Especially if she's gone with a boy.'

Sophie's forehead wrinkled in a frown. 'But I wouldn't have said she was like that. She was so focussed on her work. She wants to be a scientist – or a biologist.'

'And she's a seventeen-year-old girl,' said Fran. 'All hormones and emotion. And if she sees her family as a barrier to going to university, she's bound to see them as a barrier to everything else, too, especially love. Doesn't that make sense?'

'Except that she would want to go back to school, as I said earlier, to get her A levels. And knowing the family, if she goes back to school, they can get her back home.' Sophie laid her head on her father's arm. 'Thank goodness for enlightened parents.'

'What will Ian do now?' asked Ben, as he helped Libby and Fran to clear the table.

'What he said, I suppose,' said Libby. 'Wait for dating evidence from the experts. And follow up any missing person reports that might be relevant. I don't envy whoever has to do that.'

'And meanwhile, he still has the other enquiry.' Guy came into the kitchen.

'Well, at least that's not murder,' said Ben. 'And he knows who the victims are.'

'Not exactly who they were,' said Libby, 'just *what* they were.'

'But there's murder there, too,' said Fran from the sink.

'Well, mistaken murder,' said Libby. 'More manslaughter, I would have thought.'

'Not them,' said Fran without turning round. 'Paul Findon.'

Chapter Twenty-nine

'I'M SURE OF IT.' Fran turned round, wiping her hands. 'I don't know why, but it's just one of those inescapable facts.'

'Is this why the cellar's important?' asked Ben.

'I think we'd established that,' said Libby, still looking at Fran. 'You've been telling Ian to look into Findon and the cellar from the minute we found out about him.'

'And the estate agent,' said Fran, 'but from what we saw this afternoon, it looks as though he's already doing that.'

'Except that whoever was involved in letting White Lodge after Findon died won't still be around.'

'But they're still involved in selling the property, so they must know something,' said Ben. 'We should have asked him.'

Libby grinned at him. 'You're getting as interested as we are.'

'It has a certain appeal as a puzzle.' He grinned back.

'But it's the human cost,' said Fran, turning back to the sink.

'I know.' Libby went across and gave her a hug. 'Sophie's right. We mustn't forget the real people.'

Soon after this conversation, Ben and Libby left.

'When do you think we'll hear anything more about it all?' asked Libby, as they drove through the quiet night.

'I don't know. Ian might let me know of the results of my report and Sophie will hear about Rachita.'

'But how? If Rachanda can't speak to anyone and is confined to the house …'

'Ian's quite kind-hearted. He'd tell her, I'm sure. Or at least tell Guy to tell her.' Ben reached across and patted her knee. 'Don't worry about it. Get back to painting and working out what we're going to do at the theatre this Christmas.'

'Hoy! We know what we're going to do,' said Libby. 'What do you mean?'

'I don't mean the panto, idiot! I mean the party. We said we would have a Christmas party.'

'Oh, yes, so we did.' Libby thought for a moment. 'Are we going to do it for the whole village, or just for our members?'

'We haven't got members as such,' said Ben. 'But we should send an invitation to all the people who've worked with us. We've got most people's email addresses, haven't we?'

'I suppose we can't really have any more people than that, we haven't got room. Pity we can't take the auditorium seats out.'

'I would definitely put my foot down at that,' said Ben.

Tuesday morning was still pleasant and summery, and after gloomily pottering around the cottage after Ben had gone to the Manor, Libby took his advice and went into the conservatory to continue with the painting that sat waiting on her easel. She'd got no further than sorting out the paints and brushes when the landline rang.

'Hello, Libby,' said Campbell McLean.

'Campbell,' said Libby, furiously trying to remember how much information had leaked out about the White Lodge case.

'I wondered if you had anything for me yet.'

'For you?'

'Come on, Libby. I told you I knew what was going on at White Lodge over a week ago. And now they've started work at the other end of the estate. I must say, I never knew that barn was there.'

'I don't know anything about it, Campbell. If you want to know any more you'll have to ask the police.'

'Libby.' Campbell made an exasperated sound. 'You, Fran and Ben were seen yesterday being let into White Lodge by DI Connell. So you must know something.'

Oh, bum, thought Libby. 'Obviously I can't tell you anything about that,' she said. 'And it's really nothing to do with you.'

He roared with laughter. 'That's the most naive and ridiculous statement I've ever heard you make. I'm a journalist!'

'Well, I'm still not telling you anything,' said Libby, ruffled. 'Ian would know immediately where a leak came from, and if you print anything about the case he'll still think it came from me, even if it didn't.' She took a deep breath. 'I'm going now. If I am allowed to talk to you, I will. All right?'

She switched off the phone and immediately re-dialled Ian's private mobile number.

'Campbell McLean just phoned me. He knows about us going to White Lodge yesterday,' she said when he answered, sounding exasperated.

'Shit. Oh, well, to be expected. They've been very good about keeping quiet so far. I suppose it's press conference time.'

'About both sets of bodies?'

'Hmmm.' Ian paused. 'Perhaps not.'

'It might smoke Rachita's family out,' said Libby.

'Libby, I don't think I've ever heard such a sensible suggestion from you. Well done. I'll try and let you know if there's any progress.' He switched off his phone.

'Oh.' Libby sat down on the third step, disturbing Sidney. 'Good lord above.'

She sat thinking for a moment, then picked up the phone again and called Fran.

'Will he let you know if it'll be on the news?' asked Fran.

'Bound to be, by tonight at least,' said Libby. 'He said he'd try to let me know if there was any progress.'

'I'll tell Sophie,' said Fran.

Next, Libby rang Ben. By the sound of it, he was out and about on the estate somewhere.

'I'll come home in time for the lunchtime news,' he said. 'I'll just let Mum know.'

'Shouldn't have thought he'd have time for a press conference before the lunchtime news. This evening, I expect.'

'Just in case,' said Ben.

Ben arrived just before the Kent and Coast bulletin was about to start. Libby put a plate of sandwiches between them and settled down on the sofa. Twenty minutes later, she sighed and stood up.

'Obviously not, as I said. I expect it will be on later.'

'No, hang on,' said Ben, 'look.'

The female presenter was looking seriously into the camera. '… report that several bodies have been found at a site in Kent. An update on this story in our later news bulletin.'

'It'll be on the national news, too,' said Libby. 'It's too big a story to keep local.'

Ben went back to the Manor and Libby loaded the dishwasher and went back into the conservatory. She kept the radio on, and towards the end of the afternoon there was a short reference to the story. At this point she gave up pretending to paint, cleaned her brushes and went to make tea.

By the time Ben came home she'd put a chilli in the oven and was sitting in front of the television.

'I don't want to miss anything,' she said.

Sure enough, the third item in the national news was the White Lodge story. Ian obviously hadn't been deemed important enough to speak to the massed cameras, and Libby was appalled to see her bête noire from a couple of years ago, Superintendent "Big Bertha" Bertram, shaking her bright blonde hair back from heavily made-up sharp features, standing on the steps of the police station.

She read out a prepared statement and invited questions.

'Have you any idea how old the bodies are?' shouted one reporter over the rest.

'Some are probably more than fifty years old,' Bertram replied, 'others as little as a few weeks.'

There was a sudden shocked silence, then the noise level rose to an almost unbearable level, and there was a cut to the studio. 'Our reporter joins us live from Nethergate outside the police station …'

'So they haven't confirmed anything,' said Ben, as the item ended. 'Not that the first bodies were TB victims or the second were suspected honour killings.'

'They realised pretty quickly it wasn't a serial killer, didn't they?' Libby stood up and went to fetch a bottle of wine.

'Well, it couldn't possibly be, could it? He'd have to be about a hundred!'

Within ten minutes of the news bulletin the phone started ringing. Fran called first, then Adam, then Harry and finally Rosie.

'I want to go back and see if that man will let us have a look from his upstairs room,' she said.

'Colonel Weston?' said Libby doubtfully.

'Yes. He was rather dishy, wasn't he? And he did offer.'

'He might not be so keen now,' said Libby. 'The news has broken, and he will have been interviewed again by the police. And he's quite likely,' she added as a thought struck her, 'to connect us with the breaking story.'

'Why?'

'Oh, come on, Rosie! He already thought we were journalists or something last time.'

'All right, I'll go back on my own,' said Rosie. 'I can go for lunch in the pub.'

'Oh, all right,' said Libby with a sigh, 'I'll come. I really don't want you walking into the lion's den on your own.'

'Shall I meet you there? Or I could pick you up, if you like.'

'That's out of your way. Are you going to call Fran?'

'Should I? Or will you?'

'I'll do it,' said Libby with another sigh. 'See you there at about mid-day.'

Ben, predictably wasn't entirely happy about the proposed visit.'

'Neither am I, but I couldn't let her go on her own, could I? And she would have done. She's gone from a sensible, if manipulative, mature woman to a complete wreck and back to a regained youth in a matter of a couple of weeks. It's like holding on to lightning.'

Fran agreed to meet them there. 'I don't know how to reign her in,' she said.

'I know. If we had no conscience we'd just let her carry on on her own, but I feel sort of responsible, now.'

Fran sighed. 'I wish we'd never gone to see her in the first place.'

'But look what Ian's discovered because we did. No, we've got to stick with it now.'

The sun continued to shine on the Wednesday morning, and although a little trepidatious, Libby enjoyed the drive to Cherry Ashton. Once again, she was the last to arrive, and found Fran and Rosie already ensconced at a table with Colonel Weston.

'Ah! The trio is complete.' He stood up and indicated a chair. 'What can I get you to drink – er – Libby, isn't it?'

Libby asked for a half of lager shandy and raised her eyebrows at the other two when he went to fetch it.

'So what have you said?'

'Nothing. He was already here when we arrived and immediately offered to buy us drinks. He'd only just sat down when you came,' said Fran.

'Thank you, Colonel,' said Libby when the big man placed her drink in front of her.

'Oh, Hugh, please.' He smiled round at them all. 'Now, what can have brought you back here so soon?'

Seeing Rosie open her mouth, Fran and Libby both rushed into speech.

'The report on the –'

'The discovery of the –'

'I thought so.' The smile disappeared. 'I wasn't so very wrong last time, was I?'

'Wrong?'

'Immediately after your visit we were all re-interviewed by the police, and not a couple of uniforms, either, a Detective Inspector and a Sergeant.'

'Ian and Sergeant Maiden,' said Fran. 'Yes.'

'So what are you?' Hugh looked slightly annoyed. 'Undercover cops? Very good cover, if so.'

'Three nosy old biddies? Yes, that's what I thought,' said Libby.

He looked blank, then astonished. 'You're not?'

Libby chuckled and the other two smiled. 'No, of course we're not.'

'Then what?' He looked at Fran. 'You knew the

two detectives who came to see us all.'

'Yes. We've known them for some time.' Fran sipped her drink and looked out of the window.

Hugh frowned. 'Now I'm even more confused. You work with them, do you?'

'Yes,' said Libby, 'but we're really not allowed to say any more. Although,' she added, looking at Rosie, 'we would quite like to take you up on your offer.'

'What offer?'

'To scc what we can see from your upstairs window,' said Libby.

Chapter Thirty

DECIDING TO HAVE LUNCH when they returned to the Ashton Arms, they finished their drinks and set off after their involuntary host.

'Do you know all your neighbours in this terrace?' asked Fran.

'Yes. We have a little neighbourhood watch scheme – we're so out of the way we need to keep an eye out for each other.'

'We noticed that,' said Libby.

'Me being nosy? Sorry about that, but so were you, as far as I was concerned.'

Libby decided not to mention Mr Vindari, and hoped the others wouldn't either. She couldn't quite say why she didn't want to mention him, just that it didn't feel right.

The walked up the little drive to the carriage arch and underneath to face a long two-storey building of mellow red brick.

'Welcome to Ashton Court.' Hugh waved an ironic hand. 'Not my choice, my father converted a barn after the original house was demolished.'

'It's lovely.' Rosie beamed at him. 'You're so lucky.'

Fran and Libby exchanged looks. Hugh preened slightly.

'Come on in, then,' he said.

He led them up a wide stairway to the upper floor and along a corridor to what appeared to have been an oast roundel at the end.

'There,' he said. 'Panoramic views.'

They went over to the windows which looked out over a hundred and eighty degree prospect. Below them were obviously the gardens of the Court, to their right the back gardens of Ashton Terrace, and further over were the trees which formed the boundary to the White Lodge estate. Libby was surprised to see a much larger open area behind the barn than there had been previously. A white van, stakes and blue-and-white tape marked the fact that it was still a scene of crime and under the aegis of the police. The huge barn doors were now open, and inside she could see white-boiler-suited figures moving about.

'You can see inside, can't you,' she said.

'But not quite what they're doing,' said Hugh, behind her. 'Until yesterday I didn't know they were digging up bodies. Although when your friend the Inspector arrived it was fairly obviously something important. I thought it must be drugs.'

'That's what we thought,' said Fran.

'Oh?'

'What I meant was – that's why they went in to search,' said Fran, turning back to the window.

'I don't get it.' Hugh perched on a windowsill and surveyed them all. 'You say you're not police, but you're obviously working with them, you've admitted that. But what on? As what?'

'They're helping me,' Rosie said suddenly. 'I own the barn. And the White Lodge estate.'

'Ah.' Hugh nodded. 'I see. So my friend Mr Vindari was right.'

'He told you?' asked Libby.

'After your last visit. He also said you'd told him the police were digging up bodies. I'm afraid I told him he was too gullible.' He shrugged. 'And then when the police came and didn't say anything we decided it couldn't be murder or we'd know about it. But it was.'

Libby turned back to the window. It was interesting to note, she thought, that the two gardens belonging to Ashton Terrace between the Court and the barn both led on to a field behind, which in turn bordered the estate trees. It would be easy to gain access from there, even if overlooked from here. Although there was little sign of any disturbance to the line of trees.

'Who owns that field?' she asked.

'I do. I own all the land beyond the terrace and the church as far as the next farm on the Heronsbourne Road.'

'Is that as big as mine?' Rosie asked ingenuously. Libby narrowed her eyes at her. Surely Hugh wasn't naive enough to fall for that. He smiled, rather suavely, Libby thought.

'I shouldn't think so. The White Lodge estate, we now know, although we didn't before, runs all the way between this road and the coast road.'

'Is that the road White Lodge is actually on?'

'Yes. We call it the coast road, but it really only runs parallel with the coast.'

Rosie nodded and turned back to the windows.

Libby felt Fran nudge her shoulder slightly. About to ask, she saw Fran nod at the window. Below them, Aakarsh Vindari stood in one of the gardens looking up at them.

'Do we wave?' muttered Libby.

'Well, it was really good of you to show us, Hugh,' said Fran, moving away from the windows, 'but Brenda will have our meals ready by now.'

'Yes, thank you so much,' said Libby. 'Very enlightening.'

Hugh raised his eyebrows, but before he could speak Rosie broke in.

'I'd like to see more of your barn,' she said. 'Could you apologise to Brenda for me, girls? And don't wait for me if you've finished before I get back.' She smiled sweetly. Hugh looked surprised, and Fran and Libby aghast.

'Up to Hugh,' said Libby.

'No, of course I don't mind,' he said, looking down at Rosie for all the world as if he were going to pat her hand and call her "little woman".

Outside on their own, Fran and Libby looked at one another.

'Well!' said Fran.

'Harry was right about her. She is an inveterate flirt,' said Libby.

'And at her age!'

'You'd think it would be difficult to find men personable enough at that age to flirt with, if you know what I mean.'

'Who didn't want women young enough to be their granddaughters,' added Fran.

'Which most of them do,' agreed Libby. 'We were both lucky.'

Fran nodded solemnly and they walked back in silence to the Ashton Arms.

Libby apologised about Rosie and Brenda

shrugged. 'S'allright,' she said. 'She'd paid up front. I'll bring yours over. Stayed up at the Court has she?'

'Er – yes. She wanted to see over it,' said Fran.

'Don't know how he does it,' said Brenda, going towards the kitchen. 'Charm the knickers off a nun, he would.'

Libby snorted with laughter.

'Just right for each other then, aren't they?' said Fran as they went to sit down.

'Although I would say Rosie is what we used to call a prick-teaser,' said Libby thoughtfully. 'I bet what happened with Andrew is that she led him on and when he pounced she got the shock of her life.'

'More traumatised than that,' said Fran. 'We'll probably never know. You were sure they'd gone to bed together.'

'Mmm.' Libby watched Brenda approaching with their food. 'Ooh, I did enjoy that sausage pie. Hope this is as good.'

It was.

Rosie had not appeared by the time Fran and Libby had finished their lunch and coffee.

'Well, I'm not waiting around for her,' said Libby, standing up. 'Come on, Fran.'

Once outside, she stopped dead. 'Her car's not here.'

'Perhaps she moved it to the Court,' said Fran.

'No we'd have seen her go past the window if she went that way,' said Libby. 'She must have crept round the side and driven off towards the coast road.'

'To see how big Hugh's estate really is?' Fran

laughed.

'I expect she might already have found that out,' said Libby with a giggle.

'I wonder why she didn't come and say goodbye,' said Fran.

'Embarrassment?'

'Possibly.' Fran unlocked her car. 'I'll ring her when I get home. Ring me if you hear from her first.'

Libby drove slowly home. This, she decided was all rather suspicious. First, Rosie wanted to go back to the village and had more or less coerced Libby and Fran into accompanying her. Then there was her wish to go and see the upstairs of Ashton court, which Libby, in the end, had made happen for her. And, finally, the very obvious ploy of staying on her own with Hugh. And now the disappearing car.

'I should have gone down towards the coast road,' Libby said to herself. 'Then I could have seen if there was anywhere she could have turned off or parked. I bet she went back to Ashton Court.'

As soon as she arrived home, Libby called both Rosie's numbers. Both went to voice mail. She called Fran.

'Same here,' said Fran. 'It's odd.'

'Not if she did get back to Ashton Court through a back way,' said Libby. 'She and Hugh are probably wallowing creakily in a tangle of sheets by now.'

'I don't want to think about that,' said Fran. 'So there's nothing we can do apart from wait to hear from her.'

'She's hardly a missing person,' said Libby.

'And that reminds me, do you think Ian's found out any more about the Asian girls?'

'He might have done, but it's probably a bit early,' said Fran. 'We can hardly ask, can we?'

'No,' sighed Libby. 'We can see if anything's on the news later.' She looked out of the window. 'Bother. It's started to rain again.'

She and Ben watched all the local news programmes that evening but the only reference to murder was discovery of two dead males in an alley somewhere in the Medway area.

'Come on,' said Libby, switching off the set. 'We've got the meeting at the theatre tonight.'

'And you still haven't decided what we're doing for Christmas,' said Ben.

The meeting was, as usual, followed by a gathering in the pub.

'How's the investigation going?' asked Peter as they squashed round a table.

Libby updated him adding that she didn't think she and Fran were going to be involved any longer.

'Ben might,' she said, idly stirring her drink with a finger. 'Now he's given his report to Ian. We might find out what's happened with that.'

'Shocking business,' said Peter, shaking his head. 'I don't mean all those unfortunate TB victims, although that's sad, of course, but these honour killings, if that's what they are.'

'They're all Asian,' said Libby. 'I don't see what else they can be.'

'That's a bit of a generalisation,' said Ben.

'Hmm,' said Libby. 'And there's another thing. You know I told you about the Indian guy, Vindari,

Pete?'

'The restaurant bloke.' Peter nodded wisely and stretched out his long legs.

'His garden leads into the field at the back which butts right up to the trees surrounding the barn and he could get in quite easily.'

'Were there any breaks in the trees?' asked Ben.

'Not that I could see,' said Libby.

'Ian will have questioned him by now. And they'll have investigated the whole of the perimeter, too,' said Ben.

'They missed the signs of entry Fran and I found, didn't they?' Libby finished her drink and frowned.

'Don't worry about it.' Peter patted her hand. 'Your Ian's very thorough. Not much gets past him.'

'But it does. Sometimes it's Fran or me that tells him things he doesn't know.'

'But you've told him everything now, so he'll be on top of it.' Peter stood up. 'Come on. Have another drink and cheer up.'

Harry arrived in one of his trademark pink shirts and draped himself over his partner at the bar.

'Customers all gone?' asked Peter.

'Only a few tonight,' said Harry. 'I let Donna go early. Ad's got young Sophie stowed away in the flat, so he didn't mind staying on.' He turned to the table and swung his leg over a chair. 'Hello, my little investigator. How're things with you?'

Libby told him. When she got to Rosie's defection he snorted.

'Told you, didn't I? Right horny old biddy.'

'I don't know how you know so much,' said Libby, on her dignity. 'You're gay.'

'Oh, be still my beating heart! She noticed,' said Harry, clapping a hand to his head. 'That's why, you old trout. They often come on to us. All they see is a nice young man paying them some attention – we're so kind to our elders, you see – and not being quite as au fait with modern sexual mores as you, petal, they go all unnecessary.'

'Oh. So that's what Rosie's done, is it? Gone all unnecessary?'

'Course not. She's not that old, and she's a novelist, isn't she? She knows what's what. I bet she'll turn up all innocence, wide-eyed because she can't think what the fuss was about.'

'There hasn't been any fuss,' said Libby. 'Fran and I came to the same conclusion. I doubt if she'll tell us what happened, or why, and we can hardly ask.'

'Shame,' said Harry. 'I do love a bit of gossip.'

'If I hear anything, I'll tell you,' said Libby. 'Although I doubt if I'll hear from her for a while.'

But in the morning, the phone rang before nine o'clock.

'Libby?'

'Ian! What's up?'

'Where's your Rosie? She's not answering either of her phones, her car's missing and she's not at home.'

Chapter Thirty-one

LIBBY'S HEART SANK.

'I haven't seen her since yesterday lunchtime. She stayed behind at Ashton Court with Colonel Weston.'

Ian swore. 'What was she doing there?'

Libby told him. 'We felt we had to go over there with her, or she was going on her own. She didn't listen when we warned her to keep her mouth shut, so Mr Vindari and Weston both know she owns the barn. I don't know what she thought she was about, asking to see over the Court, but it looked to Fran and me as if she was on a seduction mission.'

'That woman hasn't got an ounce of sense,' said Ian. 'When you think about her behaviour right from the beginning, when she approached you and Fran. I don't know what she's playing at.'

'Hadn't you better go and talk to Colonel Weston?' asked Libby. 'After all, he can't deny she was there, when Fran and I were, too.'

'Of course he can't, and why should he?'

'I don't know. Will you let us know if you find her?'

'Yes, yes. Do I need to call Fran? She was with you all the time?'

'Yes, and got the same voice mail messages as me when we got home.'

'What messages?'

'I meant, when we tried to call Rosie all we got was voice mail.'

'So she's actually been out of contact since yesterday afternoon?'

'Yes. Have you tried Andrew?'

'No – I thought they'd had a row.'

'I'll call him, if you like,' said Libby. 'Oh – and why did you want her?'

'We've broken through into the cellar. You might tell Ben. And you can come and look later, but not until I tell you.' He rang off.

Libby sat looking at the phone. Ben came down from the bathroom ready to set off for the Manor.

'Who was that?'

She told him. 'And now I'm really worried.'

'Call Fran and Andrew. And don't go galloping off on your own, either. Ian's on to it. He'll do his best.'

But before Libby could call anyone, the phone rang again.

'Libby, it's Andrew. I don't suppose you know where Rosie is, do you? Only I've been trying to ring her since yesterday afternoon, and I just went over there and her car was gone.'

With the feeling that the day was going to get much worse very soon, Libby told him, leaving out any reference to the possible seduction of Colonel Weston.

'So Inspector Connell is trying to find her, too, so we can leave it to him,' she concluded.

'I think this is all my fault.' Andrew sounded miserable.

'How can it be your fault? For goodness' sake, Andrew, haven't you seen through Rosie yet? She's a thoroughly manipulative woman with an agenda that no one knows.'

Andrew sighed. 'I know she appears like that, but, believe me, she was very shocked when we found out about Paul Findon, and even more so about the legacy.'

'How do you know about that?' asked Libby sharply. 'You weren't there, and she had apparently cut all ties with you at that point.'

'It was temporary. She called me later that night.'

Libby gasped. 'You see? She's been leading everyone to believe you were completely out of the picture. She told Fran and me that she'd made a fool of herself with you.'

'Did she.' Andrew's voice was now grim. 'I wonder why?'

'I assumed,' said Libby boldly, 'that she'd gone to bed with you and regretted it.'

'Oh, she went to bed with me, all right. But we'd both got rather drunk, all in the name of ameliorating Rosie's shock, and she was quite mortified at both the drunkenness and the – well – intimacy.' He sighed again. 'I shouldn't be telling you this.'

'So she obviously got over that?' said Libby, ignoring this last statement.

'She did. Even suggested that we should try again because …'

'She couldn't actually remember it?' suggested Libby.

'Yes. And we did. Have.'

'Right.' Libby thought for a moment. 'And have you at any time got the impression that she would try and find out any more about what was going on at either the barn or the house itself? I mean, on her own.'

'Yes. I thought she was going to ask you and Fran to help her.'

'She did, I told you. But she was perfectly prepared to go to Cherry Ashton on her own, and both Fran and I thought she was quite likely to barge in where angels and all that, and could conceivably get into trouble.' She sighed. 'And now it appears that she has. What about Tybalt?'

'Eh?' Andrew sounded startled by the sudden change of topic.

'Tybalt. The cat.'

'Oh, Talbot. Of course, he won't have been fed. What should we do?'

'We?' said Libby.

'Well, I don't know what one does about cats. Should we phone the RSPCA?'

'I suppose we could,' said Libby doubtfully. 'And *I* don't quite know what one does in this sort of situation. Is there a cat flap?'

'I believe so.'

'Then he can get in and out. That's a relief. And if he's really starving he'll start catching food. Or you could go and put a bowl of food down near the cat flap.'

'Me?'

'You're the one in a relationship with her,' said Libby, suddenly irritated with the whole situation.

'I thought you were her friend.'

'I only met her a day or so before you did. And I'm not sure I want to be a friend now. I feel a bit used and abused. Although that isn't poor Talbot's fault.'

'I suppose I could go and put some food down for him,' said Andrew doubtfully. 'What sort?'

'Dried cat crunchies, then it won't go off if the weather suddenly turns warm again,' said Libby, glancing out at the drizzle.

'All right. And will you let me know if you hear anything?'

'I will. And the same goes if you hear.'

'Yes, yes, of course.'

After Andrew had rung off, Libby sat and thought. It was apparent that something had happened, but quite what was unfathomable. Had Hugh Weston bumped Rosie off because he had something to do with the bodies in the barn? And if so, why? Murdering the owner of the property wouldn't stop the police investigation. Anyway, how could Weston have anything to do with honour killings, if that's what they were? Much easier to believe that smooth Mr Vindari had something to do with it. Which was far too convenient. She sighed and punched Fran's number into the phone.

Fran was worried. 'Something's happened to her. I think she's been pursuing her own agenda all the time.'

'But she honestly didn't know about Findon or the legacy,' said Libby. 'I really believe that.'

'So do I, but it's since she found out about it she's become so strange.'

'And flighty,' said Libby. 'Do you really think she was out to seduce Hugh Weston? After all that romping in the sack with Andrew?'

'But again, why?' Fran was silent for a moment. 'Do you think we should go over and ask Weston?'

'I knew you were going to say that,' said Libby. 'Ben told me not to go haring off on my own, that Ian would deal with it, but I can't help feeling that we should try on our own.'

'As long as he doesn't think we're chasing him,' said Fran.

'Who, Ian?'

'No, stupid, Weston. Why should he? We're just concerned about our friend.

'Huh,' said Libby. 'Friend. She's caused me more trouble than any real friend has in years.'

'Shall I meet you at the pub again?' Fran sounded as though she was already halfway out the door.

'No, I couldn't bear that. Let's meet at The Red Lion. George will let me leave my car in his car park.'

'OK. Twenty minutes?'

'I'll try.'

It was, in fact, nearly half an hour before Libby drew in to the car park of the Red Lion. The doors weren't open yet, so Fran was still sitting in her car.

'Off we go again,' said Libby, climbing in beside her.

'What do you think about Andrew's confession that they've been having rampant sex?' she asked a few moments later as they set off for Cherry Ashton.

'What do you mean? Don't you believe him?'

'He seemed to be telling the truth.'

'But you're not sure? It is odd for a man to boast about it to a woman, I suppose.'

'I thought blokes did that all the time? Or perhaps they don't in these enlightened times?' said Libby. 'I'm out of touch.'

'True or not, he knew about the legacy, so someone told him, and if not Rosie, who?'

'Oh, don't start suspecting Andrew of anything,' said Libby. 'He only came into the picture after we suggested an expert.'

'I seem to remember you thinking he might be part of a plot at one time.'

'Yes, yes, all right.' Libby looked out of the window. 'It's raining again.'

'Do we park in the pub car park again?' asked Fran as they approached the crossroads.

'Couldn't we park in front of Ashton Court?' said Libby. 'It's him we've come to see, after all, and he won't be at the pub yet. It's only just about opening time.'

'It'll advertise our presence, but yes, I suppose so.'

'So would parking in the pub car park,' said Libby.

Fran drove slowly under the arch and came to a halt behind a large Land Rover.

'Here goes,' said Libby, and climbed out.

Hugh Weston appeared at the door wearing his hat and coat as usual.

'Ladies!' he said genially. 'Again! What can I do for you this time?'

'We're worried about Rosie,' said Fran without preamble. 'She's been missing since yesterday.'

His face went blank. 'Really?'

'Yes, we just wondered if you knew where she

went when she left here?' said Libby.

'No idea.' He turned and pulled the door closed behind him. 'I'm just off for a drink. Join me?'

'No thanks,' said Fran. 'Are you sure she said nothing that might give us a clue?'

'Nothing. Why should she have done?'

'How long was she here?' asked Libby.

He frowned. 'Not long. I showed her the rest of the house and she left. Didn't she come back to the pub?'

'Of course not,' said Libby, 'or we wouldn't be asking you. When we came out of the pub her car had gone.'

'So why ask me, then?' He was looking quite aggressive now. 'She obviously went off on her own.'

'Yes, but she hasn't been seen since. Hasn't been home and she wouldn't leave her cat.' Fran sighed and turned back to the car. 'Sorry we troubled you.'

'No trouble.' He was back to normal and holding the door open for her. 'Do let me know when she comes home. Rather a nice lady.'

'We will,' said Libby. 'Thank you.'

Weston watched as Fran reversed carefully back under the arch and out on to the lane.

'Well!' said Libby, blowing out a long breath. 'That was a waste of time. And obviously the police hadn't been to see him yet.'

'We don't know that. He was unlikely to tell us,' said Fran.

'Oh, he would. If the police had already been he would have greeted us with a concerned air and, "So sorry to hear about your friend, ladies." He'd know we'd know if Ian had seen him.'

'True. Where now?' said Fran, halting at the crossroads.

'Right. Let's see if we can spot a turning anywhere.'

But there wasn't, only a track leading to the farm they'd seen in the distance.

'Actually, it was a bit of a foolish idea,' said Fran. 'What on earth did we think we'd find out? We could hardly search the house.'

'Let's turn on the radio. There might be something on the local radio,' suggested Libby.

But the local news bulletin contained nothing about the White Lodge case or Rosie, only more about the two bodies discovered in the Medway area, which had now been discovered to be those of itinerant builders.

'Oh, well,' said Libby. 'Let's go back to The Red Lion. We could have a coffee with George.'

But before they reached the pub, Libby's mobile rang.

'Where are you?' said Ian.

'In the car with Fran on the way to The Red Lion. Why, have you found Rosie yet?'

'No, I've just been to see Colonel Weston, and he told me you'd beaten me to it.'

'Ah.' Libby glanced at Fran and made a face.

'When will you keep out of things, Libby? He was warned I was coming, and if there'd been anything suspicious he could have made sure there was no evidence.'

'But we didn't say the police knew,' said Libby.

Ian made an unprintable sound. 'Don't be so

naive.'

'Sorry.'

'Just don't go getting into anything else.'

'No. Sorry.' Libby took a deep breath. 'What about the cellar?'

'I don't know when I'm going to get around to that. You'll just have to wait.' The phone went dead.

'Telling off?' asked Fran, as she pulled in to The Red Lion car park.

Libby sighed. 'As usual. And now it looks as though we won't get to see the cellar.'

'You didn't say anything about the cellar.'

Libby told her as they went into the pub and across to the bar.

'I expect he'll let you see soon enough – or Ben, at least.'

'Hmm.' Libby nodded gloomily.

'Hello, ladies.' George beaming appeared at the door from the kitchen. 'Where've you been this time. Not back over to Cherry Ashton again?'

'Yes,' said Libby. 'Can we have two coffees, George?'

'How's that old cat of yours, then?' He asked as he busied himself at the coffee machine.

'Balzac's fine, thank you, George.' Fran hoisted herself onto a stool next to Libby.

'I'll tell you what, your coffee's a darn sight better than at The Red Lion,' said Libby. 'Although they do a good sausage pie.'

'I said they did good food, didn't I?' George set their foaming mugs before them. 'Funny place, though.'

'Yes. We met the owner,' said Fran.

'Oh, Colonel Bloody Weston?' George rolled his eyes. 'Thinks he's God's gift, he does.'

'Yes, his manager said he's a bit of a lad with the women,' said Libby.

'Oh, not only with the ladies.' George leant forward. 'He thinks he knows everything about everything. That manager of his – the pub wouldn't be nothing without her – yet he goes on about it as if he did it all. And I'll tell you, the ladies don't always like it. I've had a couple in here who say they wouldn't go back.'

'Why did he buy it?' asked Fran, blowing froth.

'Buy it? Lord above, he didn't buy it! It was part of the estate. He lives in the old Court barn, now.'

'Yes,' said Libby, not wanting to admit that they'd been there. 'Was it a big estate, then? I thought it was just the land between there and the coast road.'

'His old man owned the whole village.' George sat down on his own stool. 'In the family, like. At least, I think so. All those cottages an' all.'

'But we met one person who apparently owned one of the cottages,' said Libby.

'Oh, yeah. Old man sold a load off over the years, as people died. You still looking into things up there? Shocking, innit? Them honour killings is it?'

'I don't think that's been confirmed,' said Fran.

'Said on the news they was all Asian, the bodies, and all female. Stands to reason.'

'Mmm.' Libby drank more coffee and licked froth off her upper lip.

'Well old man Weston won't like that. Darkies

buried on his land? He'll go loopy.'

'He's racist?' Libby was surprised. 'But he seems to be quite friendly with another of the residents –'

'Old Vindari? Yeah, only on the surface though, I bet,' said George. 'He's all right, though. Got a couple of good restaurants.'

Libby and Fran agreed and fell silent.

'So you're involved, eh?' George prompted.

'Sort of,' agreed Libby. 'Although we've been told to stay out of it now.'

'Getting too dangerous, is it?' Seems to me you two like a bit of danger. I keep an eye on you in the paper. And that young Jane from the *Mercury* and her husband come in here sometimes. Haven't see them for a bit, though.'

'You won't either. They've just had a baby girl, Imogen,' said Libby.

'Oh, that's nice. Tell them George said congrats, won't you?'

'What did Colonle Weston's father do?' asked Fran, out of the blue. George and Libby looked surprised.

'Do? I don't reckon he did anything. Farmed the land a bit, although that wasn't him, it was the tenant farmer, I think he had what they call business interests and he'd been in the war – course, most people his age had been. I think he just came home and played the landed gentry. Sent young Hugh off to boarding school, and then into the army.'

'He's a typical product of that sort of upbringing,' said Libby.

'Any brothers or sisters?' asked Fran.

'What Hugh? Not as far as I know. And what I do know's general knowledge, anyway.'

'Business interests,' said Fran thoughtfully.

'What's wrong with that?' asked Libby, as another couple of customers came in and George went to serve them. 'People like that always had business interests.'

'I'd like to know what they were.' Fran drained her mug. 'Who'd know?'

'Bloody hell, Fran! How do I know?'

'Would you have to go to the chamber of commerce or something?' Fran was staring at the bottles behind the bar not seeing them. 'Or Rotary?'

'I thought Rotary clubs were charitable organisations?'

'But it's all local businessmen, isn't it? They'd know about other businessmen.'

'I don't think they'd particularly want to be asked questions like that.'

'Solicitors,' said Fran. 'They always know. Ian said he'd been in touch with the firm that rented out White Lodge in the sixties, didn't he?'

'Yes, but we couldn't go asking about Colonel Weston's dad! What *are* you thinking? And why, anyway?'

'I'm not sure,' said Fran, looking more normal. 'I'll have to think it through.'

'You do that,' said Libby, 'and let me know when you get the answer.'

'You do realise, don't you,' said Fran, 'that Rosie and Hugh are about the same age. They could have known one another.'

'Unlikely, isn't it? The houses are quite far from

one another, and Rosie didn't live here, she only visited.'

Fran nodded. 'Suppose so. Want another coffee?'

'No thanks. I'll get home and be a good little housewife.'

'You're not a wife.'

'Good little house-concubine, then.' Libby slid off the stool. 'Come on.'

They waved goodbye to George.

'Thanks for the information,' Fran called, and George waved back.

'Did Ian say when the cellar was bricked up?' asked Fran, just as Libby was getting into her car.

'I think Ben thought it was comparatively recent. In years, I mean. Don't think it was done when Findon was killed.'

'Oh, so you think he was murdered, too?'

'Slip of the tongue.'

'Someone, then,' said Fran, unlocking her car, 'knows about it. So the police should be able to track down who did it.'

'Should they?' said Libby doubtfully. 'No one would admit to it, would they?'

'No,' acknowledged Fran, 'but I feel sure they'll be found.'

'They?'

'Whoever bricked up the cellar. And then – who told them to do it.'

'But that's got nothing to do with the honour killings.' Libby was puzzled.

'There's got to be a link somewhere,' said Fran, and got into her car.

Chapter Thirty-two

'WHAT LINK?' LIBBY SAID out loud to herself as she drove home. 'How can there be a link between Paul Findon, the bricked-up cellar and the bodies in the barn?'

She began to review the whole case in her head so thoroughly that she found herself outside number seventeen with little knowledge of how she got there.

First, there was Rosie and the dreams. Then Fran and Libby had visited the house and heard the music and discovered the grave. That was another thing, that grave. Why was it a new grave with an old body? And who laid the flowers? After that, they discovered that Rosie had actually been to the house. Then came the advent of Andrew, the discovery of the archives and of Rosie's relationship with Paul Findon. Ian's further revelation of the legacy, Andrew's claim that he and Rosie had become rather intimate and Rosie's new, strange attitude.

Almost completely unconnected was Libby's discovery of the barn, Fran's suspicions about it and finally, the discovery of the poor mutilated bodies. And Sophie's missing friend, Rachita, of course.

No. She shook her head as she opened the door and Sidney shot between her legs. There was absolutely nothing to connect the two cases.

Except – Libby stopped and stared hard at the fireplace. All the bodies were on the same estate.

That was a given, no one had questioned it, but why were they? Simply because the barn had lain semi-derelict for years and someone knew about it? That could mean anyone in Cherry Ashton, though. So that was a non-starter.

She wandered around the cottage trying to make some sort of sense of the chain of events, then picked up her basket and left the house again. She arrived at the Manor five minutes later.

'Het,' she said following her knock into the kitchen, 'have you ever heard of a Colonel Weston?'

'Weston?' Hetty looked up from her old-fashioned yellow mixing bowl. 'Weston. Rings a bell, but it ain't an uncommon name, so I coulda known lots of Westons.'

'Do you think Greg might know? His father was a Weston out at Cherry Ashton.'

'Go and ask him, girl. You know where to find him.'

'Weston,' Greg repeated, screwing up his eyes. 'Yes, I do seem to remember a Weston. Had a son a bit older than Ben who went away to boarding school.'

'That's the one!' Libby was delighted. 'Do you remember what he did? We know he had a farm, but the tenant farmer looked after that.'

'Good heavens, Libby! How on earth would I know that?'

'If he'd been a – oh, I don't know – a solicitor, for instance, you'd remember, wouldn't you?'

'I suppose so,' said Greg, looking amused, 'but I didn't know the man. He was a good bit older than me. I believe at one time he was something to do with the old hospital –'

'What?' Libby almost bounced out of her chair. 'The sanatorium?'

'Honestly, Libby, I don't really remember. All I know is there was a hospital – all right, sanatorium – over there somewhere, and I have the feeling that he was on the board, because they used to hold fund-raising events and he was always the driving force. I don't know what happened for a few years because I was away, as you know,' Greg had been in a prisoner-of-war camp during the second world war, 'and when I came back I wasn't too well. But I do remember him trying to save the hospital.' He frowned. 'That was after the war, of course. Before the war there'd been piano recitals by someone quite famous.'

'Oh, Greg! I wish I'd talked to you earlier. The hospital was the Princess Beatrice TB Sanatorium, and the pianist was a former inmate, Paul Findon. He's our friend Rosie's uncle.'

'Is he?' Greg concentrated on a corner of the ceiling. 'Findon. Yes, I vaguely remember. We had his recording of *Clair de Lune*.'

'So Colonel Weston's father was something to do with the hospital? Oh, this is marvellous!'

'Why?' Greg leant back in his leather chair looking itercsted.

'Hasn't Ben told you anything about what we've been doing?' No? Well, you see this is how it all started …'

Ten minutes later Libby had explained the whole story.

'And you say Fran asked what Colonel Weston's

father did? That's what made you come and ask me?' said Greg.

'You were the only person I could think of, being a local landowner.'

'I'll tell you who else might be able to help, and that's your friend over at Anderson Place.'

'Sir Jonathan?'

'When did he buy the place?'

'He inherited it,' said Libby. 'Would he have known other businessmen in the area?'

'He was – and is – a landowner. That's the main point, didn't you say? There's the local hunt, for instance. I didn't ever hunt, but I had applications to cross my land.' He shrugged. 'Couldn't really refuse, although I wanted to. Sir Jonathan would have had the same and might have even hunted. Weston, I'm pretty sure, hunted.'

'So they could both have been members of the local hunt?' Libby was getting quite breathless with excitement.

'It's an idea, isn't it?' Greg watched her with amusement. 'You'd better see what you can find out on that computer of yours.'

'I will.' Libby stood up. 'Say hello to Ben when you see him.'

'Aren't you going to?'

'Not till this evening.' She went over to give Greg a kiss. 'Thank you so much. There is such a wealth of knowledge and information in this village, I don't know why anyone goes anywhere else.'

The local hunt did indeed cover the areas of both Anderson Place and Ashton Court and had an impressive website with an informative history page, where Libby was delighted to discover a Willoughby Weston as Master immediately before and after the war. It unfortunately didn't say anything about his business interests, but now she had a name to search for.

She rang Fran.

'Excellent!' said Fran. 'Are you looking him up?'

'Yes. It's mainly ancestor-type pages.' Libby groaned. 'Oh, God. We've been here before.'

'I'll do it. You go and make yourself some tea and I'll call you when I've found something.'

'Thank you,' said Libby. 'That coffee at George's seems a long time ago.'

She'd barely poured her tea when the phone rang.

'Got it,' said Fran. 'You'll never guess.'

'He was on the board of the sanatorium?'

'No, you'd already guessed that,' said Fran. 'No better than that.'

'Oh – I don't know! What?'

'He was also a director of Riley and Naughton.'

'Wh–? God! The estate agents?' Libby sat down with a thump.

'Yes. And what's more, he didn't appear until after Paul Findon died.'

'What do you mean he didn't appear? What does that mean?'

'Think about it. After Paul Findon died, however he died, the house was rented out. Then the body was discovered, the ghost was supposedly seen, and at the same time this Weston buys into the estate agency and the house falls empty. It doesn't appear on anyone's radar until it goes on to Riley's website a year or so ago.'

'After which it's taken down,' said Libby. 'But not by Willoughby. He's long gone.'

'Supposing his father left Hugh Weston not only his whole estate but business interests, too?'

Libby was silent sipping tea and thinking.

'Do you see what I mean?' said Fran.

'Yes, but that would mean that if Willoughby was involved in something nasty at White Lodge way back when, his son knows about it.'

'And why not?'

'You wouldn't confess nasties to your children.'

'Perhaps he found out? Whichever way you look at it, it's suspicious.'

'Doesn't help us with finding Rosie, though.'

'It does if Hugh Weston's guilty of covering up his father's crime, whatever it was.'

'Doing trials on those poor girls, I expect,' said Libby. 'But what does that have to do with Rosie? She only knew White Lodge after Paul Findon bought it. She wasn't here when those girls died.'

'So what do we do now?' said Fran. 'I feel we ought to let Ian know, but I'm not sure how he'd take it.'

'You never know – he might already know.' Libby thought for a moment. 'After all, he did warn us off this morning. Perhaps he was doing research and that's why we beat him to it.'

'Oh – hang on, the other phone's going. I'll ring you back.' Fran switched off.

Libby took her mug into the kitchen. This was a turn-up for the books, and thank goodness for the internet. It was a wonder how detectives ever found anything out before the wonderful web came into being.

The phone rang again.

'A bit of good news,' said Fran. 'Rachita's back.'

'Oh, thank goodness,' said Libby, going quite weak at the knees. 'Do we know where she's been?'

'Yes, apparently camping out with a friend. Rachanda's being allowed out again now, so Sophie's going to meet her. She said there's quite a lot to the story.'

'We might not get to hear about it, then,' said Libby. 'It might be personal.'

'They've had to tell the police she's home and someone wants to interview her, but there's a problem there. Appropriate adults, or something.'

'I expect they want her to be questioned without the parents and they don't want that,' said Libby. 'The parents, I mean.'

'Well, I'm sure Sophie will tell us what she can,' said Fran. 'I'll keep you updated.'

'And what do we do about Hugh Weston and Ian?'

'Wait, I suppose. That's all we can do.'

Libby wasn't surprised not to hear anything from anyone for the rest of the day. The rain stopped, so she made a pretence of weeding, and, after preparing dinner, turned the television to a rolling news channel hoping for some mention of either of the local stories. There was none. The only vaguely local item was the fact that the two builders found murdered in Medway had been named. And they were both Asian.

There was absolutely no reason to connect this with the White Lodge murders, but it was inevitable that Libby would. She rang Fran.

'Why should they be anything to do with our barn bodies?' said Fran, who was trying to control a pan full of spitting oil.

'They could be the murderers,' said Libby.

'Hired assassins?' suggested Fran. 'Oh, Libby, go back to the television and leave me to cook my stir fry.'

Hired assassins, thought Libby. Good one. I wonder if Ian's thought of that?

But it wasn't until the following day that Libby found out what Ian thought about anything.

On Friday morning Adam called.

'Can you come down to the flat, Ma? I think we need a council of war.'

'We do?' Libby's heart jumped. 'What about?'

'I'll tell you when you get here.'

'OK. I'll be there in five minutes,' said Libby, who was still in her dressing gown.

'No, Ma, not there. Sophie's flat.'

'Oh, right. OK – half an hour, then.'

Head filled with all sorts of images, none of them good, Libby dressed hurriedly and set off for Nethergate, keeping a close eye on the petrol gauge which was hovering dangerously close to the red line.

The nearest she could park to Guy's shop-cum-gallery was way beyond Coastguard Cottage. This was a Friday towards the end of August, and the holiday-makers and weekenders were out in force –

as were their cars, parked like a shiny metal sea wall all the way along Harbour Street.

Guy was in the shop on his own when Libby pushed open the door. He jerked his head in the direction of the stairs and made a face. 'They're all up there.'

'Don't you want to go, if it's Sophie …?' Libby trailed off.

'It's not Sophie.' Guy grinned. 'It's a case for Castle and Sarjeant.'

'Right,' said Libby in surprise, and made for the stairs.

In the little sitting room over the shop sat Fran, Adam, Sophie and a beautiful Indian girl.

'Hi, Libby.' Sophie stood up and came to kiss her. 'This is my friend Rachanda. She's told us some things that we think you ought to hear.'

'Me? Why me?'

'Because you know all about the case. I wanted to call you last night, but Ad said it would be better if we did it this morning when Rach could be here.'

Libby smiled at Rachanda, who smiled sweetly back. 'It's lovely to meet you, Rachanda, especially as we've heard so much about you.'

'That's why we thought you ought to know what's been happening,' said the girl in a barely accented voice. 'You see, there's more to Rachita's adventure than we first thought, and I think we must tell the police. My parents won't hear of it, though. They haven't even allowed the police to interview her.'

Libby turned to Fran. 'You said yesterday the police wanted to interview her. Why? She was a missing girl who'd turned up at home. Why would they want to see her?'

'Apparently they always do,' said Sophie. 'In case the family are lying and the person hasn't really come back, or the people who made the report weren't telling the truth in the first place or in case something awful has happened while the person's been away. It's quite normal.'

'So, what's Rachita's story?' asked Libby.

'I've heard it, so I'll go and make more coffee,' said Fran. 'Or tea, anyone?'

Libby and Rachanda opted for tea, and Rachanda started her story.

'Sophie says you all wondered if there was a boyfriend involved, although she didn't think so. But, in fact, there was.' She paused and looked into the empty fireplace. 'And the worst sort of boyfriend, too. Not that any boy, unless chosen by my parents, would have been good enough, but this one was beyond everything.'

'Amazing in this day and age,' said Libby.

Rachanda smiled. 'Not in our culture, as I expect you know. There are many women trying to change things and standing up to their families, but I wasn't brave enough.'

'Brave enough?' repeated Libby. 'Were you afraid?'

'No, no,' Rachanda corrected hastily. 'I wasn't brave enough to leave the community. A lot of women who do get away never see their families again. I didn't want that. I love my family.'

Fran reappeared with a tray and handed out mugs.

‘Go on,’ said Libby. ‘Who was Rachita’s boyfriend?’

‘He was an illegal immigrant.’

‘Oh, no.’ Libby shook her head, remembering the last occasion she and Fran had investigated the illegal workers scams.

‘Yes. Sophie says you know something about them?’

‘A bit. Not a lot. Where was this boy from?’

‘Pakistan, we think.’

‘And where did she met him?’

‘He was doing some building work at an uncle’s shop. We have several uncles who are shopkeepers. The council said the facilities at the back weren’t correct, so Uncle Jaiman had to have an extension built.’

‘Health and safety,’ said Libby.

‘Exactly.’ Rachanda nodded. ‘And this Kiran was one of the builders. Rachita used to go there on the way home from school every day –’

‘Like we did,’ put in Sophie.

‘Yes. And they became friendly.’ Rachanda shook her head. ‘I didn’t know anything about it, none of us did, even Uncle Jaiman.’

‘Is that the only place they met?’ asked Libby.

‘No. You see, the extension was finished and Kiran and the other men left. But Kiran arranged to meet Rachita at the place where he was staying.’ She wrinkled her nose. ‘My sister says it wasn’t at all nice. But then, suddenly, Kiran sent her a message saying he had to leave. He didn’t say why. And so my silly little sister ran away to go with him.’

'What made her come back? Is she disillusioned?'

Rachanda shook her head. 'No. Kiran is dead.'

Libby gasped.

'That's why I said you needed to be here,' said Fran. 'The confirmation of a theory – if not quite the right one.'

'What? You mean … one of those builders found in Medway?'

'Yes.' Rachanda nodded. 'Two of them. Kiran and another boy – they were only nineteen. Rachita says they were hiding, but they wouldn't say who from. Just that if they were caught they would be killed. She thinks it was something they had worked on that wasn't right, somehow.'

'How did she get home? Did she have any money?'

'No. The place they were hiding was some old building, and the boys went out to find food. When they didn't come back, Rachita went out at night, found a phone box and called my father. He went and picked her up. Then she heard about the two people murdered. Then, yesterday, they were named on the television news, although she'd already guessed it was them. She was hysterical.'

'And your parents won't let her speak to the police?' said Libby.

'No. They say it will bring shame.'

'Oh, *really*.'

'I know.' Rachanda sighed. 'It is ridiculous. This is why I told Sophie yesterday and she said we must tell you and her mother.'

Fran opened her mouth to correct this, but closed

it with a smile at Sophie. ‘And you did the right thing Rachanda. So now we must tell the police. And if necessary, protect you from your parents.’

Rachanda nodded. ‘They will not be pleased. Neither, I think, will my sister.’

‘That,’ said Libby, ‘is not our problem.’

Chapter Thirty-three

IAN'S PERSONAL MOBILE WAS switched off, unsurprisingly. Neither Fran nor Libby had his dedicated police mobile number in their phone books, so Libby phoned Ben to ask if he still had Ian's business card.

'Yes,' he said. 'At home. Why?'

Libby sighed and told him.

'Wouldn't it be quicker just to phone the station? At least they would leave a message for him. Or you could ask for the other bloke.'

'Sergeant Maiden. The trouble is, the police switchboard is just that – it doesn't go through to the actual station. Oh, never mind. We'll sort it out.' Libby switched off the phone.

Adam stood up. 'Sophie and I will go round there. It's only five minutes from here. And if he's in the station he'll see us, or we'll leave him a note. Or speak to someone else. After all, he's not the only person on the enquiry, is he?'

'Don't talk to that dreadful Big Bertha,' said Libby.

'She's County,' said Fran. 'She'll have gone back to Maidstone or wherever she comes from.'

'Good idea, though, Ad. You OK with that, Sophie?'

'Yes, fine,' said Sophie. 'Rachanda can stay here with you, can't she?'

'Of course,' said Fran.

'You are all very kind,' said Rachanda when

Adam and Sophie had gone. ‘I wish my parents were more – more –’

‘Liberal?’ suggested Libby.

‘Yes. I love them, but they are very strict.’

‘Do you know,’ said Libby, ‘I was reading an article the other day about integration in this country, which said that things had often changed completely in the home countries of cultures like yours, yet people in this country didn’t realise it. They were keeping to traditions that had been outdated for several generations.’

‘Libby!’ said Fran, but Rachanda shook her head.

‘No, Mrs Wolfe. Mrs Sarjeant is quite right. Many people of my generation know this, that is why people feel free to break away and go to university, or get good jobs. But my parents’ and grandparents’ generations are still living as though they were at the beginning of the last century. My grandmother still hardly speaks any English.’

‘It’s so sad, when you think of all that has been done to integrate our different communities,’ said Libby.

‘Yet there are still people here who are openly racist,’ said Rachanda.

‘There are, but not so much towards the better integrated,’ said Libby. ‘And there are examples of whole communities living side by side and respecting each other. Look at the terrific Sikh Temple in Gravesend. It’s there for the community.’

‘Yes.’ Rachanda looked thoughtful. ‘Perhaps because we keep ourselves to ourselves people think we are somehow different from them.’

'But you *are* different,' said Libby, 'but we should be celebrating that. Teaching each other.'

They were still debating the issue ten minutes later when they heard steps on the stairs. Fran went to open the door. 'Oh,' she said.

Ian came into the room and stopped in front of Rachanda, who stood up and bowed her head. Libby wanted to shake her.

'Miss Sharma,' he said. 'I'm Detective Inspector Connell. I believe you have some information for me?'

'We'll go,' said Libby, turning to shepherd Adam, Sophie and Fran from the room.

'No, please stay,' said Rachanda, a note of desperation in her voice. 'They may stay, Inspector?'

'Of course, if you want them to.' Ian looked round at the others with a smile. 'They already know everything anyway. Please sit down.'

And Rachanda began her story once again.

'And your sister has no idea who they were hiding from? Or what?' asked Ian when she'd finished.

'She says she has not.'

'Then I'm afraid I'm going to have to speak to her whether her – your – parents want me to or not.' Ian frowned. 'Has anyone tried to speak to her?'

'My father told them on the phone it was out of the question. I don't think they have been to the house.'

'Do you know who they spoke to?'

'No, but it was the local station. They were not pleased it was reported in the first place.'

'I'm sure they weren't,' grunted Ian. 'I suppose I'm going to have to bring in the big guns on this, and a Community Liaison officer.' He sighed and stood up. 'Would you like to be taken home, Miss Sharma?'

Rachanda looked confused, and Fran stepped forward. 'She can stay here for the time being, Ian.'

'Thank you,' said Rachanda.

Ian left and Libby stood up. 'Shall I go and get us all a take-away for lunch? I don't suppose anyone feels like cooking.'

Everyone agreed, Rachanda admitting she had a weakness for pizza and was never allowed it at home. Adam volunteered to go with his mother.

'Seriously, Ma, what do you think's going on here?' he said as they walked along Harbour Street. 'And is it anything to do with your bodies in the barn?'

'I'm not sure,' said Libby. 'I can't see the link at the moment.'

'If Rachita had been kidnapped I would have said yes and had serious doubts about the parents. Now I don't know. It looks as though this Kiran was on the lam, but why and who from I've no idea.'

'On the lam?' Adam frowned at his mother.

'On the run. Running away. Anyway, someone was after him. I bet he wasn't exactly thrilled when Rachita ran after him!'

'But Rachanda says they were in love.'

'From what I hear, Rachita is a headstrong young woman who, as far as she's able, does what she wants. And what she wanted for a time was Kiran, so when he upped and offed, she went too. You notice she didn't hang around long after he'd disappeared from the hideout.'

'No, I noticed that,' said Adam, looking pleased. 'Thought it was a bit odd.'

'And now she'll do anything to get out from under the parental controls, you watch.'

The truth of this was proved an hour or so later when Guy appeared in the flat, a worried frown on his face.

'Ian's downstairs with Rachanda's sister,' he said. 'May they come up?'

'What?' Everyone stood up and Rachanda made a rush for the stairs. Sophie gently pulled her away.

'Yes, show them up,' said Fran, and everyone looked at each other in silence while they waited for the unexpected guests to make an appearance.

Rachita exploded into the room in a flurry of brightly coloured sari and flew at her sister.

'Sorry,' said Ian, looking grey and harassed.

'What happened?' said Libby, while Fran once again went to put the kettle on.

'The father wasn't there, luckily, but the mother and grandmother were not prepared to let me or anyone else in. If it wasn't for the young lady quietly letting herself out of the house at the back and being stopped by one of our policewomen we would have had to get a warrant, which was precisely what we didn't want. And now she's refusing to go back home or talk to us. All I could think of was to bring her to her sister.'

'Very sensible,' said Fran, putting a steaming mug into his hands. 'But she can't stay here, there isn't room.'

'I know that, and to be frank, I don't think I'd fancy either sisters' chances if they went back home. Can I just talk to her here, then we'll see what can be done? PC Donnington is looking into accommodation for them both, and Maiden is fielding the family's complaints at the station.'

Eventually Rachanda calmed her sister down, not an easy job as Rachita was quite obviously thoroughly enjoying being the centre of attention, and persuaded her that she need to talk to Ian. This however, she refused to do, looking pointedly at Adam, who, with an exasperated 'For fuck's sake' stomped downstairs to the shop. Rachita smiled sweetly.

'Miss Sharma,' Ian began, 'you are not under arrest, I am simply asking you a few questions about the man with whom you – er – ran away.'

'Kiran, yes.' Rachita nodded.

'And you have stated that he was hiding from someone or something.'

'Yes, but I do not know what.'

'Or why?'

Rachita wrinkled her brow. 'When they talked about it together and they thought I wasn't listening – this is Kiran and his friend, you know? – they said it could be either of them.'

'Either Kiran and his friend?'

'No, no, either of two people who were after them. I don't think they knew which it was.'

'And you have no idea who either of those people were?'

'No, I told you.' Rachita looked annoyed. 'One was the boss they worked for, I think.'

'And you don't know who the boss is?'

'No!' Libby got the feeling that Rachita was just stopping herself from stamping her foot.

'Did you ever see the boss at Uncle Jaiman's shop?' asked Rachanda.

Rachita shrugged. 'No. The only person I saw there was Uncle Aakarsh. He organised for Kiran and his friend to do the work.'

The silence that fell in the small room was almost tangible. Ian kept his eyes steadily on Rachita, who began to fidget.

'Miss – Rachanda,' he said. 'Is your sister referring to Aakarsh Vindari?'

'Yes,' she said. 'We call him Uncle, although I think he is only a distant cousin of my father's. He owns two restaurants.'

'Yes, we know him,' said Ian. 'So do Mrs Sarjeant and Mrs Wolfe.'

'You do?' Rachanda looked at them in surprise. 'How do you know him?'

'We met him in the village where he lives,' said Fran.

'So, Rachita – Miss Sharma – do you think it was Mr Vindari who they were afraid of?' Ian leant forward, elbows on knees.

'Uncle Aakarsh?' She stared back, wide-eyed. 'Of course not.'

'Do you know if he organised any other work for them?'

'I think he had recommended them in the past, but I don't know who to.' She looked round at the four other women. 'What is this all about? I am over sixteen. My parents have no legal control over me in this country. I can't be prosecuted for running away. And now,' she let her voice wobble tragically, 'my Kiran is dead and I am being persecuted.'

Ian sighed deeply. 'Miss Sharma, you are not being persecuted, but someone murdered your Kiran and we have to find out who. You are the best chance we have of finding his murderer, who is still at large, and –' Ian paused dramatically '– knows that you are still alive.'

Rachita's expression changed from tragic heroinc to frightened child in an instant.

'You think she's in danger?' asked Rachanda, putting her arm round her sister's shoulders.

'I think she could be, yes,' said Ian. 'So, for the time being, I want you both to stay in accommodation that we will find for you. The first place whoever it is will look for you is at your parents' home.'

There was a knock on thc outer door of the flat and a young woman police officer put her head round the door.

'Sorry to interrupt, sir, but we've found a small hotel with a nice en-suite double for the young ladies, and Sergeant Maiden says Mr Sharma and a friend of his are playing merry hell at the station.'

'Thank you, Donnington,' said Ian with a grin. 'Perhaps you can organise an unmarked to take the ladies to their hotel?' He turned to Libby, Fran and Sophie. 'I don't want to send any of you with them, or you could well start getting unwanted attention, but you could perhaps buy them any essentials they need and we'll see they get them.' He turned back to Rachanda and Rachita. 'Will you give your friends a list of things you might need?'

In under ten minutes the sisters had gone.

'I don't think we've got time to visit the cellar today,' said Ian, 'but I'll give you a ring tomorrow. I'm going to tackle Mr Sharma and his friend, now. Thanks for all your help.'

'What about Rosie?' said Libby. 'She's still missing.'

'I know.' Ian's face held a strange expression. 'I don't think you need worry, though.'

Fran and Libby exchanged puzzled frowns as he left the flat. Sophie sighed and stretched.

'Well, if this is the way things go when you're on one of your cases I wonder why you carry on with them,' she said. 'What a performance.'

Chapter Thirty-four

'WHY IS IAN NOT worried about Rosie?' asked Libby, as she and Fran walked back down Harbour Street.

'He must think she's gone off for some reason of her own.'

'But she left the cat.'

'There was a cat flap. Presumably she thought he could fend for himself for a bit.'

'So it must have been something she found out while she was at Hugh Weston's. Something that suddenly hit her?' said Libby.

'Unless she found out something and he had to silence her,' said Fran

'But you said –'

'Ian thinks she's gone off on her own. I know. But has she?'

'Where would she go?' They stopped in front of Coastguard Cottage.

'White Lodge,' said Fran, opening her front door.

'Really?' Libby grabbed her arm and Fran turned in surprise.

'Yes.' She frowned. 'At least, I think so. I was sure when I said it.'

'Hurrah! A moment!' crowed Libby.

'I suppose so.' Fran shook her head with a small laugh. 'Don't get so many these days. Should I tell Ian?'

'If you can get through to him. I wonder how

he's getting on with Mr Sharma?'

'Badly, I should think. That was a real facer when Rachita told him about Uncle Aakarsh, wasn't it?'

'I know! Couldn't believe it. Do you think he's the actual boss?'

'I don't know. I think Ian thinks he could be. And fancy him being related to the Sharmas. Are you coming in?'

'I'd better get back. Will you let me know if you hear anything?'

'What do you think?' Fran grinned, and, to Libby's surprise, leant forward and kissed her cheek. 'Go on. I'll talk to you later.'

Libby drove home puzzling over the various revelations of the day and the strange disappearance of Rosie. Ian hadn't taken it seriously from the start, simply been annoyed that she wasn't available to answer questions. So there must be some reason for that. She heaved a sigh of frustration and parked outside number seventeen.

The rain began again before it got completely dark. Libby was standing at the sitting room window looking out at the sodden landscape when her phone rang. Ben handed it to her.

'Libby, can you get away?'

'Fran? Why? What's going on?'

'I can't get through to Ian, and I'm sure Rosie's at White Lodge. There's something wrong, Lib. I want to go over there.'

'Have you tried her mobile?'

Fran made an impatient sound. 'Of course I have. Will you come?'

Libby looked over her shoulder at Ben, who was sitting watching her, an amused expression on his face.

'Yes, I'll come straight away. See you in about twenty minutes.' She switched off the phone.

'Another council of war?' said Ben.

Libby decided not to tell him the exact truth.

'Yes. Fran's thought of something else. Perhaps Sophie's heard from Rachanda.'

'Go on, then.' Ben stood up. 'I'm going to have a production meeting with Peter about the pantomime, anyway. Try not to be late.'

Libby put on her new hooded jacket, hardly the most inconspicuous garment, being bright turquoise, but better than her very old blue cape or Ben's old anorak. Also, aware of the almost-pond now forming in front of the Renault, she put on her pink flowery wellingtons.

'I look like a bloody clown,' she muttered to herself as she splashed across the road in the twilight.

The night got darker, the wind stronger and the rain heavier as Libby drove through the lanes.

There appeared to be no other cars near White Lodge other than Fran's little Smart car tucked into the hedge. Libby pulled in behind her, having switched off the headlights a hundred yards back. She climbed out and went towards Fran, who was standing just outside the gate. She pointed up.

Above the wind, Libby could hear the piano. The wind blew grey clouds rimmed with silver across a dark sky and the house was revealed in a flash of lightning. A light shone briefly from a window on the left, turned into a flickering strobe by a whippy birch. The music came to a sudden stop and the light went out.

'What's going on?' she whispered to Fran.

'I don't know, but I was right. Someone's here.'

'It might not be Rosie.' Libby pulled her hood firmly over her head, aware of rainwater trickling down her neck. 'Is that the actual piano or the recording? I can't tell in this wind.'

'I don't know.' Fran began moving slowly towards the gate.

'Fran, you're not going to go in?' Libby shivered. 'It might not be safe.'

Fran turned back to her. 'Look, I'm scared, too, but if Rosie's in trouble and we can't get hold of Ian, what choice do we have?'

'She might not be in trouble. Ian wasn't worried, was he?'

'I'm not so sure.' Fran turned away and sidled along the hedge. 'I'm going in, anyway. If I can get in.'

Swallowing hard, Libby followed. Inside the gate, blue-and-white police tape fluttered, still attached to the front door on one side, but not the other. Fran paused, flat against the wall at the side, and listened. Libby scuttled up behind her, legs shaking.

Gently, Fran pushed the door. It swung creakily open on to darkness. Libby caught Fran's arm.

'You can't go in there!'

Fran ignored her and crept round the door. With a groan, Libby followed once more.

Inside, they could hear nothing. After a moment,

Fran moved forward down the passage which led to the cellar, hugging the wall. As they passed the door to the piano room, Libby peered inside and gasped. Fran stopped.

The piano lid was up. On top lay sheets of music, lit by an old-fashioned candelabra.

'We couldn't see this window from the front,' hissed Libby. Fran put her finger to her lips and began to slide cautiously along the wall again. At the corner of the passage she made for the cellar door, now unblocked and surrounded by a certain amount of rubble.

'There's obviously somebody here,' she whispered.

'Well, dur,' said Libby.

'Yes, yes, but I think Rosie's here *and* someone else.'

'That's what I've been worrying about,' whispered back Libby.

'Shall we try down here?' Fran began to ease the cellar door open.

'No!' Libby tried to stop her, but Fran continued to pull, and the door came back suddenly, nearly knocking them both flying. They both froze.

No sound was heard, so Fran, producing a pencil torch from a pocket, shone it on the stairs. She beckoned and pointed.

At the bottom of the steep stairs, another door. Closed, and blocked by what was obviously wood and brick from the now unblocked door at the top.

'Deliberate, do you think?' said Fran, close to Libby's ear. Libby nodded and hit Fran's nose with her forehead.

Fran followed the thin beam of light down the stairs, Libby clinging like a toddler to the back of her coat. Then they heard the footsteps.

Libby thought she was going to faint, but Fran pulled her the rest of the way down the steps and pushed her into the recess behind them. The footsteps came to the head of the stairs and stopped.

'Shit,' said a voice.

Fran and Libby clutched each other as Hugh Weston began to descend the stairs. He was so close when he reached the bottom, Libby could have touched his waxed coat sleeve almost without raising her hand. She didn't.

He began to move the bricks and wood away from the closed door, then dragged it open.

'Who's here with you?' he said into the darkness.

'No one,' came Rosie's voice, cold as the stone around them.

'The door at the top of the steps was open.'

'I can't help that.' Rosie cleared her throat. I've been shut in down here for the last twenty-four hours, just the same as I was all those years ago. As you know.'

'It was nothing to do with me.'

'It was your father. Your father killed my uncle.'

'He pushed him down the steps. It was an accident.'

'In that case,' said Rosie, and now Libby could hear a tremble in her voice, 'just let me out. Nothing more need be said.'

'I told you it's not as simple as that.'

'So what do you intend to do with me? Wait until

you're told what to do by that Vindari man?'

Fran nudged Libby violently.

'I don't have a choice.'

'I don't understand.'

'You don't have to understand. Just keep quiet.' Hugh Weston came out of the room, shut the door and began piling the rubble in front of it. Finished, he stood up straight, brushed his hands together and climbed the stairs. Libby waited in agony to hear if he would shut and lock the door at the top, but apparently he was no longer worried and left it wide open. They heard his footsteps retreating.

'Quick!' whispered Fran, and began pulling at the rubble. It took them much longer than it had taken Weston but at last they had the door open.

'Sssh!' were Fran's and Libby's first words, as Rosie came to her feet. Fran flashed her torch quickly to see where they were. Rosie was still in the clothes she had been wearing when they left her at Weston's house.

'Come on,' whispered Fran, 'we're getting out.'

'He's still in the house,' said Rosie. 'How will we get past him? And that bloody Vindari man – she took a deep breath '– Weston must have called him. He followed me here and shut me in, and then –' another shuddering breath '– he said Vindari would decide what to with me. And now he's here too –' she began to sob.

Fran looked helplessly at Libby.

'Come on,' said Libby. 'He'll find it much harder with three of us, and we got here without him seeing us, didn't we? We'll make it.'

They supported Rosie up the stairs and up to the

corner of the passage, where they waited and listened, Rosie sagging between them.

Then – more footsteps. Slower, this time, and softer. Coming down the stairs. Libby looked round wildly for cover and saw another door. She pointed, and they all but dragged Rosie into the room, where she sank to the floor and Libby and Fran stood listening by the door.

'We should have piled the rubble back,' breathed Libby.

'No time.' Fran looked over her shoulder. 'There's a long window over there. I'm going to see if it will open. You stay here and listen.'

Libby glued her ear to the crack. Now she could hear two male voices. Luckily, they didn't appear to be coming any closer, but they were getting louder.

Fran came back, nodding. 'It's moved a bit. We might be able to shove it a bit further together.'

'OK,' whispered Libby, 'but just listen.'

'It isn't,' Aakarsh Vindari was saying, 'as if you haven't done it before.'

'It was fucking different and you know it.' Weston's voice was harsh.

'How? Just because she's not black?' Libby could almost hear Vindari shrugging. 'So, she's a white woman.'

'There'll be a hell of a police investigation about her. She hasn't got a family who'll cover things up.'

'So what do you propose to do? And no one's come here looking for her so far, have they?'

'Oh, yes they have. Yesterday. There were two police cars.' They heard Weston move. 'They didn't go down to the cellar.'

'And yet you risked playing the piano?'

Weston mumbled something the listeners couldn't hear.

'If the police are interested you don't start drawing attention to the house.'

'We've been playing the recordings for over a year. What difference would it make?' shouted Weston, and Libby clutched Fran's arm. 'He taught me to play.'

'The pianist? Sentimentality. He's dead. Your father killed him.'

'Shut the fuck up.'

There was a short silence, then Vindari began again.

'So. You have to get rid of her. Take her away from here. And kill her.'

Fran glanced down at Rosie, but she didn't appear to have heard.

'Those women will be looking for her,' said Weston.

'Tell me, my dear Weston,' Vindari's voice was like treacle, 'how many women have you killed so far?'

'You know how many. I don't,' said Weston gruffly. Libby felt sick.

'And it's worked well. I kept quiet about your father's silly little mistakes, and yours, we protect the barn between us and we get paid by the families. Don't tell me you're going to let three more women get in our way now?'

Libby and Fran looked at each other in horror.

'The window!' mouthed Fran.

Trying to push the casement window out while

listening for the terrible voices coming nearer and nearer was one of the most terrifying things Libby had ever experienced, but at last it gave under their combined weight. Libby went back and dragged Rosie to her feet, and together they got her over the sill.

In the fresh rain-washed air outside they stood listening for signs that their escape had been noticed, while Fran keyed in a 999 call and then called Guy. Libby was unable to press the buttons on her own phone until her fingers had stopped resembling sausages.

They dragged Rosie round the side of the house, keeping low, out of the gate and down the hedge until they came to the cars.

'Into mine,' said Libby. 'We won't all get into yours.'

They all bundled into Romeo and sat breathing heavily.

'And now, Rosie,' said Libby, 'I think it's time you told us what's been going on.'

Chapter Thirty-five

BUT ROSIE WAS IN no state to tell them anything. They bundled her in their own coats and sat shivering until out of the darkness a large dark car slid noiselessly alongside the Renault.

'I'm not going to ask what you thought you were doing,' said Ian, as a policeman and DC Donnington half-carried Rosie into the back of the car and two marked police cars stationed themselves silently in front of the house.

'We only went to find Rosie,' said Libby, in a voice that still held the suspicion of a shake.

'I thought she might be here,' said Fran. 'We didn't know anyone else would be there. You weren't answering your phone.'

Ian sighed. 'All right. I should really take you both back to the station and question you, but Maiden can come and take a statement from you both here, then you can go home. All right?'

They both nodded, and waited, huddled together in the back of Renault until DS Maiden's fresh and cheerful face appeared at the window.

'You do get yourselves into some messes, ladies, don't you?' he said as he settled himself in the front seat. 'Now just tell me everything in your own words. I'll stop you if I need to.'

Halfway through the recital the house was suddenly lit up like a stage set. Through a confusion of police uniforms and yellow jackets they could see Weston and Vindari being escorted to the two police cars. Ian turned and gave a thumbs-up in their direction and disappeared.

'Now,' said DS Maiden as the account of the evening's adventures petered to a halt. 'I'll just get you to sign this – yes, each page, please – and you can get off home. I'm sure DI Connell will need to speak to you again, but he knows where to find you.'

'Always,' said Libby wearily. 'Thank you, Mr Maiden.'

The both got out of the car and stretched.

'Are you OK to drive?' asked Fran.

'I'll have to be,' said Libby, wondering if she could.

'Don't worry.' Fran nodded over her shoulder. 'The cavalry's coming.'

The big 4X4 stopped behind them and Guy and Ben leapt out.

There was a confusion of 'Are you all right?', 'What the hell did you think?', and 'Bloody women', and both women were held in bear hugs.

'Let's get you home,' said Guy. 'You look as if you need a drink.'

'Is there time to get to a pub before closing?' said Ben.

'Just.' Guy peered at his watch. 'What's the nearest?'

'The Fox at Creekmarsh,' said Fran and Libby together.

'Is there a pub in the county you two don't know?' said Ben.

'Very few,' said Libby smugly.

Ten minutes later they were sitting in The Fox

with drinks before them. Fran and Libby didn't know the barman, which Guy said was a good thing.

'Come on then,' said Ben. 'Tell us what was going on.'

Once again they told their story in tandem, this time with far more condemnatory comments than before.

'So what do we think was happening?' said Libby.

'I really don't know.'

'Murder is what was happening,' said Guy. 'It sounds as though Weston had been killing women as a sort of hired killer for Vindari.'

'So they *were* honour killings. Just not committed by the families themselves,' said Libby.

'That way the families could all have alibis,' agreed Ben.

'But what was Rosie doing there? Did Weston take her? Or did she go on her own?' Libby looked at Fran.

'I'm sure she went on her own. I think she'd remembered. I'm sorry she had to go through all that. And I can't understand why Ian wasn't worried about her.' She sighed. 'I trusted her, even though she's turned out to be a bit of a –'

'Flake?' suggested Libby.

'I suppose so,' said Fran with a smile. 'I know I've been wrong before, but never that wrong. And what about Andrew?'

'What about him?' said Libby. 'A poor deluded soul like the rest of us? I think he's genuinely fallen for her. She's played him like an old boot, though.'

'Your similes are quite without parallel,' said

Ben, patting her arm. 'But yes, it would appear she's not been entirely open with poor Andrew.'

Libby sniffed. 'Serve him right. I hope he remembered to feed Tybalt.'

'Talbot,' said Fran.

'And him, too. Come on, I'm cold and wet and fed-up with speculating.'

She wondered why the other three laughed at her.

Libby was awake early on Saturday morning. She and Ben had arrived home damp and dejected, had a large whisky each and gone to bed. Libby had thought she wouldn't be able to sleep with everything that had happened that day churning over and over in her mind, but in fact she had slept almost immediately, and it was now that yesterday's events were dominating her thoughts. She carefully slipped out of bed and padded downstairs.

The thunderstorm had cleared the air, and everything outside was sparkling under a clear blue sky. She fed Sidney, made a cup of tea and went into the garden to sit under the cherry tree, taking her phone with her. At six-thirty it was a bit early to ring anybody, but she thought she might send Fran a text.

However, it was a text from Ian she received first, at just before seven.

'I'm going to sleep. Do not call me. I'll buy you all a drink at your pub this evening.'

She called Fran.

'Yes, I've had it, too. What should we do?'

'Try and call Rosie?'

'I don't think so,' said Fran.

'Oh, I don't know,' said Libby, exasperated. 'I suppose we just wait until summoned. Did Ian mean the pub here?'

'Yes. Shall we eat there, too? And we'll bring Sophie shall we?'

'Ad will be working at the caff, but he can join us afterwards. I think they need to know all about it, too.'

Libby tried to spend Saturday as normally as possible. Ben didn't go to work, but did go up to the Manor briefly to explain why he'd taken the Land Rover the previous night. Libby pottered down to the eight-til-late and the butcher and popped in to see Flo and Lenny in Maltby Close, and Peter to say sorry for disturbing his meeting with Ben.

'If you're about tonight, I don't suppose Ian will mind if you sit in on the revelations,' she said. 'You've been there every time before!'

'He does like his little Poirot gather-them-in-the-library moments, doesn't he?' said Peter.

'Except it's only explanation not accusation,' said Libby.

'Your time might come,' said Peter, pointing a long finger. 'Give me a call when it's appropriate.'

It was almost eight o'clock before Ian made his entrance into the snug, where his audience was assembled.

'Yes, please,' he said to the chorused offer of drinks. 'Peter has kindly offered me the spare bedroom, so I can.'

'I sent him a text,' said Peter. 'I've still got his private number from last winter.'

'Well, tell us,' said Libby, when Ian had been provided with a pint of bitter and a whisky chaser. 'We've all been on tenterhooks. What's Rosie guilty of?'

Ian smiled round at his listeners. 'If I'm going to tell this, it will have to be in my time and my words. It's difficult enough to understand forwards, impossible if you take it out of sequence.'

Baffled, Libby shook her head. 'So were none of our conclusions right?'

'I said, Libby, let me tell it.'

Libby subsided under a chorus of 'Shhh!'

'We have to start with the Princess Beatrice sanatorium. Willoughby Weston, Master of Foxhounds, Justice of the Peace and general VIP, was on the governing body. Despite the NHS, fairly new in those days, people paid to go there. But the incidence of TB was lessening, and antibiotics were proving effective. In the fifties the NHS began sending patients there, but that meant less money. Weston was approached, as far as we can make out, by a drug company who had a new drug they wished to try out. Weston agreed, and they paid him. However, the drugs, which our forensic anthropologists have managed to isolate, proved fatal to the patients.'

'See, I said so!' said Libby and received another round of 'Shhh!'

'Yes, Libby, you were right.' Ian gave her a grin. 'So they buried these poor unfortunates in their back garden and used old gravestones from the graveyard of the chapel that belonged to the estate, I suppose to deflect attention.

‘Then the sanatorium closed and Paul Findon, who’d been doing his bit as a former patient by raising funds performing charity concerts, bought it and returned it to a private dwelling.’

‘What about the barn?’ asked Fran. ‘Sorry to interrupt.’

‘As far as we can tell, the barn was used for isolation purposes, and Paul Findon, if he knew about it, did nothing with it at all,’ said Ian. ‘It was at this time that Findon’s sister Sheila and he began to see each other again and she used to bring young Rosie with her. As we gathered, he introduced her to music, Debussy in particular.

‘And then, one day, Weston came to pay a visit with his son, Hugh.’

There was a subdued rustle from the audience.

‘At the time, Paul was in his little music room, the cellar, with Rosie. She stayed there while he went up to talk to Weston. She heard them arguing. Then she saw her uncle toppling down the stairs. He caught the edge of the door, which slammed shut, locking her inside.’

There was a collective indrawn breath.

‘We gathered that yesterday,’ said Libby, and shuddered. ‘Just thinking about being shut up down there gives me the horrors, So she remembered at last?’

‘She remembered. Things were beginning to come back, you realised that. It was her screaming that finally alerted her mother, who had been away overnight and came back to find her daughter, as she thought, missing. Rosie, as you can imagine, was thoroughly traumatised and was even in hospital for a time. She had completely expunged the whole thing from her memory, though, except for a terror of cellars. Sheila wanted nothing to do with the house, and left it to a local agent, Riley and Naughton, to rent out.'

'And Weston was a partner?' said Fran.

'A director. He put money in at around the same time. Also around the same time, young Hugh was sent off to school.'

'He would have seen what happened!' said Ben.

'He did.' Ian nodded. 'As far as we can work out, talking to Hugh and from other sources, killing was a necessary part of living. Willoughby was a military man, had seen active war service and Hugh went straight into the school army corps and from there straight into the army. But one thing apparently stayed with Hugh. Paul Findon had taught him to play the piano.' Ian shook his head. 'I don't know what part that played in his extraordinary psyche, but it affected him.' He looked up at Fran. 'He actually used to go there – to White Lodge – in the middle of the night and play the piano. No wonder the rumour spread that it was haunted.

'But back to the house. The people who rented it turned it into a hotel – not a very grand one, I think, and they wanted to put an extension on the back. It was during excavations for the foundations of this that the body of the poor TB victim was unearthed.'

'Hang on a minute,' said Libby. 'You said Uncle Paul fell down the cellar steps, so presumably Willoughby pushed him. But why?'

'We can only assume that it was something to do

with the deaths from the poisonous medications. Perhaps there were records left somewhere. The police saw the other gravestones hidden in the undergrowth and assumed they were all victims of workhouse and sanatorium, reburied the little body –'

'Was it –? interrupted Libby.

'No. They buried the body in a new grave, not the one you saw when you first went there.'

Libby subsided.

'Then there were reports of a ghost being seen either inside or outside the house. No one quite seems to know where these came from, but we think Willoughby Weston must have paid a maid at the hotel to say she'd seen something, or sent anonymous tip-offs to the media. Anyway, the story spread, the hotel people gave up and left and that was that. Willoughby made sure that the details of the property never made it into the current files of the agency.

'When he died, his whole estate went to his son, including his interest, now a controlling one, in what had now become just Riley's. Weston won't say how much he knew of his father's misdeeds, but he's hardly as pure as the driven snow himself.

'A year or so ago, a new manager came to Riley's. Being a good, decent, hard-working sort, he went through the files and came across what he saw as a very decent property, updated the details and put it on the website and in the local paper.

'Weston saw this and, thinking quickly, because he had been in comms –'

'What?' said Fran.

'Communications,' said Peter, 'which means he was probably a bit of an electronics whizz.'

'Quite,' said Ian. 'He went and rigged up his Debussy – he knew all about Findon, you see – and then set about bricking up the cellar, where the equipment was.'

'Why didn't he just make sure the house details went back into the vaults or wherever they were?' asked Guy.

'He did, but they'd been out there already and somebody might have seen them and asked to view. Which in fact they did. Rosie wasn't the first.'

'But why? Just because of the mistakes his father had made? Or had he already started killing women for Vindari?' asked Guy.

'Luckily Maiden gave me your report before we started questioning Vindari and Weston,' Ian told Fran and Libby, 'so we knew roughly what had happened.'

'What?' said several voices together.

'Weston – in Vindari's terms – defiled a female member of his family and unfortunately killed her in the process.'

There was another collective gasp.

'Vindari found out and, not particularly interested in the outdated mores of his fellow countrymen, nevertheless spied an opportunity. The barn made a perfect hiding place for girls who had, according to their families, transgressed. He organised the imprisonment and death. He forced Weston to bury the girl in the barn, and then blackmailed him into killing the other girls. Which Weston was well suited for.' Ian shook his head. 'It was this that Weston needed to cover up. He had to keep people away from White Lodge.'

'So the hauntings began again.' Libby looked across at Fran. 'But not proper ones.'

'No. Then it was easy to tell the staff it was a complicated probate sale and not to push it. Because Weston actually had no idea who owned the estate.'

'And then Rosie came along,' said Fran.

'Yes, and she was telling the truth, you know. But fragments of memory had begun to return and she was getting scared. So she recruited you, thinking she ought not to appear in the business herself, although she wasn't quite sure why.'

'Hang on – what was the connection with Rachita?' asked Libby. 'Is there one?'

'Think about Rachita's story,' said Ian. 'Where did she meet the young man she ran off with?'

'At her uncle's, and Mr Vindari was there.' Fran nodded.

'And he'd organised work previously for Kiran and his friend.'

'The cellar!' shouted Libby, and the whole of the pub turned to look.

'Right. It was Kiran and his friend who had been recruited to brick up the cellar. When we came to break into it, we found it hadn't been done skillfully, and it looked as if it had been done in a hurry. The more we found out, the more interest there was in White Lodge, the more dangerous things were becoming. So Kiran and his friend had to go.'

'What about Rachita?' asked Fran.

'She really did run off with Kiran, but there

would have been no chance for her if Vindari had found her before her father. The boys were killed to stop them talking about bricking up the cellar and revealing a connection between Weston and Vindari.'

'Who killed them?' asked Guy.

'They are each saying the other,' said Ian. 'We'll probably never know.'

'What about Rosie, Ian?' asked Fran. 'What was she doing there last night? And why did she disappear?'

'Her memory had fully returned by now and she went to see if she could find any sort of proof that Willoughby Weston had killed her uncle.'

'Why didn't she tell anybody where she was?' asked Fran.

'Because she thought if Weston got to know he'd come after her.'

'Why weren't you worried about her?' asked Libby.

'Because she told me she was going away to think things out,' said Ian. 'I should have known she would be up to something.' He looked at Libby and Fran. 'She knows you two.'

'But she's all right?' persisted Libby.

'She's perfectly all right, and Professor Wylie is staying with her. She wants to see you both, but I said to give it a day or so. We'll have more questions for her.'

Silence fell around the table.

'And Weston and Vindari?' asked Peter after a moment. 'What will they be charged with?'

'Murder and whatever else we can dig up.'

'Ian,' Fran said suddenly. 'Whose was the reburial in the new grave?'

Ian smiled. 'I wondered when you'd get round to that. According to Weston, it was the maid who said she'd seen the ghost. When he found her body – and we don't know where he found it – possibly somewhere in his own home – she was wrapped in something of his father's and he put two and two together. He decided, for what reason we don't know, but with some kind of idea of doing it for his father, that she should go back to the garden. So he buried her. His downfall, or one of them, was keeping the grave clear.'

'And putting flowers on it.' Fran nodded.

'Why did Rosie stay behind when we left her at Ashton Court?' asked Libby.

'She says she was looking for proof. Photographs of his father, anything. I'm not sure she really knew herself.' Ian shook his head. 'Her main idea was to get to White Lodge without anyone knowing.'

'She did use us a bit, you know, Fran,' said Libby.

'She did.' Fran sighed. 'I'm not sure I want to go on with the creative writing classes now.'

'Oh, go on with you,' said Peter standing up. We want you to write down all your adventures. Think! You've got material for loads of books. Anyone want another drink?'

And somewhere in the darkness, the music began again.

Ex-actress Libby Sarjeant's fresh start in a picturesque Kent village includes an exciting new venture – the Oast House Theatre. She never expects it to include a new romance in the form of Ben, but who's complaining? She just isn't expecting ingredients three, four and five: mystery, intrigue and the shadow of old murder…

ISBN 9781905170159 £6.99

Once again, Libby Sarjeant finds herself involved in a mystery, this time because of the death of her friend Fran's Aunt Eleanor. Echoes of the past clash with very 21st century motives, and once again, thc Steeple Martin posse are on hand to give encouragemcnt and advice.

ISBN 9781905170845 £6.99

The third in the Libby Sarjeant series sees Fran consulted by Bella Morleigh, who has been left a derelict seaside theatre by an unknown relative.
Bella wants to know more about her family, particularly when a body is found in her local theatre. Despite being deep in pantomime rehearsals at The Oast House Theatre, Libby and Fran are soon involved in another murder investigation.

ISBN 9781906125028 £6.99

When a body is discovered on a rocky little island in the middle of Nethergate Bay the media swoop on the seaside town. Soon an enquiring hack discovers that local resident Fran Castle, has previously aided the police using her psychic abilities. Brought into the investigation, Fran naturally asks her friend Libby Sarjeant to help, but they soon find themselves up to their knees in more mud and murder than they could possibly have anticipated.

ISBN 9781906373306 £6.99

When television personality Lewis Osbourne-Walker buys Creekmarsh Place, near Steeple Martin in Kent, Libby Sarjeant's son Adam is employed to help with the renovation of the garden. What he doesn't expect is to uncover a long buried corpse. Libby, naturally, wants to know more about it, but the police aren't going to tell her, and with her friend Fran's mind on other things, she has to go it alone, with interesting and possibly catastrophic results.

ISBN 9781906373771 £6.99

The sixth in the Libby Sarjeant series sees Libby and her friend Fran involved in the strange rituals of the local Morris Men, when one of them is found dead on May Day and another seems to have vanished into thin air. Libby goes out of her comfort zone as far as Cornwall in search of the solution, which, in the end, is found much closer to home, turning out to be the most unpleasant case she has dealt with yet.

ISBN 9781907016080 £6.99

The seventh title in the Libby Sarjeant series finds her distracted from involvement with her local pantomime by her friend Harry, who asks her to help a friend of his who has been receiving threatening letters.

At first she believes it to be a simple case of prejudice, but soon Libby uncovers links to particularly nasty crimes in the past, revelations that have catastrophic results.

ISBN 9781907016462 £6.99

HOW TO WRITE A PANTOMIME
by Lesley Cookman

This book clearly explains how to plan and deliver a successful, traditional pantomime script. There are thousands of pantomimes staged throughout the world every year, most of them in Britain. Most groups, whether they be amateur drama societies, schools, Women's Institutes or Village Hall committees are constantly on the lookout for something fresh and original. This is often a matter of economics, as professional pantomimes can be costly in terms of performing rights, let alone the cost of scripts. This book is aimed at those people who take part in this increasingly popular hobby, and at the writer who wishes to write a pantomime, either for a local group, or, indeed, for mass publication

ISBN 9781906125127

£9.99

Also available from Accent Press

The HEARTBEAT Series
by Nicholas Rhea
a much-loved TV series

"...an account of the hilarious happenings to the county's rural policemen" **Yorkshire Post**

"Rhea's strengths are his sharp portraits of people and absorbing detail of a country copper practising his craft." **Northern Echo**

9781906373375 9781906373405 9781906373399 9781906373429

9781906373382 9781906373412 9781906373368 9781906373351

About The Author

Born in Guildford, Surrey, Lesley spent her early life in south London, before marrying and moving all over the south-east of England. Lesley fell into feature writing by accident, then went on to reviewing for both magazines and radio. She writes for the stage, she has written short fiction for women's weekly magazines and is a former editor of *The Call Boy*, the British Music Hall Society journal. Her first Libby Sarjeant novel, *Murder In Steeple Martin,* was published to much acclaim in 2006, followed in 2007 by *Murder At The Laurels* and *Murder In Midwinter*. In 2008, Lesley's ever-increasing number of fans welcomed the publication of *Murder By The Sea*. 2009 saw the publication of *Murder In Bloom. Murder In The Green* and *Murder Imperfect* made their appearance in 2010.

Her passion for the theatre is reflected in her first non-fiction work, *How To Write A Pantomime,* also published by Accent Press.

www.lesleycookman.co.uk